A Deadly Place to Stay

Josephine Bell

Walker and Company ✺ New York

First published in the United States of America
in 1983 by the Walker Publishing Company, Inc.

ISBN: 0-8027-5496-1

Library of Congress Catalog Card Number: 82-51304

Printed in the United States of America

10   9   8   7   6   5   4   3   2   1

A Deadly Place to Stay

Other Walker novels by Josephine Bell
Wolf! Wolf!
Treachery in Type
A Stroke of Death
The Trouble in Hunter Ward
A Question of Inheritance

1

The girl woke when the warm June sun reached her bare arms and dried the mingled dew and spent tears on her pale face.

She felt the warmth as a blessing now, on the third morning of her solitary, secret walk; her escape, she called it to herself, half believing it had succeeded, half inclined to call herself a sissy to think she could throw off all the fear, all the dread of a future she had at last decided she could no longer endure.

Well, she seemed to have succeeded; she praised herself for her quiet decision to walk out of that unendurable straight waistcoat, the so-called home, that cage. She felt she was at least a hundred miles from the discreet, neat, trim, white-washed, rose-gardened villa; the town, sprawling into tower blocks and glass-windowed factories along the grassy canal, the iron bridges, the wasteland stuffed with rubbish dumps, where stray dogs and straying, neglected children rootled for food or other treasure.

She turned to lie on her back. The sun was stronger now. She opened her arms to allow the warmth to cover her neck and breast and as the vigour roused energy in turn to her limbs and mind, her thoughts moved to the future. She felt in her pockets, in her soft bag of small belongings, where the almost total emptiness brought her softly from self-praise to self-contempt.

Two days of walking, two nights sleeping rough and not a penny left of the five pound note she had taken from the till the day before she left. Not a penny and the last sign-post she had passed the night before she had turned into this little copse off the narrow lane had pointed the way, two miles ahead, to a village very well known to her!

By name, that is, she reminded herself. In the car her so-called mother had driven through this village to reach the nearest motorway. They had never stopped there. Why should they? They had barely left home.

The tears she had shed the night before, as, tired out, lonely, hungry, afraid, she had collapsed on to a dry patch under spreading bushes, began to fall again. From now on, this third morning, she was still only ten miles or so from the town centre, therefore no more than fifteen from that less than happy home on the west side of it and the elegant, popular, prosperous, general grocery store, so convenient for the villa dwellers, so popular, being small, apeing a real village shop, stocking exotic foods and foreign delicacies in frozen packets. She cried because she had no means whatever to do more than walk, on and on, on and on.

Or go back, defeated? Never. The challenge, not wholly repelled, grew louder, more insistent, the more painful her circumstances became. The question, at its loudest yet, drove her to her feet, stamping them free from the cramp that attacked both legs as she stood up, but only deepened her resolve as she stamped and rubbed and writhed herself free of the sickening pain. She pushed herself away from the bushes and tramped off along the road towards the village.

Old Mrs Tavern, struggling slowly up the hill from the village Post Office, reached her cottage about a quarter of an hour before the girl, who came from the opposite direction.

Mrs Tavern unlocked her front door and locked it again on the inside. She put her shopping bag on the table and began to unload its ample contents. Her purse, with her week's pension, cashed in the village, fell out with her bag of flour as she pushed it under. Normally she undid the clasp to see that the notes were all there. Twenty-five pounds left. With the couple of quid left over from last week and the odd fifty pence of this week, as well as the 'social security' she'd just renewed for old Tom she'd stocked up for the week, a good supply of everything she enjoyed.

Mrs Tavern's happy thoughts were broken into by a loud knock at her front door. She dropped her purse on the table, clapped a hand to her chest, sent up a desperate plea to the Almighty, "Please God not them! Oh, my Lord, let it be the Welfare, *not, oh not them*!"

The knock came again, but unexpectedly less loud, not louder.

Mrs Tavern was surprised, even astonished. Very unusual. Authority knocked ever more loudly, impatient like, not less, surely? She crept up to the window and peered out between the half-drawn curtains. She saw a slim, tallish girl, 'bit of a scarecrow' she described her later, raising a hand that trembled violently, to knock again before the stranger collapsed, sliding down the door to the ground, while still feebly to implore for attention, for help, for relief.

Mrs Tavern was in two minds what to do for the best. If the girl was ill, even dying, which God forbid, and she was discovered, dying or dead, on the cottage doorstep, there would be all manner of disturbance, fuss, the papers, enquiries. Not that, not that, please God! If, on the other hand, she let the girl in to recover, was not that a more instant, a more certain danger? She took a quick look round at her stores, her *purse*, Lord save us! She swept the lot together, pushing the purse under the bag. Creeping back to the window she peered out again. The girl was gone! No, she was up against the door again. Another knock, feebler still, but insistent. Drat it all, she'd have to let her in, or better, ask her to go away.

There was no question of that. As soon as the bolts were off and the key turned the door thrust Mrs Tavern back as the girl staggered forward.

"You can't come in!" the old woman shouted, anger over-riding her fear. "You can't — "

"Water!" the girl gasped, leaning back against the door, shutting it behind her with the key still in the lock. "Please, oh please, just a glass of water!"

"Sit down," Mrs Tavern said. "Who are you? Where've you come from?"

The girl had already collapsed on to the nearest chair, a

rickety upright, rush-seated one, of great age and old-fashioned, but sturdy still, home-made to last. It shook as she sank down on it, but did not collapse under her light weight. She let her head sink forward, covering her face with her hands, but peering round the room from behind her latticed fingers.

"Lost yer tongue, 'ave yer?" Mrs Tavern grumbled, unwilling to accept genuine distress. "Why should yer be in want of water? Your lot drinks coffee, don't ee? Or summat stronger?"

The girl raised her head slowly.

"I've left home," she said. "I've come a long way. Further than I hoped when I started. The job had gone I was going for. That was three days ago. I've been walking since. No food or drink since the day before yesterday."

"I've nothing for yer," Mrs Tavern said, disbelieving the bulk of the story.

"I meant to get something in the village," the other said. "Then I began to feel faint. If you would just — "

This was true at any rate, Mrs Tavern decided. The girl had evidently not seen her at the window, or she would have appealed to her direct. In this she was wrong. It was because she had caught sight of the old, sour face and small mean eyes between the window curtains that the girl had decided to try for help. There would be no welcome but a strong wish to oblige and get rid of her.

Mrs Tavern decided to oblige, unwillingly, with the gift of cold water wrapped in an ungracious lecture on the dangers and difficulties of throwing away parental advice and care, the strong necessity of going home again at once.

"I'll get you what you ask for, though it won't do you much good, I'm thinking. 'eadstrong, I should think and ignorant, though better-spoken than I'd expect from yer appearance, with those everlasting jeans, frayed a-purpose like they allus do, I'm told, and that heavy jumper, that's not seen the tub in months."

She got no response, only the blank unnerving stare she was accustomed to from her young neighbours. So she tottered off into her little back room where there was a sink and a rack and an old copper boiler where she still did an occasional wash for herself but no longer took in washing from any of the larger houses of the neighbourhood, where, in former times and another part of the country, she had been used to find custom.

Left alone, the girl took instant action. Silent, practised, she was beside the shopping basket in a flash. As she reached into it the old woman's bulging leather purse rolled from underneath. It had fallen open as it was being thrust out of sight. Inside, the folded wad of notes was immediately visible.

The girl snatched at the outside one, brown, large, fairly crisp. Ten pounds. Surely not! Impossible to change safely in her present untidy, dirty state!

She snatched again, blue fivers this time. More like it! Stuffing them up the sleeve of her sweater she was easing the shopping bag over the purse when Mrs Tavern's cracked screech sent her jumping back from the table.

"Young devil! Might 'ave knowed it! Bloody hippy! Liar!"

The girl stood quite still, recovering herself from the assault as she had learned to do over the years. Waiting for the other's rage to subside into weakness as it nearly always did on these occasions of attack.

As it did now, but not quite as she expected. Mrs Tavern was holding a mug with fluid in it. Water probably, what she had asked for and what the drops looked like, splashing over the shaking old fingers that held it, while from the other hand the clumsily cut tail of a loaf fell to the floor.

Mrs Tavern needed a free hand to secure her shopping and her purse. Succour for the girl impeded her: she discarded the bread, but the girl snatched the mug: drank eagerly, gulping great mouthfuls, gasping for air as she denied that need in favour of her parched mouth and throat.

"Get out of my house!" shrieked Mrs Tavern, still rootling among her parcels in her bag, still keeping it covering her purse, for she was now in worse terror lest the girl she hoped she had forestalled in her thieving should snatch the cash and bolt.

But the young slut showed no sign of moving. Nor did she

stoop to pick up the bread. All that about starving, lies, every word of it, she'd been right.

"Get out! Get out!" she screamed again and turned on the girl, who now had the mug upturned in her hand to secure the last drops from the bottom of it.

Mrs Tavern's old hand first drove into the girl's soft right breast. In her yell of pain she swallowed those last drops the wrong way, choked, coughed and brought the mug down on Mrs Tavern's head, where it cracked and split into a shower of ancient crockery.

The old woman fell backwards. Her head met the floor with a sharp crack not unlike the sound just made by the mug. No other sound followed.

The girl waited. The old woman lay still. She did not seem to be breathing but it did not occur to her attacker to find out or to help her in any way. After all that fuss she had got her water to drink and the bread, but that was spoilt; she couldn't eat if off the filthy floor, could she? If the old bitch hadn't made all that bother —

Ought she to get help? How could she explain! Better just go.

She pulled her sweater straight and heard the notes in her sleeve crackle and felt them prick her arm. No, she couldn't get help! What if the old girl had knocked herself out, tripping up like that? Well, she had tripped, hadn't she? The mug was old and cracked to begin with. She'd hardly done more than tapped the old cow with it.

Bracing herself, excusing herself, she peered at the still figure on the floor, satisfied to see no blood appearing. 'Pools of blood' it always was in the papers.

The girl found her own empty purse in her haversack and slipped her two five pounds notes into it. She left the cottage very quietly, closing the front door carefully behind her.

She remembered that the signpost was back along the lane to her left, so she walked firmly to the right. She was still hungry: perhaps more so, since her thirst, now eased, had taken precedence before. But distance and speed were more than ever urgent. The alarm over her absence must surely be widespread by now, she thought. And soon this other trouble would be added to it. She still did not allow herself to call it disaster. In any case it was not her fault. She had not really struck the old bitch, just stopped her finding out about the cash. She smiled faintly as she walked briskly through the straggling cottages, past the single dingy shop with its Post Office sign over the door, past the untidy garage where a clear-eyed boy was making a poor attempt at sweeping the drive-in to the four self-service pumps. Cash was the word she always used for coinage, because that word applied to the till in their shop at home, to its contents and so to the source of her pilfering, from the time she was first capable of reaching it and of understanding how it worked.

Passing the village shop she wondered if she could find a few biscuits there, possibly a sausage roll and so change that unlikely five pound note. But she decided, in spite of her now renewed hunger, that this would not be safe. She would be remembered. She had been lucky so far. Only a clutch of schoolchildren had appeared from house doors, swinging satchels and brief cases, struggling to do up blazer buttons as they tried to run, to catch up other children, shouting recognition, warning they'd be late, punching, snatching at caps, fighting in a half-hearted desultory manner. The more responsible set up shouts of "The bus! Give over! We'll miss the bloody bus!"

A bus, she thought. Just a school bus? What time was it after all? Her watch had stopped yesterday and she had failed to wind it. If the kids were aiming at nine o'clock school, how had the old woman managed to get her shopping done so early in the day? If so, where had all that money come from?

She hurried herself to keep up with the children and very soon came to a cross-roads, where to her joy she saw a bus-stop and a group of more children with a few adults waiting. She joined the latter.

The bus arrived in a very few minutes, a country bus, not a school one she saw with some relief. As she discovered, again most thankfully listening to those in front of her in the short queue, they were aiming at Northampton. She took a single ticket, cursing herself for not planning her escape more sensibly and in more detail. That impulse to run away, carried out with childish simplicity, had been a right nonsense.

Northampton. Only as far as that in three days! All that walking down leafy paths, sheltered lanes, avoiding the high land because it was so bare and open. Fool! Did she suppose her keepers, (she would not call them parents) would be searching for her with a telescope?

Even more ravenous, she was first off the bus, pushing past the schoolchildren, not caring if they remembered her or not. The bus station had a cafeteria. She was maddened by the sight and smell of several hot dishes, swimming in large, flat containers; plates of made meals, keeping hot on shelves behind glass; and a great variety of cold foods, also on display behind glass.

With great self-restraint she bought a sausage roll, a lump of cheese, a bread roll and a cup of coffee. She forced herself to eat and drink very slowly, while all the time she considered the next move in the journey she now knew she had barely begun.

Only Northampton. All her former visits to the place had been on the shop's half day, a Thursday in her home town. Certainly she had never seen this bus station before, nor the part of the town it occupied. Quite sure her keepers would travel long distances by car or by train she determined to go as far as possible by coach.

She felt much better when she had finished her meal, so she went outside again. There were the various local buses, mostly painted red. And far away, at one side of the row there was a white coach with National painted on the side and at the front its destination London.

That was it, the girl decided. Old-fashioned, old hat? Dotty to think London would hide her, help her to a job, shield her from further harm, set her truly free from the hypocrisy, the false piety, the dishonesty, the snob talks, the scolding, slave-driving, suppression, and punishments, called training? Set her free, or drown her?

She checked her wild flood of inward complainings, suddenly aware that people were looking at her. She fumbled for a handkerchief but found only a torn tissue and a very grubby headscarf, which she screwed into her eyes as if to wipe away tears. After that she moved away to find the 'toilets'.

She was appalled by her appearance in the lavatory mirrors. She repaired the state of her face and hair as well as she could, before going out again to find the National coach office. The fare to London would take most of her remaining money, but it was possible. She had convinced herself that London would make her disappearance certain and secure, unbreakable.

The office was able to advise her on that afternoon's possible journey. The ticket, single only, would cost most of one of her notes. Her name? Without thinking the girl said Lesley. It was the private name she had always called herself, because she disliked Miriam, her adoptive name and also because Lesley had been her best friend at her primary school, but had been lost to her when she was moved to a small private school nearer to her home. She gave the name but said she had not quite decided if she would go that day.

The National coach office assistant stopped preparing a ticket but said, "Well, your coach will be in any time now, so if you want to travel ask the driver for a ticket."

"Where does it come in?" Lesley asked.

She was told, directed where to go and abandoned in favour of the next customer, an impatient man with a complaining wife at his side who wanted to reach Cheltenham before dark.

The coach was reasonably punctual. Lesley was waiting at the head of the short queue and spoke to the driver at once. He gave her a single ticket. She was fortunate in finding a window seat and sank into it very thankfully, keeping her face turned away from the window until they moved off. She would look at the countryside when they were blessedly in motion.

But when the countryside was indeed moving past Lesley's eyes drooped shut and remained so. She roused a little when the coach began to meet other traffic in the outskirts of London, but only came fully awake at last as her fellow travellers began to pull their hand luggage from the shelves and climb into their outer coats or mackintoshes as the coach moved slowly into the great covered bus station at Victoria.

13

2

Lesley got down from the warm shelter of the coach into a scene of terrifying confusion and ear-shocking noise.

She had expected London to be bigger than any town she had ever visited. But she had slept through the now far-off outer country suburbs, the growing wide mainroads, gradually merging one into another between continuous immense rows of dying terraces of houses split into office blocks and shops; historic railway terminals over which the mainroads soared on higher and wider bridges: finally, to the famous landmarks of Victorian London, much altered indeed, but still recognisable: Marble Arch, Hyde Park Corner, finally Buckingham Palace Road, with Victoria Railway Station at one side and Victoria Coach Station on the other.

Lesley, if she had watched the approach, might have been better prepared for the pandemonium of extended travel. But she was not, and she was terrified.

At first she followed her fellow passengers off the coach, shaking her head when someone, seeing her bewilderment, told her the driver was handing out the baggage from the boot at the back. She had no luggage, except the loose bag she clutched firmly in one hand.

Most of her recent companions scattered before they reached the wide pavement, but a few continued and like herself stood still, turned round and looked about them for their next objective. She felt waves of anger and envy as they all, in due course, made up their minds and moved away. She herself had no objective: she felt she had no mind left to use on her own situation in this petrol-laden, moving, grinding, shouting, swinging, arm-waving, hurrying, pushing, screaming, mass of machines and mankind.

But if her mind was numbed, her body, newly awake from a long, deep, satisfying sleep, was roused and demanding. She boldly joined a short queue beside one of the small newspaper and magazine stalls that lined the outer wall of the Station. When her turn came she asked for the Toilets. The woman behind the stall, annoyed by this unprofitable interruption of her business, at first ignored her. But Lesley's need was great: she stood her ground and repeated her request. The woman pointed across the concourse. Lesley thanked her and moved on.

It took her fully five minutes to thread her way round, but she was encouraged by seeing, fairly soon, the notice high on the glass door announcing Ladies Waiting Room. Twice she had to dodge and sidestep and squeeze past a solid block of those held back from a coach that was moving into position to take them aboard. A little later she was forced to venture out among the coaches to get round another solid block, this time not attempting to queue but settled down to sit out their waiting time on their large suitcases, some with children sitting beside them or a baby in a pram or simply in a harness on a father's back or a mother's bosom. But she got there in the end, relieved to find a kind of peace inside, though she had to pay for her comfort, a few pence only, but she resented it for diminishing her tiny capital.

This reminded her of the extent of her poverty. She had to find a job, but how? Not in this bedlam, that was for sure! This lot, every single one, it seemed, was just changing coaches or else taking off for the wide expanse of London. The names on the boards at each coach stop reminded her of parts of England, Scotland, Wales and the West Country; names she had found exciting when she was at the grammar all those four weary years ago. Well, it had got to be London for her. Surely in this place alone, a tiny bit of the whole outfit, she guessed, it would be next to impossible for *them* to find her. But already she dreaded the moment when she would have to leave it:

dreaded to find herself alone, an easily marked stranger. She feared to be alone and yet longed for the peace of solitude, that peace she had welcomed with astonishment in the shelter of the inner field hedge where she had spent the second night and the first rest of her flight.

She had been standing just outside the Ladies Waiting Room, so intent upon her problems that she had not noticed the individuals who found her an obstacle in their path. For the most part they avoided her by a quick movement or ignored her in pushing past, even bumping into her. But one stout figure, after a slight collision, said, not angrily, with authority, "You are blocking our way, my dear."

Lesley was shaken into apology, but too late, for the woman had disappeared behind the swinging door. However, she was startled into movement and looking desperately about her, caught the sign of half the title REST, with the end of it AURANT coming into view as she moved towards that welcoming sign.

She found herself inclined to giggle as the glass doors, the well-filled tables, the piles of parked luggage came into full view. Yes, she must buy food again or be incapable of plan, decision, even physical movement. She pushed through the doors and waited for them to close behind her.

On a smaller scale she was used to this set-up. Tables covered with pale green formica tops, seats four a side, the chairs fixed at that uncomfortable distance that had, years back, been too far off the table and now were usually too near. In the distance, behind more glass walls, the food and the queue moving slowly, choosing a meal as they went along. The menu, printed, so the same every day, was on the wall behind the food. Plates of prepared dishes stood on glass shelves, salads first, then hot meals. Just like Northampton.

Lesley drifted to the end of the queue. She was trying to remember what money she had left without getting out her purse to discover it.

A man in front of her, looking back said, "You'll want a tray, love." He had pity in his eyes when she said, in her midland voice "Of course, thanks a lot," and snatched one off the pile

16

at the beginning of a long enclosed counter, reaching across the arm of the customer behind her, without apology, without even looking at the person behind the arm.

She loaded fish and chips and peas, a choc ice and a cup of coffee. She would have liked to add a roll and butter and cheese, but she dared not. She must keep something for a lodging that night and supper or at least breakfast the next day.

Lodging? Supper? Breakfast? Where? How? Without giving it all up. A complete, humiliating failure. Already she could hear so-called Dad's growling abuse, sickening pinch or arm-twist. And so-called Mum's high-piercing cry of rage and never-ending tale of her wickedness, her ingratitude, her bad heredity, her criminal inborn nature and so-on and so-on.

Lesley paid for her meal and carried it away, looking for a single empty place, preferably at the end of a table. She found one with a vacant seat opposite and planted her tray, standing to unload it before sitting down.

Again she was blocking the fairway. Again a voice, vaguely familiar, asked to get past. Again she saw the woman who had accused her before, but this time with a hearty laugh and a voice grown fruity as she said, "You again! My dear, you really must keep out of people's way if you need to day-dream!"

"I'm sorry," Lesley said. She flopped into her chair, began rapidly to move her meal into some sort of order on the table and then, with the empty tray held in front of her like a shield saw to her surprise and disgust that the stout woman had taken the empty seat opposite and was in turn unloading the contents of her own tray, a plate of sandwiches, a small glass of orange squash and a banana.

"You didn't really want to get past me, did you?" she found herself saying indignantly, as she began to eat.

"I did at first, but then I noticed this place was empty, so I thought we might have a little chat as we ate our lunch."

Lesley made no answer, not even any sign she had heard what the fat old cow was saying. But she *had* heard. And as she forced herself to eat slowly and carefully she glanced across from time to time to see what the woman looked like.

She was not surprised to find a dark blue very plain over-

17

coat, perhaps linen, probably polyester, a sort of uniform, since it buttoned up to the neck, though it carried no badge of any sort to show to which organised body it belonged. Perched on the owner's grey curls was a headdress with a veil attached. Salvation Army, Lesley wondered, but decided it was not quite right for that. Religious anyhow, she guessed. One of the cranky lot, those who kept wandering into the shop at home with collecting boxes, until Dad had put the fear of God into them instead of the other way round.

"Travelling alone, I see," said the fat woman, in a kind, but quite casual tone. Lesley did not answer, did not appear to have heard.

"This place has grown up like a mushroom over the last few years," the kind voice went on. "I'm not surprised you were a bit thrown, as they call it, by all that hullabaloo outside. People have taken to coaches since the rail fares have gone up so much and have so many strikes."

The people in the two seats next to them at the same table got up to go. Almost at once a young man, tall, with fair curly hair, profuse but not overlong, and a well-shaved face, planted his tray beside Lesley's right arm, which she had rested on the table.

"Excuse me," he said, in a pleasant voice, "this place is vacant, isn't it?"

"Oh, yes," she answered, startled and annoyed with herself for showing it. "Didn't you see those others leave?"

He laughed which confused her more. So much so that she got up, saying, "I'm coming back. Keep my place, will you?"

"Sure," he answered, quite serious again.

The stout woman also rose.

"If you are staying in London and have nowhere booked for tonight — "

"The Y.W. — " Lesley began, defensively.

"Of course. But also my organisation — Nearer, and close to facilities. I mean a Labour Exchange — "

She was holding out a card. It had printed words on it, a prominent title in heavy black letters THE HOLY GROUP. Below that an address. Above in pencil, Sister Brook.

18

Lesley muttered, "Thanks a lot," and moved away, still holding her cup and saucer in her other hand.

As she waited again in the queue, discarding the used cup when she saw disapproving faces staring at it, she told herself she had been right, the woman was a do-gooder and the religious kind as well. Holy Group! Holy balls! Fat lot of good she'd be to anyone, fat old Sister Brook!

But before she had secured her second cup of coffee Lesley had looked again at the do-gooder's card and had second thoughts. When the fat woman had started talking Lesley had realised that she herself had made no further plans. Though it was still light, being late August, the afternoon was well advanced, almost evening, there could not be more than another couple of hours of real daylight. It was high time to begin finding a lodging and already too late to find a job, for that day at least. When she had blurted out about going to the Y.W.C.A. she had thought it a very bright idea. But now she wasn't so sure. Wouldn't that be the first thing *They* would think of at home. Y.W.s had all the warnings put out by the police. Of course they would suspect her story. Of course. And the old woman in the cottage, who hadn't believed her. If she wasn't — If she hadn't — When she came round and someone found her, as they must have by now, whether or not —. They would get her description, they would find the money missing — They would search the Y.$\overline{W}$.s all over, all over the country and get her description when they found there was money missing. It always came back to the same thing.

By the time she was back at her table Lesley had made up her mind. Sister Brook might be scatty, but this Holy Group couldn't be worse than the Y.W. and would have to do for tonight, for a couple of nights most likely.

The young man was still there. He did not seem to have got very far with his coffee. He looked up at her before she sat down and said, "What did the old dame want?"

Lesley was surprised into answering naturally.

"To slip me the address of her place. If it *is* her place. One of those crackpot religious outfits, it looks like."

Having sat down she showed him the now rather

crumpled card. He looked at it and smiled before handing it back.

"Do you know where that is?" Lesley asked.

"Actually I do. Battersea. South of the river."

She shook her head.

"No dice. Never been this far south before."

"Take a taxi."

She shook her head again.

"Bus then."

"Which one?"

He stared at her so straight and hard that she had to bury her face in her coffee cup to hide her blushes. She was ignorant, yes. Helpless, yes. So what the hell! But she had to know. Who to ask? Not anyone of the types in this god-awful bus station. Not the police, Christ no!

The young man was going: he was getting up slowly.

"It's only a short bus ride to that place," he said carefully, looking away from her now. "I'm going that way myself. I'll show you if you like."

"O.K," she said, recovering and gulping down the rest of her coffee before scrambling to her feet.

"Your bag?" he asked as they left the table together.

"I've got all I need for a day or two," she answered.

He looked sideways at the small haversack and seemed to resent its inadequacy. But all he said was, "What's your name?"

"Lesley," she answered.

"Lesley what?"

Desperately she searched for something totally unlike the truth. She could only think of the do-gooder, Sister Brook.

"Rivers," she said. "Lesley Rivers." It had rather a pleasant sound, she thought.

"Mine's Reg Bridge," he said.

She felt a small suspicion dig into her mind. Was that true? Brook, Rivers, Bridge. True, or as false as her own invention? And if false, why so? Why on earth, for God's sake?

But she smiled, one of her blank, meaningless smiles, as they walked away from the coach station. She let him guide her

20

across the busy road, but hesitated as he turned off to the right where traffic was moving into the railway station or so it seemed.

"Train?" she asked. "I thought you said bus?"

He laughed.

"Quickest way to the local buses." He gave her another sideways look. "You are green, aren't you? Where've you been all these years?"

"I've never come to London before if that's what you mean? But London isn't the world," she answered, with indignation.

There was no time to justify herself further, because they had already crossed the station to emerge where a continuous stream of taxis was setting down and picking up passengers with luggage of a kind that made her small soft bag look right daft, she knew.

"Over here," Reg said, taking her elbow again as he had done to cross the road.

It was dusk now: though the sky was still blue above the houses, at street level the lights were needed. London, seen thus, was at its most magical, most alluring, had the solitary, clueless waif from the Midlands but known it, been capable of seeing, of feeling, anything outside her immediate, animal needs. But she was by now thoroughly exhausted and utterly confused, so she followed Reg on to the bus he chose, squeezed past him under his direction to the window seat and sat in silence as they moved away down Vauxhall Bridge Road.

When they passed over the river she did exclaim in total surprise and some alarm.

"It's only the old Thames," Reg told her. "That address is south of the river. Didn't the old — didn't that old lady tell you?"

"She just gave me the card. How was I to know?"

How indeed? Matter of fact, Reg had said 'south of the river' but it hadn't registered. Anyway he hadn't said it was the *Thames*. Well, what the hell! Would she find a job south of the river? How far did it go? How soon? — Reg was on again.

21

"Look, I'm going farther than you are. I'll tell you when to get off. Here's your ticket. No, don't pay me for it. My pleasure."

He was grinning at her as if he knew quite well she had not made, had no intention of making, any effort to pay him. She mumbled "Thanks a lot."

"When you get off, wait till the bus goes on. Then cross the road. Best to stop halfway over, lights go green when it's safe for you."

"I do know about traffic lights,·' she was stung into interrupting.

"Fine. On the opposite side walk the same way this bus is going and turn right at the second turning. About two blocks of houses along it the shops give up and there's a row of private houses. Some of them have boards outside. One's a photographer, I think. Wedding photos and kids. In colour. Soppy. Then this place you're aiming for. Holy something."

"Group. Holy Group. Sister Brook."

"That's right. Show them your card. You've still got it?"

"Of course."

"Good. Better change places with me, now. We're nearly there."

She obeyed without argument, trying to fix his directions in her mind as he repeated them just before he gave her a gentle shove.

"Off you go now! Good luck!"

"Thanks a lot."

There was no time to say more and she felt no inclination to do so. His manner had been very peculiar, something she had not met before. But kind, really, except for that dig about the bus fare. Before she crossed the road, waiting to do so until she got the green light, she glanced at the bus ticket she still held. Twenty p. Quite a trip. Well, he didn't have to pay if he didn't want to. She'd have been bound to produce the money if he'd asked for it.

Lesley managed to find the road; the row of shops, the sleazy, stucco-chipped, dirty-windowed houses, standing a little back from the pavement behind low brick walls. In their long-neglected front gardens, with coarse grass crowding the wooden supports of the advertising boards, she recognised the photographer's studio from the display of his skill, both in black and white and in colour. Next but one to it Miss Bellaire, on a discreet plaque, notified customers in need of massage and kindred activities. Two houses beyond this again the house was well lighted, behind curtains in all the front windows, from the wide front gate up three white steps to a pillared porch and on either side of a sign held up on an iron frame over the gate, which carried the inscription in large square-cut letters

THE HOLY GROUP

and below, in smaller script

all friends welcome

Lesley felt a wave of relief that nearly overwhelmed her. As she pushed her way in through the gate she had difficulty in not giving way to tears. But she managed enough control to say, when the door was opened very soon after she had pressed the bell, "I'm looking for a room for the night. I was advised by Sister Brook at Victoria coach station."

"Come in, my child. Greetings, Sister. Greetings."

Lesley's response to this was mixed. She moved across the threshold. She accepted a chair in a wide, bare, agressively clean hall and immediately stood up again on an impulse to reject that sickeningly effusive welcome.

But the portress, or whoever she was, had gone and the front door was not only locked but had two chains across it, top and bottom.

She sat down again. She still had a little money left. She could pay for one night if she had to. There was no other way open to her and she knew it.

3

After an interval, in which Lesley found herself drifting off again into a half-conscious, muddled doze, she suddenly became aware of another presence, standing quite near her, rock still, silent, regarding her from clear, steady eyes in a long, calm face.

Lesley struggled to stand up, she began to mutter excuses, explanations, in the rapid, almost inaudible slang and cliché of her generation. But a firm, a very firm, hand on her shoulder sent her back on to her chair as the tall woman said, not unkindly, but with quelling authority, "You are exhausted, my child. Tell me where you have come from and how we can help you."

"From the coach station," Lesley said. She had prepared this start to her account of herself, and went on, "I'm in London to find work. I've only just got here. I need a bed for tonight. I was given this card in the buffet."

She held out Sister Brook's directions, but the other did not take it, only said softly, "Our good friend, Sister Brook. And you followed her advice and found your way to us. Praise the Lord!"

The fervour with which she spoke astonished Lesley. Once more she wondered where she had landed herself, whether they were all bats in this joint. Until her grinding fatigue and the growing ache of renewed hunger told her she would be batty herself to leave, perhaps incapable of doing so.

So she looked up at the tall woman and put on the smile that had never failed in the shop when she managed to sell something at a price above the normal, where she could keep the excess for herself. She held out the grubby wallet where she had counted her tiny pile of cash and said, "I can pay you for a bed and breakfast if it isn't too much, Miss — Mrs — "

"Sister Manley," she was told, "I am in charge of this particular centre. The Group has other houses in different parts of London. Our creed is belief in God and our leader. Our aim is succour of the homeless, like yourself, my dear. We make no charge, but we hope for domestic selfhelp from those who stay with us."

While Lesley tried to find suitable words of thanks for this generous news, Sister Manley took her by the arm and brought her to her feet very smartly indeed.

"Supper first," she said, "then a hot bath and bed. You will be sharing a room with two others of your age. You may not see them tonight because I am sure you will be asleep before they come back from a choral service they have been at with one of the other houses. So come along."

The supper was plain, but hot, ample and tasty. The bath was also hot and deep, though the towel was thin and the borrowed pyjamas made of coarse material and too big for her.

Her eyes were closing again as she was shown her bed in a sparsely furnished room with two other iron frames and their mattresses, but she was in no state to criticise, but only to sink under blesssedly heavy blankets in a mood of total surrender, in honest thankfulness.

Lesley woke the next morning to the sound of high girlish voices, some laughter, some complaints.

She opened her eyes. The electric light was on: a single bulb without a shade, hanging from a short flex at the middle of the ceiling. The other two beds were occupied. In one a girl with long, mouse-coloured hair hiding most of her face, sat rubbing her pale cheeks and bemoaning the chilly autumn weather. In the other a dark, bushy mop of curls hid the rest of the second girl's head and face. She had pulled her blankets up to cover her ears and was clearly trying to postpone the moment of rising.

Lesley turned on to her back, rubbed her eyes and pushed her own hair away from her face.

"What time is it?" she asked. Her watch was on her left wrist, where she had put it back again after that super bath, but she had forgotten to wind it up. God, she'd been tired. Flaked right out!

"When do we get up?" she went on, not waiting to hear the time.

The dark head suddenly erupted. In a burst of energy the owner flung off her bedclothes, jumped to the floor.

"*Now*!" she declared vigorously, pulling a long nightdress up over her head. "Seven, isn't it?"

"My watch stopped," Lesley tried to explain.

"Another wet like you, Sue! I'm Fran Harmer," the dark girl said, in the same grating, decided tone, steadying her ample breasts in a tight bra and pulling up a pair of bikini briefs. "What's your name?" she asked, peering at Lesley from small black eyes in a notably plain face.

"Lesley Rivers."

"Les. *She's* Sue Ford."

"Susan?" Lesley asked, turning to the third girl, who still sat with her face in her hands now, making no move to get up. But hearing Lesley's voice, clearly asking her a question, she did reluctantly answer, "Of course. But it makes no difference."

"To what?"

"They all call me Sue. *She* makes them."

Fran by this time was in her jeans and a very wide, polo-necked sweater. She was in front of one of the three small chests of drawers, the only furniture in the room beside the beds. She was pulling a stiff small brush through her curls, making the mop stand out further than ever from the snub nose and wide mouth.

She turned, snatched Sue's blankets from her weak grasp with such violence that the girl fell forward and rolled off the bed on to the floor.

"Up!" she shouted and turned towards Lesley.

"You too!"

But as she snatched at Lesley's bedclothes the new girl caught at her hand, twisted it sharply and brought the attacker to her knees.

26

The latter's face darkened, but she got up without attempting to retaliate.

"Judo, eh?" she said in a quieter tone.

"That's right."

Lesley got up from the bed, turned her back on Fran and pulled her own pile of clothes towards her. She fumbled in her grubby sack for her single unsoiled jumper. The spare bra and briefs looked about as scruffy as those she had discarded the night before. She would have to ask the tall bitch in charge here where she could find their washing machine and use it, hopefully without charge. When she turned round again she saw that Fran had left the room, but Sue, also dressed, was waiting, with a shy smile on her pale face.

"You put the wind up her, proper," she said. "Can you really do Judo?"

Lesley laughed.

"Want me to show you?"

"*No, no!*"

Lesley decided to ignore that faked terror. Sue surely couldn't be serious.

"I'm starving," she said. "Lead the way to breakfast."

"We're late," Sue muttered. "We won't get more than bread and marge. Fran'll see to that."

If the young bully had had any such intention, it was not evident. There were only six other girls in the austere dining room, where a stern-faced young woman in a plain grey overall stood near a hatch where she took cups and plates from unseen hands in the kitchen beyond.

She ignored Sue, who reached for an already poured out cup of tea, dropped sugar into it and took it away. The server turned to Lesley.

"You came to us last night, Sister. I hope you slept well and feel better for it."

"Yes," Lesley answered and remembering a training in basic manners she had long discarded, added rather awkwardly, "Thank you," and waited.

"Here is your tea," said the server, pulling another prepared cup forward.

"Is that all?" Lesley asked. "I mean, I'm not on a diet of any kind." She attempted a laugh that was not shared.

"Bread and butter, or cornflakes?" The server's voice had grown sharper.

"Both really," Lesley answered and added quickly, "I can pay all right. I've been travelling the last few days, not having proper meals, you know." She was disturbed by the hardening expression on the grey-overalled young woman's face. "*Please!*" she implored.

The response was a plate of very dry-looking cut loaf with a dab of margarine on each slice. There were only two.

"We have rules here," the server said. "Late-comers at meal times interfere with the routine of the kitchen staff. We provide for the delay in this way."

"I didn't know what time to get up," Lesley persisted. "There was a girl shouting insults at me and the poor little wet over there." She pointed at Sue sipping her tea at a table near the hatch. "That delayed us. Called herself Fran. Proper bully, that one. Why can't I have cornflakes as well, if I pay for them?"

She had not noticed that the server had touched with her foot a bell push on the floor just under the table. So that Lesley jumped round in a fright when a firm hand fell on her shoulder and the voice she remembered from the night before said, "Sister Lesley, why do you make trouble at the breakfast table?"

It was the boss Sister, looking all kinds of forfeits, Lesley saw and trembled inwardly. She mumbled an apology, then turned on the half-smile that had sometimes worked at the grammar school three years ago.

It did not work with Sister Manley.

"We do not want your money," she was told. "You will keep it for more important purposes than stuffing your stomach with unnecessary artificial luxuries. Take what you have been offered. Our Group morning prayers are held in the Great Hall at nine o'clock, for all those whose daily work for the Group does not begin at eight o'clock. There you will be received publicly: afterwards I will discuss your future in my study. Be patient, Sister."

She was gone, leaving Lesley totally bewildered, empty of any and every kind of response. To such massive authority, conveyed to her without anger, without argument, without criticism, the girl felt reduced to nothing herself. She stood at the serving table silent, shaking all over, until the women there, with a nod of understanding and a smile of easy contempt, pushed the plate of despised bread and butter against this young newcomer's hand.

"Better get on with your breakfast, Sister," she said, quietly.

This time Lesley accepted the frugal meal and took it away to the table where Sue still lingered.

"Now you see what it's like," the girl whispered. "I saw Sister Manley come. I knew she'd turn up when you raised your voice. They can call her in her office from the hatch."

"How? I didn't see anything."

"You wouldn't. There's a bell push under the table or some-where. I don't know, but I've seen it happen. To Fran, just after she came."

This could be true, Lesley thought. Then how?

"So Fran got the message, did she? And copies it, I suppose?"

She nodded, looking interested.

"Could be. Sister Manley does talk a lot about training and self-discipline. All that sort of thing."

Lesley ate her simple meal in silence. There was not much time before nine o'clock and the server, whose name Sue told her was Sister Gordon, was making signs to their table to bring in their crockery to be handed through the hatch for the washing-up machine.

"We're supposed to make our beds before prayers," Sue announced as they left the dining room. "I'll help you with yours if you like."

"Thanks a lot. And show me this Great Hall she said I was to go to at nine."

Certainly the Great Hall was large, far bigger than one would expect from looking at the front of the house from the street outside. But the house was semi-detached and though the front next door bore another board with a placard announcing 'Madam Sanssoufrance Chiropody, Superfluous Hair, Etc,' the back part of that similar attached house was now part of the premises of The Holy Group and had been altered together with its next storey above, into a very spacious room. The ground floor windows had been boarded up, those of the next storey were filled with small fixed panes of coloured glass and had shutters that could be closed at night. The hall was ventilated by air conditioning and warmed by central heating.

The meeting in this hall was less formidable than Lesley had feared. The Ruler, so-called, did not in any way live up to that name, she decided. A short man, white-haired but smooth-faced, with a high voice and a tendency to break off in the middle of a sentence when he spoke to anyone directly. Not that he addressed any single member of the small gathering, but only Sister Manley.

There was no break, no hesitation in the actual words of the services he conducted, which reminded Lesley forcibly of those non-conformist church attendances her foster parents had taken her to regularly in her early childhood, less frequently as she reached adolescence and after she left school only if she decided to join them, which she hardly ever did.

She followed the present ritual automatically, until she was startled by the Ruler stepping forward to announce in his high monotone.

"We have a newcomer in our midst! Welcome, welcome, Sister! The Holy Group bids you welcome, wishes you peace, happiness, fruitful strivings, joy in toil, success in grateful endurance."

Sister Manley was beside her now, that very firm hand on her arm, urging her towards the low dais on which the Ruler now sat in a great oak chair with a high back and carved arms.

"Kneel!" ordered Sister Manley.

The pressure was now on each shoulder. Lesley knelt on the bare boards of the dais.

The Ruler put both his rather small, but elegantly long-fingered hands on the acolyte's head. Lesley stared up at him, astonished rather than impressed. The Ruler bent her head forward into a more submissive posture.

"Repeat after me," he ordered. "I promise I will keep the rules of my group — "

"*Repeat*" urged Sister Manley.

"— the rules of my group," the Ruler's voice took on a steely note.

Lesley gave in. This religious shit meant nothing to her one way or another. But she dared not leave this mad house until she'd found herself a job. So she began to follow the rigmarole, and after she had made another couple of promises she did not mean to keep she found the rest of the congregation joining in and the repetition, the companionship, the breathy, warm, ill-spoken support all round her carried her back to those early school days, softening her resistance, filling her eyes with most unaccustomed tears.

The meeting ended with the Ruler helping her to her feet, shaking hands with her, turning to the dozen or so girls, three older women and two bearded young men to present her as Lesley Rivers, before turning away towards the door.

Lesley tried to smile at the new friends surrounding her. They did not seem enthusiastic, but neither were they hostile. In fact most of them showed complete indifference, just stood looking at her, until she began to feel embarrassed and turned away to find Sue just behind her. Instinctively she took the hand thrust towards her by her room-mate.

"Let's get out of here," she muttered. "Worse than a bloody church! Did they do all that to you when you came?"

"Oh yes. But I wanted it. I needed it then. That was what I came for."

"But you know better now?"

"Hush!" Sue looked terrified. Lesley let out a great laugh as they crossed the main front hall again.

A door opened. Sister Gordon, the server of meals, appeared.

"Sister Susan," she said in an urgent voice. "You are excused outdoor work today. Your typing class is to be held at eleven o'clock this morning in the study. Sister Lesley, the wardress wishes to speak to you, at once, in her study."

The girls parted in the hall, going their directed ways.

31

For Lesley it was a slow and detailed ordeal. Her false history had not been invented with anything like the care and detail it needed for the Holy Group. At first Sister Manley kept her standing; she seemed anxious to discover what effect her public presentation had had in softening, as against hardening, her mood, her attitude to her surroundings. But Lesley had spent many years keeping herself to herself, building and preserving a firm barrier between all those put in authority over her.

"I understand you have run away from home. You cannot be here in London without means or luggage with the consent of your parents."

"I have no parents. No real parents."

"Foster parents? Or an institution?"

"Foster parents. But I'm nineteen. Of age over a year. They can't have me back. I'll never go back!"

"You have come to us. We shall guard you. But they may be setting up a search, notifying your absence, calling upon the police for help. Would it not be better to give me their address, so that we can give them news of your decision and relieve their minds."

"No," Lesley said, very calm, totally obstinate.

The questions went on, in groups of enquiry relating to her childhood, her schooling, her religious upbringing, which had been sparing, but persistent.

"I had to attend chapél," Lesley conceded, "for the look of the thing at the shop. After we moved into the house on the private estate."

"Chapel, you said. Was that methodist?"

"Could've been that, or baptist, or congregational. Don't know, I'm sure. Never took all that interest."

Sister Manley considered this a tiresome lie, which it was, but she kept her patience and moved on to questions of health, illness in hospital, any operations?

Lesley boasted she had never been ill, properly ill, in her life. After this statement, given in a rough, loud tone, she was silent. Sister Manley was silent, too.

Then Lesley said, in a small, but urgent voice, "I came to

32

London to find a job, Sister Manley. I must really start looking. Where do you go to find the nearest labour exchange?"

It was the first sign of breakdown, of weakness, as usual, the wardress thought. She said gravely, "You are not yet ready, Sister, either mentally or emotionally, to take up any paid work. Oh, I know you have told me you are fully trained as a shop assistant, but you have no references and can give me no name or address of any employer. So we cannot recommend you yet."

"But I can't just sit on my — can't just *stay* here — "

Sister Manley turned to her desk and began to write on a wide loose-leaved file. Lesley, tired of standing, moved slowly to the door and reached for the handle. Sister Manley's voice made her jump.

"Lunch is in the dining room at one o'clock. Before that you will have made your bed and swept and dusted your room. At three o'clock there is a dressmaking session in the work room. At five there is tea and biscuits; at six you will attend a lecture in the Great Hall. At seven-thirty there is supper. You will find a notice of all these times in the hall near the front door."

Lesley had listened in total astonishment. She had the door open now, pulled it towards her, to splutter some indignant refusals of all such idiotic rubbish.

But Sister Manley's voice overwhelmed her efforts.

"That will be all, Sister. Go now. Close the door. *Close the door.* Go now, Sister. Go!"

4

During the next few days Lesley found herself rushed through an unconcealed crash course of information, mental and physical instruction, in all manner of useful knowledge, semi-professional crafts and domestic skills. In fact the whole basic structure of a regulated way of life, attached most firmly to a system of religious belief that remained vaguely Christian, in a curious, distinctly uncaring puritan mode.

Through it all the girl remained almost completely unimpressed, or rather unmoved. But more than ever warned of the need to hide her real feelings and intentions, whenever they were threatened. To resist, too, as she had done from the moment she was handed over to her foster parents' care from the Home where she had passed her infant years.

This attitude to life had prevented her from ever understanding her fellow men, except in a very wary sense her schoolmates, both boys and girls. She understood in time their ability to wound or frustrate, never their softer or more intelligent attitudes. She was aware of evil as it was applied to herself. She was totally innocent of good, which she invariably considered weakness, if she considered it at all.

Her practised technique of hidden resistance was largely understood in the Holy Group, but not to this degree, for she had shown them so far nothing but rude and hostile behaviour. Sister Manley, practised in all the skills of will-breaking, was stimulated rather than annoyed by Sister Lesley's underhand ploys, her excuses that did not sound like the lies they really were, her unembarrassed attitude to disclosure, her loud,

34

clearly impertinent laugh with the seemingly sincere apology.

Of course the problem of her future was not a simple one. No one was more sure of it than Lesley herself during all the time they were trying to break her in to their peculiar ways. All this time she was trying to make *them* find her a job, or at least put her on the way of discovering one for herself. She had moments of real alarm when she did try to understand why the Group was so bent on ruling its followers. And why so many of them were girls. She had never seen more than three or four young men at the services in the Great Hall. Sister Manley said this was a Sisters' House; that there was a Brothers' House in a neighbouring road and more in the northern districts of the capital.

When she heard about the extent of the activities of the Holy Group she was amazed. She began to realise her own ignorance. Was it the fault of her upbringing? Was it her non-parents, as she had chosen to call them at school to her class-mates? Well, live and learn. It was a rum world, and no mistake. But she must find herself a job soon. Or cut loose. She found she was already becoming reluctant to do so.

At about this stage Sister Manley, aware of ultimate defeat in regard to Sister Lesley, decided to recommend to the Ruler that she be allowed to join a collecting party.

"It is imperative she be allowed more activity," she explained to him, in his comfortable office at the neighbouring male Group House. "It is surprising that she seems to have had a good grammar school education but has no standards of any kind, no means of acquiring any, either. Reasoning powers, I think I mean."

"The peasant mentality? That should be profitable, surely?"

"Oh no, not peasant. And not practised; that should go with it. That should respond to order, to ritual, to community magic. But she is hopeless at manual skill, too. Except in physical self-defence, I'm told."

The Ruler's little eyes had an instant gleam in them.

"Perhaps she is not yet trying to learn?"

"That, yes. But at her grammar school. She says she got five

O levels there. But left at sixteen to be trained as a shop assistant. In her foster father's shop, only, though."

"And that is what she wants to be here in London, a shop assistant?"

"Yes. But even so she seems to be totally unable to consider the real facts of her position. Unaware of them. No method in her thought. How did they manage to teach her, to get those O levels?"

"I think," said the Ruler, after a pause, "that they were trying to nurture her 'creativity', don't they call it? These same ignorant teachers, with their false ideals and their jargon and their ill-temper when criticised."

He chuckled softly, a mirth so cold, yet so venomous, that even Sister Manley felt chilled by it, her devotion to duty, however arduous, weakened.

The Ruler noticed her discomfort. He became brisk, helpful. His long, graceful fingers shuffled Lesley's small file of papers together and pushed them over to the wardress.

"It might help us to find out where she comes from if we could discover more about those O levels," he suggested. "I think she lies. I think she is not using her real name. If no Lesley Rivers appears to have attended any Midland school, grammar or comprehensive with an achievement of five O levels three or four years ago, we may be justified in accusing her of lying." He paused, smiling again as he stroked the file in its blue cover. "And then you may suggest that she tells you her real name, with a hint of sanctions if she still refuses to speak the truth."

"And until then?" Sister Manley herself was all submissive now. 'Sanctions' always upset, her, taking her back to that —

"Meanwhile," the Ruler continued, quite aware of the effect of his words upon his loyal wardress, "you may send her out upon our collecting mission in Upper Polson Street and Brindley Square. Show her the list of collectors in those parts and let her choose her companions. Three go together, I think you always arrange?"

"That's right. No trouble from trios. I don't know why not?"

"But I do," said the Ruler, without explaining himself.

Though she was annoyed by the further delay in her search for a real job, real wages and the end of her stay with the Holy Group, Lesley did welcome her new activities and her excursions into the streets near her temporary home. She realised, with a distinct sense of shock, that she had not been more than a few yards from its dreary little front garden in all the weeks, in fact a couple of months, she had stayed there.

Her companions for the collecting tour were Susan Ford and a girl with a smooth lightish brown face, black eyes, an aquiline nose, a black pigtail and a name that sounded like Nana, but looked different written down. She had joined the bedroom of the other two in place of Fran, who had demanded the move. A second encounter with Lesley had sent her screaming with rage and panic to Sister Manley, who had shown no sympathy. To Fran's horror she had expressed merely contempt, but she had moved the defeated bully, warned Lesley to control her hooligan expertise, as she called the latter's practised self defence.

On their first begging expedition the three girls were provided with neat, plain dark blue overcoats to wear with light blue berets, a uniform, Sue told Lesley, they were always given to wear when they went out officially.

"And on our own? Our own things, I suppose? Only I left all mine behind."

"We don't go out on our own," Nana said. She spoke the usual fluent correct English of the Indian sub-continent, with its clipped, staccato accent.

"Not *ever*?"

"We don't need to," Sue added, looking anxious.

Lesley laughed at them both. Pointless one way or the other. She knew where the coats had come from. Sister Gordon had shown her where to find them and taken her also, to unlock the cupboard where they hung on coat hangers.

Turning to the left when they shut the gate behind them, the three girls soon passed the few business establishments, using similar houses to the Holy Group, but single for the most part,

37

not semi-detached. They reached the end of the street, where its name was fastened under the last of the untidy garden hedges. Upper Polson Street, in black on a white ground, but scratched and dented by the abuse of years as the neighbourhood sank from its original Victorian respectability to its present near slum.

"When do we start collecting?" Lesley asked, bored by their silent, slow march. There were few people about.

"Now," said Sister Gordon, who had seen them on their way but now turned back to go home. "Sister Susan, you understand you are in charge? You will take this side of the square first, all together, with old Mrs Trevelyan. Show the others how to make the approach, then split up. You are to complete the square before the lunch hour. You must not be late back."

She grinned at them, adding cheerfully, "Roast pork today, girls! *Crackling*!" She rolled the R to make them laugh, which Lesley thought 'wet' in the extreme. Then she left them.

"You heard what she said about the collecting," Sue told them. "Come on!"

Mrs Trevelyan lived in the corner house. She seemed to be alone there, for she opened the door to them herself and smiled to greet Sue, whom she knew. She was surprised to see her young friend with a tall, very pretty girl beside her and a small coloured girl just behind.

"How time flies!" the old woman said in a kind elderly voice. "Is it really a month since your last visit?"

As Sue nodded, mumbling "Yes, Mrs Trevelyan" she went on, "Wait while I get my purse," then paused, "No, say your piece, dear. I see you are to instruct your friends. I'll stop while you do it."

Sue said, "Thank you, Mrs Trevelyan" and then, clasping her hands and shutting her eyes she went on in a high monotonous tone, "We seek your help, Sister, in our work to the glory of God, the care of the needy, the instruction of the ignorant, the succour of those in danger."

"Wait now," Mrs Trevelyan said. "I will get my purse."

She disappeared into the house, leaving the front door closed

38

but not fastened. Sue gestured to the couple behind her.

"Now you know," she said, more firmly than Lesley had ever before heard her speak. "You start on the other side of the square to this and work up round to meet me halfway across the top end."

"Do we have to get out all that spiel?" Lesley asked.

"Yes, you do. Whichever of you knows it by heart. You've been practising it, haven't you? Anyway you've been given written copies, haven't you?"

The two girls nodded and moved away slowly. Mrs Trevelyan came back with a small sheaf of notes. She handed them to Sue, who counted them before putting them in the small grey velvet-covered wallet she carried.

"Thank you and bless you," said Sue, in the same, clerical, intoning voice she had used before.

"Make it a full month before you come again," Mrs Trevelyan said and shut the door before Sue was fairly down the steps. They heard the lock turn and the bolts snap home.

"Does she really live alone in that great barn of a place?" Lesley asked as they met later before turning home.

"Yes, as far as I know," Sue answered. "How did you get on?"

"All that rigmarole!" Lesley was scornful. "I nearly laughed and wrecked it."

"And you, Nana? Was it all right?"

"They gave me *nothing*," the little Indian girl said bitterly.

Lesley explained that their luck had varied. At one door they pushed the bell, they heard it ring clearly, but no one came to answer it, nor when they repeated twice, at short intervals.

"They may have been out," Sue said, doubtfully.

"Someone was watching us from the next floor up," Nana pointed out. "I saw her behind the curtain. She was looking at me. She did not want to speak to me."

"Better than coming down to send you away or shout at you," Sue tried to console the race-conscious girl. "They can be nasty. Not all are like dear old Mrs T."

"That's right," Lesley agreed, unaware of the impatient contempt in her own voice.

39

Nana made no answer to this. Certainly it was better not to get into quarrels with the neighbours, Lesley thought, and who except funny old crackpots like Mrs T. as Sue called her, would want to waste money on the Holy Group, an outfit she was beginning to have very serious doubts about. This money raising lark? What was the point, for heaven's sake? At the present rate she and the other two had been at it for nearly an hour and made just about ten quid, probably. Nana nil. She, herself, four and a couple of ten pence bits, Sue perhaps six quid or so, counting in those four pound notes Mrs T had passed her. Ten or eleven quid and no more would come out of Brindley Square. This money was gross. She had already decided that the net sum handed in would not quite correspond. How she wangled that would take some working out, but it could be done.

From the top of the square they moved towards the Group house down a road parallel with Upper Polson Street, working the houses turn by turn about. Most of the owners provided no response, like so many in the square. Three of them drove the supplicants away with acid rejection or open abuse that called for a spirited answer from Lesley, quickly suppressed by Sue. But the last house on their side of the road was occupied by a number of separate flats, with an open outer door merely closed and a line of named bells beside it. Four flat-owners appeared: all were friendly and though their individual gifts were less than Mrs Trevelyan's their total sum from the house came to twelve pounds, given in small notes and some coin.

Lesley took the money on this occasion, dealt with it, made a note of the amount, while Sue pronounced the usual blessing. At the end of the whole outing Lesley decided that a small profit was certainly possible and that asking for donations was a good deed, less effort than selling goods over a counter and far easier to win her desired cut out of the takings.

But of course it did not, could not, last long. The Holy Group, as a predatory body, experienced, highly skilled, used to dealing among its inmates with every kind of petty crime, was not to be raided in this childish fashion. There came a day when Lesley was called to Sister Manley's office, that small room, formerly the downstairs cloakroom of the original house. In her innocence and total ignorance of the real inner meaning of the Holy Group, she went there expecting praise for her work with Sue, or perhaps news of some agreeable job that would end her very restrictive stay in the place. Her reception astonished her.

"Sister Lesley," the wardress began as soon as Sister Gordon had ushered her into the office and had shut the door behind her, "Sister, it has been made clear to me, that you have been meddling with the sums collected on your charitable rounds. We know what was given to the cause by our well-wishers. Money presented to the leader of your collecting party, that is Sister Susan, she takes, together with your own and Sister Nana's collectings and stores in the Group wallet. At the same time she records the amount in a separate small book she carries. The same procedure with Sister Nana's collections. So that — "

"Nana never gets anything," Lesley broke in indignantly.

"So that," Sister Manley repeated, disregarding the interruption, "so that we know how much each of our kind friends contributes."

"Typical!" Lesley could not help commenting aloud.

Sister Manley's eyes glowed with justified anger at this second interruption, but she ignored it as completely as before, only went on to say, "We find the sum in the wallets does not correspond with that in the recording machine. Can you account for this discrepancy?"

"This what?" Lesley asked, stalling for time.

"This loss. We think you may have taken it."

"I never!"

It was an answer she had learned in her earliest years. From her mother, weak, stupid, dishonest, unhappy, handing her over to the social worker who rescued her from her total neglect in a one-parent home, so-called. It was an answer that never convinced anyone but the social worker that it was an adequate solution of the sad problem of her unwanted existence.

Sister Manley ignored this response.

41

"You should remember," she said, looking away from Lesley now at the file on her desk, "that we have looked after you now for nearly two months, housed and fed you, free of all charge, tried to train you in useful skills. We have met with a poor response, and now this. Open stealing! Theft of gifts given in blessed charity!"

"It was work," Lesley protested, not in the least abashed by the failure of her denial, which had been automatic, the usual start while she rustled up the excuses. "It was work, all that traipsing round and the blarney! You give Sue some back, don't you? And she's here for good, isn't she? Came to you on purpose, poor little — "

"She came to us for peace and comfort and spiritual enlightenment, for communion of spirit, for sacred companionship. We offer her a little pocket money from time to time."

"Why not me, then? Pocket money."

"Because you have been allowed to keep what you came with. We have not asked for payment in cash, only in kind."

"To waste on stamps and letter paper. Why can't I get out on my own to the nearest labour exchange? Why do you always put me off? You know my writing isn't all that good, no more my spelling."

Sister Manley made an impatient gesture. This girl, Lesley Rivers, or whatever her real name was would never in any way be profitable to the Holy Group. That would be her personal recommendation to the Ruler. He must take what action he saw fit in her case'

She dismissed the girl, who went away unchastened, but thoughtful. She quite genuinely had no conception of the real meaning of the word 'steal'. To her stealing meant burglary, house-breaking, big raids on banks. Not petty snitches of cash in handbags, tills, pockets, cheating the Income Tax. Not following the foster parents' own behaviour in their shop, raiding the till as they felt inclined, a habit they must have known she followed, though they never accused her of it, perhaps because they understood what went on, how complicated, how impossible to unscramble. When is your property not your own? Lesley's average intelligence, poorly

42

taught, could not tell her.

But the Ruler, outraged by the revelation of her guilt, taught her the first of the lessons that had come her way. In a lecture on the principle of Mine and Thine, the nature of living by a system of Principle, enforced by Discipline, he showed her very plainly, in very plain, unflattering words, that her behaviour had been bad and that it would not be tolerated.

Lesley was appalled. Not only did she have to stand in his presence while he sat in his carved armchair on the dais in the Great Hall, but he did not shout at her, any more than Sister Manley had, but spoke quite softly; only the words stung and smarted, they gave her no opportunity for counter abuse.

In the end he broke her. She collapsed into bitter tears and dry sobs, humiliated beyond endurance and for the first time for many years driven into honest confession.

This called for and received a formal pronounced forgiveness, followed by a kind of purification ceremony, for which several members of the staff and older group members came into the Hall, summoned by the Ruler's bell. Lesley found herself promising never to steal again, to understand and obey the laws of property, to live an honest life. She would repay what she had taken and also pay a fine from her remaining private means.

When the company had broken up, the Ruler said to Sister Manley, "That girl is properly afraid, but she is not repentant. She has very little natural understanding. A pity, since she is healthy and strong and not over-emotional. And with her looks, considerable attraction. But watch her carefully, Helen. It will be a long battle, I think. But a challenging one."

Sister Manley knew what that meant and regretted it. She believed in the Holy Group and its work with all her cold, power-loving heart, but she had witnessed some dangerous excesses on Brother Mervyn's part. Even before he became Holy Ruler in place of the old leader. Girls like Lesley Rivers were bad for Mervyn Grant, very bad. Better to let the girl go, to encourage her to go. But very quietly, very carefully.

There must, at all costs, no, not at *any* cost, she corrected her thoughts, be any more nicking of the collecting box.

5

After what she considered, though she did not to herself use the word, that outrageous piece of play-acting on the part of the so-called Ruler, Lesley took her wild indignation to her friend Sue Ford. As she poured out her story of the row, "Got up to sound like a bloody trial," the overall injustice of the cruel things he had said to her overset the original cause of the trouble, while the indignation grew, until Sue interrupted her at last to protest mildly. "But Les, you did nick some of the takings, didn't you? You did keep some of it back for yourself and mix the bags to look all alike. Only we were all supposed to keep separate lists of what went into our personal bags. I did anyway. I don't know about the others. Nana never got much."

Lesley could not help laughing.

"You little sneak!" she cried. "And I never noticed you! Nana got damn-all. That I do know."

"You were too busy at your own stealing," Sue protested, defending herself. "Didn't anybody ever tell you it was wrong? Nobody ever explain about fraud and burglary and robbing banks and that?"

"Oh, real crime! Of course they did. Always on about the shop's insurance — how much the premium had gone up. But more for damage and breakages than for stealing. But Uncle takes out of the till whenever he feels inclined."

"I suppose the money there is his? Uncle is what you call your foster father?"

"That's right. Uncle and Aunt. Oh yes, he helped himself. So did she."

"Did you ever take any from there?"

"No fear." She saw the unbelief in Sue's eyes. "Well, yes. To come away with."

"Didn't you? Earlier on? You can't mind telling me."

Sue's eyes filled with tears. Lesley gave in.

"Well, yes. Now and then. But I stole from home in the end. Out of Aunt's handbag. To get away. I had to."

Sue said nothing. After a minute Lesley said, in a casual voice, hiding her genuine curiosity, "Were you just fed up at home or was it a row?"

Sue's tears fell freely.

"Not a row! We never had rows, but strict! Always had to say what time I'd be in and an almighty shindy if I wasn't exactly on time. So I had to get away for a bit and I saw this advertised in the local paper and then one of the girls at my school said she'd come with me, so we asked our families . . . "

"Who said no, I suppose?"

"Not all of them. My mum called it nonsense, but Dad said I'd best find out for myself and he'd pay for a month and that'd be long enough."

"When's it up?"

Sue bent her head; the tears were still flowing. At last she said, miserably, "I liked it at first, the seriousness, the services, the straightforward companionship, the old Ruler, kind, explaining, strict, of course, but most of us needed it because we'd had no rules at home that made sense, only this fear of letting us go about on our own, with friends, of course. I never had to go on my own. I mean with a boy-friend. I hadn't got one. Only girls."

"So what went wrong here?"

Sue dried her eyes, pulling herself together, clearly frightened of her own outburst, her unseemly heart-pouring.

"Didn't you report back to Dad when the month was up?" Lesley asked, as no answer seemed to be forthcoming. What a poor little nut Sue was. She'd chicken out of anything.

"Not at once." Sue's voice was low, despairing.

"But when you did?"

"My letters never reached them."

45

"Why not? How d'you know?"

"They came back undelivered." Sue shivered.

Lesley was puzzled.

"I don't understand. Changed their address or something?"

"I don't know. I don't *know*!"

Sue broke into terrified, rapid speech. "At first I thought they were angry, then that they'd given me up. But I'd written at once when I got here, so they knew my address. Besides, I gave Dad the brochure about the Group right at the beginning. But not a word! Never a word! So now I'm wondering, no, I think I believe, *They've done it*! Sister Manley always wants converts, as she calls the new people who come. She means the ones who don't absolutely need to stay, because they've nothing to live on or anywhere to go. But people dedicated, as they call it. Only I'm not now. Not any more. Oh, not, not . . . "

"How long has this been going on?" Lesley asked.

She was embarrassed by the other girl and wished she would stop telling her dismal story. It sounded particularly silly, coming from someone who had real parents she liked and a home without privation or rows of any kind. So she repeated her question.

"Nearly two years," Sue sobbed.

"Good God!"

This brought Lesley's casual indifference to an abrupt stop. This was serious. Here was a kid she judged to be about her own age, who had tried something that didn't work and seemed to be unable to reverse it. Not altogether her own fault, either. She might have seen earlier this was a rum set-up, with a lot of half-scatty characters in charge. Why hadn't she simply got on the blower to her family, months ago?

In a quieter voice after her shocked exclamation, Lesley said, "Couldn't you insist on using the 'phone, or sending a wire by 'phone or simply walking out to the nearest police station?"

Sue answered wearily, "I think they've given me up. At least Mum has, I think. I don't think they've had any of my letters and so I think they don't want to disturb me and they think it's better to leave me alone."

46

Her eyes filled again, but she had exhausted her grief for the moment. Lesley, watching her and thinking over what she had heard, began to plan more carefully and fully on her own account. She did not believe Sue could be as helpless as she seemed. It simply wasn't natural. So she decided that more serious effort on her part ought, and surely would, have results. She would study advertisements in the papers, the commercial ones, like those they used to have in the shop at home. With a pang she blamed herself for not consulting them before she ran away from home. Nothing to be really afraid of there. Not like this Ruler, as he liked to call himself. All that palaver over her keeping some of the takings. Hadn't she worked for them? It wasn't everyone who'd want to throw away good money for a crazy set-up like the Holy Group. Holy balls!

So Lesley set about collecting names and addresses when she was given back her collecting box and allowed to go out with a different set of girls on their charitable mission. Where possible she took a newspaper from an untended stall; sometimes she asked leave to look at the jobs list; she occasionally bought a paper, tore out the pages she needed and threw the rest away. She used her remaining store of cash for this, carefully, reluctantly, but without raiding her collecting box as long as her small store lasted.

She applied for several posts as shop assistant, for which she knew she was quite well trained. To her bitter disappointment she had no answers. She posted her letters in the box on the outer wall of the corner shop at the end of the road, which sold tobacco and sweets and was a post office as well. But she had no answers to any of her applications. Nevertheless, she continued her search. When Sue, who knew what she was doing, suggested the Labour Exchange as the right place at which to apply, she objected, first, because neither she nor Sue knew where to find it and secondly, more importantly, because Lesley guessed that the people at the Labour Exchange would never be satisfied with her story but would suspect that she lied and might start the ball rolling to drive her home again, which she swore she would never risk, even if the Group held on to her for ever.

Sue, confused and terrified by her own helplessness, made no more suggestions, except to say that she often wondered if Sister Manley sorted the post every day when it arrived and perhaps kept back letters she did not approve of.

This was a new idea for Lesley and she found it a suggestive one. She took to going into the main front hall early in the morning when she judged the postman might be expected to push mail through the wide letter box and perhaps she would be quick enough to find it unsorted and so could test Sue's suggestion.

It was on one such morning that she came across two people in close and active conversation. She recognised them both and stopped at the foot of the stairs, staring.

"Why!" plump Sister Brook said, advancing, while her companion turned his back, but did not move away! "It must be, let me remember, Sister Lesley, Lesley . . . "

"Rivers," said Lesley. "You spoke to me at the coach station. You got me into this place."

Sister Brook's face contracted. Nervous alarm showed in her little eyes, together with a certain spiteful anger.

"You are looking very well," she said, remembering her mission, her salary. "You are happy, I trust?"

"I'm looking for a job," Lesley said. "That was nearly six weeks ago. I haven't found one yet and I don't look like finding one either. They don't help" she added. "In fact quite the opposite."

"Why do you say that?"

All Lesley's real frustration destroyed her caution.

"I write letters for jobs. I don't get answers."

The man behind Sister Brook turned round abruptly and made for the door. But Lesley had recognised him. It was the bloke who had helped her on the bus, helped to push her into the trap that had swallowed Sue and had a grip on herself.

She called out, "Reg! Stop! I want to talk to you!"

But he only grinned broadly at her and disappeared into the street.

Sister Brook laid a hand on her arm. Her face had recovered its benevolent shape and expression.

48

"Patience, my dear," she said as kindly as when they first met.

"Patience and gratitude for the safety of your living here. Work will come to you in time. And now I must speak to your wonderful Sister Manley."

Lesley watched her go. This encounter had been a shock for the insight it gave her into the Group's method of recruitment. It was clearly wider and more organised than she had imagined. Why did they do it? To save girls like herself from the streets? If she hadn't been choosey she could have started on that line while she was still at school. Most of her boy-friends in the early days had expected it. She knew all the gossip, correct and false, that travelled round any secondary school at the adolescent level. Her own affairs had never gone further than very uninspired petting and kissing sessions. They had done nothing to break her overall obsession, which remained the longing to leave the shop, and her foster parents, those two guardians who had never shown her any real affection and did not now try to hide their growing dislike of her. They had not disapproved of her boy-friends, rather had encouraged them.

Lesley stood in the hall for several minutes after Sister Brook's solid figure passed into Sister Manley's office. Her mind was filled with memories of former failure; failure to accept the foster parents from the very beginning, failure to love them or be loved by them; too old at five, to settle as an only child, anywhere. Failure to love any of those diffident boy-friends, the ones her own circle called 'dim'. She had never been aware of her dissatisfactions so sharply as now, after meeting Sister Brook again, but she had never understood them in words, having very little knowledge of words, having heard since she was born only a poor, limited number of them at the Home of her babyhood and having understood less than their total, even so.

Sister Gordon, bustling through the hall, found her standing there.

"Waiting for someone, Sister?" she asked.

"Me? No." Lesley hesitated. Her perplexity was still with

49

her, her need clamorous. "Only — " She gulped and went on. "That fat old woman! Brook, she calls herself. It was her got me in here!"

"You've seen her, I suppose?" Sister Gordon nodded several times. Old Brook has this effect sometimes, she thought, the cunning old devil.

Sister Gordon said, "Not to worry. Look, I was just going to run out to the corner for a packet. Old Ma Dill keeps my kind for me. You go and fetch them, dear. Just say for Sister Gordon. She puts them down to the House. You don't need any cash."

Lesley went at once, her small mind clearing with Sister Gordon's instructions, for they were the first familiar-sounding words she had met since she entered the Holy Group. Small errands to a corner shop, no cash but a little addition to a small account. Those rough bits of paper, those entries on margins of cash books, that major entry called 'Sundries', she knew it all. And she saw a loophole here for her own urgent need to find some solution. It would take time and great care to work it out. But if she could line herself up with Sister Gordon in Mrs Dill's good books and favour, get her replies to letters of application addressed to the corner shop, then there might really be some genuine answers. And a few perks on the side put down to the Group as if by Sister Gordon. All worth a trial, anyhow.

Lesley put on her best manners at the corner shop. Mrs Dill, wooden-faced but sharp-eyed, summed her up without difficulty. The message and request from Cissie Gordon was nothing new, but the messenger was unexpected. Midlands accent, she decided, judging from tele, so another of these 'left home' strays. She must have a word with Cissie, must know what she meant to do for the kid. Genuine help to find a job, genuine mail, or phoney introduction to Sam's lot. Well, that business wasn't doing too badly. It wasn't her own job to interfere. The girl's looks were O.K. if the manner was a bit off-hand, well, northern, rough. Could you wonder at it? Cooped up in that place — Holy Group! Holy shit! —

Lesley's traffic with the corner shop prospered. About once

50

a week Sister Gordon sent her on an errand, to which she added her own small wants, putting them in on the same list and posting her letters of application at the same time. Most of these letters went unanswered but occasionally now Ma Dillon had a typewritten envelope for her, though in each case the position she sought was already filled.

It was inevitable that Lesley's new friendship, her obvious connection with Sister Gordon, should attract the attention of Sister Manley, who marked the girl's improvement in manners and seeming contentment.

"You are having a good effect on her, Sister," she said to the chief supervisor and server of meals. "I have discussed this with the Ruler and we think she is ready to be employed, but not where she must handle money."

"What did you think of?" Sister Gordon asked meekly.

"The organising of menus, the arrangement of the main meal," Sister Manley said vaguely. "I would introduce her as your assistant."

"I think she should really find genuine work outside," Sister Gordon insisted. "She will never be really one of us."

"You may be right. But Brother Mervyn does not agree. He is determined to win her to our faith."

Sister Gordon shivered, but did not dispute the Ruler's right to have his wish prevail.

Lesley was told of her promotion. It gave her the privilege of a room of her own, which she felt was promotion, though Sue was upset to be left with Nana and a newcomer of Welsh extraction, though the latter had been put in charge of a knitting machine section of very backward girls and had lost interest in getting to know her room mates, now that she had gained fuller scope in her daily activities.

"She'll never help me as you did," Sue complained tearfully.

"Let me know if this one copies Fran and I'll sort her," Lesley answered.

She meant what she said, but she did not take any trouble to find out if Sue actually suffered by her absence. For she had a real purpose again and she was pursuing it with all her renewed energy. Success was still delayed. But she continued to put applications through Ma Dill, and got back more answers, so far all negative, but at least she was in touch with the outside world. The trouble was the outside world wanted to know more about her history and her background than she was prepared to give. How could she? She had run away, taking money from the till. She had struck down, perhaps killed, an old woman and taken money from her victim. She could not give references, not even from the Group, because Sister Manley had said that stealing was worse than a sin, it was a disease with her. Rubbish, that! Everyone nicked things. At the Home, then with the non-mum and dad, even now with Sister Gordon, (Cissie, she called her in private), at the corner shop. Surely in time someone would turn up who didn't make such a fuss over references, who would want to see her for an interview, when she could pull it off, she felt sure.

The trouble was the waiting. And the need for stamps for her letters and those stamped addressed envelopes Ma Dill advised her to put in with her letters of application. Also the talc and the scent and the eye shadow, in preparation for the interview.

She practised making up her face, but without powder or lipstick, which were forbidden indoors, though a minimum of each, just sufficient to look young, fresh and appealing, as judged by Sister Manley, was allowed on the begging round, especially to Mrs Trevelyan in her house at the corner of Brindley Square. The old lady's eyesight was failing, but not her charitable inclination. She was a property to be pursued as the Ruler, Brother Grant, insisted. Let the girls who went to her house with their boxes look well in every sense of the word. He authorised the purchase of the make-up powder and lipstick, issued by Sister Manley. Lesley refused to wear it as well as her eye-shadow.

"I'd feel a right Charlie," she explained. "That muck's been out of fashion for years, Sister Manley."

Brother Grant had to be told of this minor rebellion. His deprecating little chuckle saddened Sister Manley, but she agreed to make no objection to Lesley's refusal of face powder and continued to obey him in this as in all of his commands.

So Lesley continued to strive for some work with a wage that would provide her with a living, and she became so used to managing the payment for this struggle in ways familiar, but totally unapproved of, that it came to her with no sense of shock, but merely surprise, when Sister Manley sent for her one evening.

"In the office," Sister Gordon said, bringing the message.

"Why not her room? It's after tea, Cissie," Lesley objected.

"Don't call me that, Sister. And you ought to know, you bloody silly little bitch!"

"Well, I don't. You'll have to tell me."

"Sister Manley'll tell you. In her office."

Sister Manley was unlike herself: nervous, almost tearful.

"We thought, after your promise on your knees, there would be no more of this trouble, stealing. But Sister Gordon's audit yesterday showed discrepancies that indicated you, as her assistant. I'm not going to give you the detail. You must know it all yourself. A more wicked, callous, theft of charitable funds . . ."

"Not me!" Lesley shouted. "Not fucking well me this time! Who orders us make-up to get money from the poor in the big houses? Who orders this and that on the quiet and the Group pays for it? So can't I have a bit, too? To get myself a job when you try to stop me all the time. Why . . ."

Sister Manley got up from her chair, took a quick step forward and with her flat hand struck Lesley across her open mouth.

The girl, who had jumped up from her chair as she began her protest, staggered back and was caught and held by strong hands on either side. The room seemed to have filled silently since the interview began.

"To the Hall!" Sister Manley ordered and Lesley found herself pulled and pushed along the corridors and into the great meeting place, darkened now except for the upper end, where Brother Mervyn Grant sat robed and majestic on the wide chair of office, high on the dais.

Furious, but terrified, her lower face smarting, her lip

53

bleeding where it had been caught between her teeth, Lesley found herself forced once again into a kneeling position before the Ruler. Only this time her right arm was seized and bound quickly to a board wheeled forward on a tripod. One strap fastened her hand, palm down, another fastened her arm about eight inches above the wrist.

The Ruler, leaning forward, his little eyes gleaming in his plump, pale face, began to speak.

The same old god-awful shit, Lesley thought, — must be bonkers, rank, raving bonkers — thinks she's scared — I won't scare — can't do —

"You have proved yourself incorrigible," the Ruler concluded, "You have promised and broken your promise. You must be taught in such a way that you will never forget, but always remember. Every time you will look at your right arm you will see the sign of your guilt, the sign of a thief. For that is what you are, a THIEF!"

From the room in darkness voices moaned, "A thief! A thief! A thief!"

And now Lesley saw a red glow appear at Brother Grant's side as a figure in a long black gown stepped forward and the Ruler rose, holding out his right hand, pointing to her bound right arm.

"I order, as a meet punishment for your sins, repeated after promises and warnings made, those promises broken, to suffer branding with the letter T upon your flesh, so that forever more you may be reminded of your sins and may sin no more!"

Lesley, appalled, saw the branding iron, glowing brighter and brighter, brought close, by the black-gowned figure. She opened her mouth to scream and found a thick pad forced against it, stopping her breath.

The glowing brand came down. Unbearable pain struck her wrist, darting up her arm, across her neck, while the smell of burning, her own flesh, her own skin being destroyed by fire, horrified and sickened her. In an extreme of fear, despair and shock, Lesley slid into unconsciousness.

6

Lesley's recovery from her collapse in the Great Hall followed
a very unusual course. That she should faint from the shock
and severe pain of her punishment was only to be expected.
The occasion had been managed with the intention of making
a lasting deterrent impression upon her. A full muster had
gathered of all the thirty brothers and sisters making up this
particular Group, which was one of six Houses in various outlying parts of London devoted to the cult they followed. Since
they lived by charitable gifts and grants and had no other solid
means of survival, it was essential to their continued existence
that stealing, in whatever form, must be severely put down.
The Holy Group called themselves a Christian body, so
Moslem punishments for theft, such as the loss of a hand,
could not be given. Branding, as applied by Brother Mervyn
Grant to the erring Sister Lesley Rivers, was intended to have
a terrific effect upon the whole community, gathered to
witness it.

And so it did. There were five faintings beside Lesley's; two
mentally weak Sisters went into hysterics, one Brother, known
to suffer from petit mal, had one of his minor epileptic fits, and
young Brother Benjamin Shaw, who had, following exact
instructions, applied the branding iron, suffered an immediate
revulsion and flung the still-hot weapon in the direction of the
Ruler, only missing his sandalled foot by a bare inch.

Lesley was expected to come round from her faint if turned
on her side and left lying on the floor. She did so, but after a
few sobbing breaths, sank again into unconsciousness, from

which she did not at once recover but stayed, eyes shut, scarcely breathing, her pulse faint, her body limp.

They carried her to her room and put her to bed. The Hindu girl, Sister Nana, who still shared the bedroom with Sue, was moved into Lesley's new room to look after her. Nana had escaped to the Group from her family in Bedford because they wanted to marry her to a Hindu man recently arrived in England, whom she had not yet met, but knew to be over thirty years old.

Nana spoke very little English because she had come to England too late to profit at all by attending a large state school for only two years. Her mother knew no English, nor would ever try to learn any. But Nana knew of a few simple remedies for burns to the skin, particularly cooking burns on hands and arms. So, supplied with a variety of dressings and antibiotic ointment and bandages, she wrapped up Lesley's ruined wrist and roused her enough to make her swallow pills and fluids.

For three days Lesley remained in a state of near coma, watched over by Nana, impassive but careful, who gave way to Sister Manley and Sister Gordon, but to no one else. And particularly not to Sister Susan Ford, whose loud screams before Lesley's collapse at the branding ceremony had been heard in the street outside. A small crowd had gathered and watched as Ma Dill, fetched from her shop, and Constable Torch from his beat, had consented to go up to the front door and ask for Cissie Gordon.

It had been a near thing and continued to be talked of in the local pubs, Cissie had explained afterwards. The people thereabouts knew quite well they had in the Group a fair lot of crackpots, near loonies, likely to go off their rockers if overexcited.

"They'd better not go really round the bend," Sister Manley said indignantly, as if she had any power to arrange the matter. "Not with Mervyn in his present mood," she added. "Keeps wanting to lecture the girl to confirm her repentance. Won't listen when I tell him it's a doctor she needs, not a lecturer."

"She spoke to me today," Sister Gordon said. "Not like

herself, very weak and listless, if you know what I mean."

Sister Manley nodded. She knew very well this symptom of spiritual defeat, this painful conversion to humility, to contrition. But she doubted its permanence in Lesley's case. The girl had an unusually strong ego, totally self-directed. She might always be a source of danger to the Group, as her basic ignorance of ordered moral behaviour had shown very clearly. In her confusion of mind, of how best to regulate the girl, Sister Manley decided to consult old Mrs Trevelyan in the big house at the corner of Brindley Square.

"Brought up by young parents who were killed in a car crash, she says now," Sister Manley explained. "But I think all that is lies. Her attitude to authority of any kind gives her away. Institutionalised I feel sure, or fostered. Real relations very unlikely. She agrees she has run away from home. We have checked with the principal Midland Homes for missing inmates, but have had no luck so far."

"Might she not have been adopted?" Mrs Trevelyan asked.

She was puzzled by Sister Manley's evident distress. Usually so clear and competent and such a blessing to the local bench where Mrs Trevelyan served as a magistrate. On this occasion Sister Manley seemed to feel she was out of her depth. Not like her. Not like her at all.

"If she had adoptive parents they don't seem to want her back," Sister Manley went on. "In any case we have not traced her and she will neither give us her true name, nor her home address, nor any useful information. She pilfers whenever she can. She has been — reprimanded, — punished — and now refuses to make any effort, but lies in bed demanding to be found a job and leave us."

"The punishment," asked Mrs Trevelyan thoughtfully. "What form did that take?"

Sister Manley had mentioned punishment once before when she had come to her for advice. That had been over a case of mugging by one of the young Brothers. The Ruler, new to the position at the time, had beaten the lad with a school-master's cane and the boy had run away a month later. He had not come back to the Group, nor had he returned to his parents, who had twice been in trouble with the police over him.

Mrs Trevelyan remembered this case and the distress Sister Manley had shown and which she showed again now over this girl, Lesley. So she asked again, "What was the punishment, this time, Sister?"

But Sister Manley, pale, desperate, but now in full command of herself, would only repeat that the girl wanted to leave them but must have a good steady job to go to before they could advise her to do so.

Mrs Trevelyan sighed. The Holy Group, dubious as it might be in the eccentric beliefs and organisation of the cult, did have its uses in the local community. It might have many of the faults of other mushroom religious groups, but it took off the streets a number of misfits, petty criminals, fanatics and other unemployables, fed, clothed and housed them, kept them out of prison, off the rates, most important out of the public eye. And all with the help of a minimal charitable grant. Mrs Trevelyan remembered with pleasure the meek, well-spoken, well-mannered girls who came to her door. She also remembered the occasional stories of acolytes who wanted to leave the Group, who spread tales of coercion, bullying, brainwashing, even forcible physical imprisonment.

"You would be best pleased if the girl Lesley, *did* leave?" she asked finally.

"Oh yes. At least, *I* would be pleased. I'm afraid Brother Mervyn would be very disappointed. But I'm afraid if we can't place Lesley, though she seems to be a trained shop assistant, but has no written references of it, she will either force her way out and perhaps try to make a scandal with the police or else go on lying in bed and refuse food or in some other way make us send for a doctor."

"You have Dr Hastings, I believe?"

"We did. But he gave us up. At least, he does come if any of our Group is on his list, but he won't take emergency calls."

"Are you trying to tell me this is really an emergency?"

Sister Manley burst into tears.

Later, restored by strong tea and with an additional charitable gift of fifty pounds in her handbag, the Group

58

Wardress went home. The new gift, she was determined, would be spent in forwarding a plan Mrs Trevelyan had suggested and so it would go into the Reserve Fund, that she had herself set up to cover correspondence and perhaps travel in connection with the case of Sister Ford.

Not Lesley at all. Her friend Sue. How the former would laugh, Sister Manley thought, as she hurried past the Group House on Upper Polsen Street to find Mrs Dill at the corner shop. Here she wrote and despatched a brief bulletin to Mrs Ford describing the health and happiness of her daughter, Susan. Sue had had a slight relapse in her recent happy acceptance of the whole life in the Holy Group, but was getting over it. She advised a continuence of the silence from home. Sue's dedication was genuine, her work in the Group was most valuable. It would be a pity to interrupt it. Mrs Ford might rely on her to report any important change in Sister Susan's behaviour and general progress.

While occupied with her report in Mrs Dill's little back office behind the Post office counter, Sister Gordon came into the shop and Ma Dill moved into the main part of the store to serve her. As she reached the part opposite Cissie Gordon she jerked a thumb back towards her office.

"In there," she whispered. "Another put-off for the Fords. Nobody's not told the girl they're ignorant of all that tripe. Wicked shame, I call it."

Sister Gordon shook her head, sadly.

"High jinks up the road, Monday," Ma Dill went on. "Knew they'd have the fuzz in when I hear that screamin' and saw people stop. And so they did."

"Excitable, some of them," Sister Gordon said, not showing any inclination to explain the incident. "I came down to see if you'd got any further over placing young Lesley. She's in a pretty bad way just now."

"How come?" asked Ma Dill calmly, fishing a sweet out of a bottle she had open on the counter beside her, then licking her finger and wiping it on a duster at her elbow.

"Got across Brother High and Mighty? 'Ad wot was coming in a big way?"

59

"That's right'"

"Scream was her, was it?"

"No."

"Friends of 'ers?"

"Sue Ford, of course."

Ma Dill nodded. That letter Sister Manley was writing.

"But Les copped it, did she?"

"In a big way, yes. That's right."

"So wot?"

"So we need the job. Got to get Les away. By now she won't be particular. Persuade her between us. Go halves, if you fix it."

"O.K. dear," Ma Dill saw it was likely to be serious now. She was ready to do her best. But she was never ready to risk damaging her own small business in any way, however great the immediate financial reward, as she called her sordid little bribes.

"O.K.," she repeated as Cissie Gordon seemed to hesitate.

"You have something in mind already?" asked Sister Gordon cautiously. "You understand I'm not a really free agent over Lesley. In fact it's just because she's got more guts than most we get in. And because she's so green, poor kid. Won't tell us why she's come south. You can tell by 'er accent — midlands, but not Brum. And not real north, either. Hasn't a clue. But scared of the Group."

"Can you blame 'er?"

"No. I certainly can't! Now. I'd have gone to the fuzz and showed them up straight off. Only she passed out and when she came round she went into a sort of coma."

Ma Dill's thin lips drooped.

"Conned you all, 'as she?" she asked, fishing up another sweet from the bottle on the counter. But this time she offered the bottle to Sister Gordon, who felt obliged to take one because she feared to insult so useful an auxiliary.

She decided not to press Ma Dill any further. So, with renewed expressions of gratitude in advance, she left the Post Office-Newspaper-Sweets shop and went back to the Holy Group.

60

Sister Manley, after finishing her letter to Mrs Ford, had listened to all she could hear of this conversation in the shop. It was obvious to her from the moment the caterer-house-keeper, arrived that she came, not as a customer, but on behalf of that trouble-maker, Lesley Rivers. Sister Manley did not hear enough to make it worth while to disturb Sister Gordon's plans, as she described them to herself. Besides, the caterer was a shrewd and careful business woman, doing an austere, unglamorous job and doing it very economically, too. Perks for herself, no doubt. Who, except a religious fanatic, was not marginally corrupt. Except Mervyn, she thought savagely, who was both, and at times seemed to be totally evil, if not mad. Or were they the same thing? Not in law, still. Did not most of the confessed murderers plead not guilty on grounds of irresponsibility? Was an insane killer less evil than a sane one? Neither would hang. Which would be the more dangerous after ten years in jail? If they survived that long?

Sister Manley pressed down the flap of her self-sealing envelope and fixed on the cheaper stamp. She did not consider Sue's case to be wildly urgent. The girl had come to them in a fit of exasperation with a couple of frivolous light-minded parents. She had found the Holy Group altogether too austere, too totally lacking in either emotional or intellectual, or essentially religious fulfillment and naturally wanted to go back and start again in her search for happiness. Her friendship with Lesley was a blind alley. The stronger girl had jolted her out of her simple home-sickness. That could not be reversed either. What a perfect nuisance this Lesley was, Sister Manley decided. Her cold heart, her devotion to order, to discipline, revolted against the confusion brought to the Group in the last few months. This must end.

Ma Dill saw Sister Manley standing just inside the back room of the shop as she turned to wave to Sister Gordon, passing by the window in front.

"I'm not too late for the post, I hope, Mrs Dillon?" Sister Manley said, holding up her letter.

"Give it 'ere, Sister," Ma Dill answered. "I'll see 'ee takes it."

She noted the second-class stamp and thought, 'Stingy bitch!' but her smile remained fixed.

Sister Manley went away happy.

In Lesley's room at the Group house, Nana was changing the dressing on the other girl's arm, just above the wrist. All the swelling had gone down from the hand and lower arm, but the red-hot iron had burned more than the skin; it had destroyed the fat beneath and injured the coverings of the tendons and the wrappings of the wrist joint. Where serum, early infected, (but held in check by the dressings Nana had demanded and been given), had begun to dry into deep, hard scabs, the Indian girl found she could not persuade her patient to attempt the slightest movement. The fingers twitched from time to time. The girl refused even to lift her arm from the bed.

At the end of the first week after the branding, Lesley was fully conscious, her breathing and heart beat normal again, quite vigorous, in fact. But she lay on her back, staring at the door, submitting to Sister Gordon, who came to see her, to lift her into a sitting position, while Nana propped her with pillows; who fed her with a spoon, since she could not lift either hand to feed herself; who neither spoke, nor cried, nor complained; who seemed to be fully conscious and fully in possession of her normal senses, but at the same time gave Sister Gordon a chill feeling of having to feed a dummy, a live person with a recognisable, pretty face and figure, who ate and drank all that was fed to her, who performed the bodily functions in the correct receptacles, who could be washed and dried and combed and brushed in all the usual ways and positions, but was not in the control of any inward spirit, but empty as a worn-out rag doll.

"I've said all along you ought to have had the doctor in to her from the start," Sister Gordon complained to Sister Manley. "Shock, that's what it was. More severe than even *he* bargained for."

"Exactly," Sister Manley answered. "So how could we possibly have had anyone in from outside with her arm — " She made a face of great repugnance, but could not bring

62

herself to describe what she had first shown to Nana.

However, Sister Gordon refused to consider the matter closed. "Shock or mental breakdown or hysteria or whatever," she persisted "I'm not spoon-feeding her ladyship another day. She's fit and ready to pull herself together. It's high time Nana gave over those daily dressings, too. The scab's been dry the last four days. Needs air to loosen it. And exercise to get the hand working again. And some sort of handwork to make her use it."

"Such as?"

"Feeding herself for a start," Sister Gordon shouted, losing control. "Rousing her bloody limbs to get dressed, speaking naturally, not in a whisper. Taking an interest in other people."

"That," said Sister Manley, "I think she never has done. Since we know nothing about her people, except that she has been fostered or adopted, we don't know which, we can't work out how much her unfortunate manners and habits and appearance are inbred and how much the result of her apparently unfortunate upbringing."

The two women continued to argue round and round Lesley's difficult behaviour, each trying to move the responsibility and the treatment from one to the other, perhaps even to an acknowledgement of defeat.

"Mr Grant would never agree," Sister Manley insisted. "I may get him to release Sue Ford because Mrs Trevelyan is interested in her and he's always careful not to let her know about our more severe treatment. But just now he's very disappointed in her for screaming at the punishment service. It was her scream that was heard outside in the road."

Sister Gordon nodded gravely. Then she said, with slow emphasis, "It might not be a bad thing to get Sue to go up to Lesley and try to persuade her to act normal again."

"I wonder." Sister Manley was doubtful and she did not want to link those two very dissimilar natures again. No good had come of their growing friendship. No good, possibly more unwanted obstacles in the way to the timid girl's return home. To keep her now could only spell danger.

"Well, can I or can't I?" Sister Gordon persisted.

"Can you what?"

"Oh, for Christ's sake! Can I send Sue up to her to tell her to get dressed and come down to supper?"

"Yes. And tell her they all miss her."

"That's a bloody lie! They're all scared stiff of her."

"Sister, I cannot have such language in my office."

"Bugger your office!"

"Don't be ridiculous!"

Sister Gordon swept out, slamming the door. She wasn't taking orders from that starchy spinster. But she met Sue near the garden door and Sue asked for news of Lesley.

"Just as sulky as ever," Sister Gordon told her. "Why not go up and see what you can do for her?"

"May I? When I tried before they said not this week, anyhow. She must have been really ill at first. The shock would have been terrific. Can I really go now?"

"Yes, you go. Tell her there's cake today."

Lesley received this news with simple pleasure, as she had also greeted the first sight of her friend.

Sue did not waste time on aimless chat. She went straight to the point.

"You've been very ill," she said. "It was an appalling shock."

"I thought I was dying," Lesley said. "Really and truly, dying. I couldn't move, I couldn't breathe, I couldn't feel my pulse. That was after I found myself in bed. They must have carried me upstairs. I don't remember, only that I kept fading away, not sleeping, fainting I suppose. I felt terrible. I'm sure I was really ill."

"But you've got over all that?"

Lesley smiled, a little careful, wise smile, that offended Sue, because it implied that she, Susan, was silly to be taken in by such old hat.

"I don't think deceit is funny any more than lying or stealing," she protested. "Grinning like that! You mean you're really putting it all on?"

"No I don't! Honestly, Sue, I did feel bloody awful for days.

Nana wasn't much good, but she was there which was a help. It would have been worse without her."

"So now that she's gone you'd better begin to look after yourself again. I've been sent up to help you. Nana brought her things back to our room today."

Lesley stared at her friend, her eyes filling with tears. This astonished her as much as it did Sue, but neither girl took any notice for fear of starting an outburst that both knew would be long, painful and probably profitless.

All the same Lesley did get out of bed and began to dress, opening drawers in the single chest across the room, to sort out some clothes to put on. Meanwhile, Sue discovered a brush and comb and some make-up bottles and pots, pushed into a drawer and arranged them on the rickety little table that stood against the near wall under a mirror.

They did not speak much. At one point Sue, pointing to the bandaged arm said, "Can I see it? Has it healed?"

"No." Lesley was firm. "It's still a mess. Rough scab, drawing up now. Still red all round."

"But what — ? How — ?"

"What will it look like, for the rest of my life? Why, the letter T. Capital T for Thief, of course. To remind me, for ever, when I stretch out my hand to nick something from the shelf or the stand or the till, to beware, to draw back, or next time it will be, not a maiming, but the whole hand, gone for ever!"

"Don't!" Sue shuddered, covering her eyes.

"I'm not quite a fool," Lesley told her. She found the sling she had got Nana to make for her and slipped it over her head and round her opposite shoulder. Then, with her free hand in Sue's and Sue's arm round her waist, the two girls went downstairs to find their supper.

7

The convalescent Lesley Rivers, still in the care of her friend Sue, did not realise at first how differently those in authority at the Group now regarded her. They were expert in hiding their true intentions at all times. In fact, as Sister Manley often warned herself, they, or some of them, seemed to be unsure of what those intentions were. She reminded herself that the Ruler had the last word in all matters of belief and in the enforcement of discipline. Also in all matters of appointment to outside, remunerative work by the inmates. Therefore to anything they were able to find for Lesley, daily becoming stronger, livelier, more dangerous, both to herself and to them.

Sister Gordon was aware of her superior's growing unease. She tried to push Ma Dill into quicker action, but had no success. Until one morning Lesley, sent to post a small parcel for Cissie, came back with a verbal message.

"For Sister Gordon," she said to the door minder as she went in. "No, not written down. Word of mouth." She moved towards the dining hall. "Where shall I find her?"

"Didn't she say?"

Since she certainly had given her probable whereabouts, Lesley moved away with a short contemptuous laugh. This everlasting mystery was enough to make you scream.

"Perkins, is it?" Sister Gordon said.

"Who is Perkins? What does he do?"

"Last couple of months he's kept a health shop in the precinct."

"Where's that?"

"St Andrew's Place — pedestrian precinct. On beyond Brindley Square, down from the bottom of it. Called after that old church, shut up now, presbyterian it was, I believe."

Lesley waited. She asked no more because she did not want to be disappointed.

"What about Perkins?" Sister Gordon asked when Lesley seemed to have dried up.

"Wants to see you, Ma thinks. Or me. Both, to start with."

"Mr Perkins wants to interview you and me? Perhaps for a job in his health food shop," Sister Gordon said firmly. "That it?"

"I wouldn't know." Lesley did not sound very eager. "Did you say health food shop? Another crank, I suppose?"

Sister Gordon stared at her.

"A possible job for you! Hadn't you better go after it, young Lesley? Or shall I tell Sister Manley you don't want . . . ?"

The girl shrank into a white trembling mass.

"No. NO! Health food store? Shop? O.K. I'll go! Perkins —?"

"That's right. Mr Edwin Perkins, Eddie to his friends. Ma Dill thinks he wants an assistant in the shop? Right?"

"Told me to tell you, and to go along with me for an interview, like I said before."

The girl's colour had come back. She put out a hand like a little girl.

"Come with me, Cissie. I don't know how to find this precinct. Can we go now?"

Sister Gordon gave a short laugh.

"O.K. Put on your outdoor coat and tidy your hair? Don't overdo the eye shadow, but the shop won't be another nunnery, of course."

She laughed again, at some private joke, for Lesley had already hurried away.

In St Andrew's place Mr Perkins stood just behind his window display, watching the crowd moving up and down outside.

Not many of them came inside his store, but most of them stopped to look at the window. For it was unusual, as he meant it to be. A sloping board carried a varied display of plants that had nothing whatever to do with health foods, but had a vaguely countrified, natural effect. They were ranged along the front edge of the board, small compact plants in pots, having nothing to do with the dishes of dry grains and fruits behind them. But they appealed, as weekly street markets always appeal, to the stifled natural instincts of the urban citizens milling round flower stalls at all times of the year. Behind the plants, immediately behind, there were a few well-arranged, if rather limp and faded, eatable green vegetables, the more durable root vegetables, the remains of the season's green beans of various kinds. In the centre of these a small cluster of books was crowned by a volume on herbs, history of same and a brief account of their uses over the centuries.

It was a subject to attract any knowledgeable customer and his own early studies made him capable of explaining it to the ignorant.

At the back of the board a row of large dishes held a variety of rice grains and above them, topping the display, there was a short row of exotic fruits, to appeal to immigrants, and which had suggested the name of the shop which was 'Mangoes'.

Mr Perkins did make a few sales of these latter foods to local dwellers, but he knew he would never develop this part of his trade, because there were established greengrocers not far away who supplied the bulk of the foreigners living in those parts.

Inside his shop Mr Perkins had lined one wall with shelves to hold the packets of all those products designed to fight the chronic constipation of a people living in a cold, damp, climate artificially warmed with dry air, taking very little exercise of any kind, and addicted to tobacco and sweets.

Behind his counter on the other side of the shop Mr Perkins had several locked drawers, from which he dispensed the needs of other addictions. Earlier in his career Mr Perkins had been a bright lad, passed from a grammar school to a polytechnic and earned a qualification as a dispensing chemist. But he had not kept in touch with the various changes in the Law respecting drugs, and from being licensed to supply certain narcotic addicts with stated amounts on a doctor's prescription, he

68

found himself without any licence at all and in fact no longer a chemist, but merely a shopkeeper.

Mr Perkins was still, however, an unusually bright lad. So after a while he had picked himself up and with the help of new friends, had started trading again, moving at intervals as convenient, until a short time before he came to settle in St Andrew's Place he was already known to Ma Dill and to the lady tenants in the big house in Brindley Square and to other groups as well.

Mrs Dill had got to know Mr Perkins just as soon as he came to order his newspapers to be delivered at his health shop. He bought sweets from her too. He also got her to stock his miniature cigars for him and after a time she agreed to keep a special line in cigarettes that some of his friends smoked. He brought these cigarettes to her in bulk in the big box for his little cigars: they made the exchange in her office. But when his friends came for the cigarettes, they brought their own empties, which she took from them and went away by herself to fill in her office and give back over the counter.

After a short while Mrs Dill made a different arrangement over the cigarettes. She told Mr Perkins she was going to take a month's holiday from the shop and thought her crippled brother would take charge for her but he could not manage any extra work at all. It was then that she suggested he ought to have an assistant in his shop. If he agreed she could probably put him in touch, without the need to go to the Labour Exchange.

Mr Perkins was disappointed at first: he had been pleased with the arrangement at Mrs Dillon's shop. He wanted to know her real reason for giving it up, without either of them having to discuss it in depth.

"You haven't found it, well, a nuisance?" he asked sadly.

"Oh no, nothing like that," Ma Dill answered. "It'd be a girl from along here," she added.

"You mean that Loony Group, people call it?"

"That's right. Holy Horrors. They've got their hooks into a runaway girl from up north. No family. Stranger in these parts. Cissie wants her fixed with a job. If you was to take 'er

69

into your place, give you a chance to see those friends of yourn outside."

She waited to see this idea sink in through the surface film of fear and suspicion. To her annoyance an obstinate look began to spread over Mr Perkins's face.

"I'll think it over," he said, "But really, Mrs Dill, I'm perfectly satisfied with our present arrangement and I'm quite willing to increase the amount of your er - commission on the cigarettes."

Ma Dill expected this. It annoyed her to learn that he could afford to be more generous, because it meant he must have underpaid her hitherto. It annoyed her even more to be fool-hardy in this undertaking. Her success, all her business life, had been due to caution. She would go to the brink of danger, time and again she had done so, but never beyond it. Some-thing told her, every time, when to stop. As now.

"I'm sorry, Mr Perkins," she said, and she really looked regretful. "But no. Tom's been a cripple ten years. 'E'll only come if 'e can bring one of 'is kids to fetch and carry in the shop. You wouldn't think much of that, would you?"

Mr Perkins did not bother to agree. He simply said, "When d'you go?"

"Fortnight tomorrow."

"Until?"

"End of October."

"And this girl you mentioned?"

"Any time, Cissie Gordon says. They want to fix 'er up."

He turned to go.

"Good-looker, this one is," Ma Dill threw out in a casual voice.

Mr Perkins turned a wry face in her direction. "You don't say," he snarled, spitting juice from his miniature cigar on to the doorstep.

It had been two days after this that Lesley had conveyed Ma Dill's message to Sister Gordon.

They set off together, Lesley very tidy in her uniform over-coat, her hair well brushed out, her eyes fashionably marked. Her skin, profiting from a well-designed, if frugal diet, had a healthy glow not often seen in that part of London.

70

Mr Perkins receiving them politely but without enthusiasm, could not but agree with Ma Dill that the girl had looks. She was also well-grown like so many girls of her age, and well-spoken, as many were not. She looked capable of work in the shop. Not that much of it was any weight to lift or move about.

"I need," he said, looking directly at Lesley, "a second pair of hands in the shop, to take the telephone or the customer when both happen at once. I understand you have some experience in shop work?"

"I've worked in one shop, general grocery," Lesley answered cautiously.

"Groceries," Mr Perkins said, thoughtfully. "Much the same sort of thing here. I don't carry a very varied stock. Many of the items are already packaged in several sizes. Some of the customers like to see the stuff weighed out, though. Especially the different brands of rice. Those people often buy for neighbours as well as themselves and in separate amounts. Large amounts, too. One or two wanted to take away a whole sack on their heads. Disappointed when they found it had come to me in very large cartons and the sort of size they wanted was in thin, soft nylon bags. One of them still comes to get several bags at a time and brings an old pram to wheel the bags away in."

As he described these features of his business Mr Perkins guided Lesley about the inside of the shop, while Sister Gordon stayed near the cash desk, watching their progress and making her own observations. She had not been inside Mr Perkins's shop before. She was able to note dates on some of the perishable foods, by which time they should be sold. All were in order. She remembered that Sister Manley wanted to have a careful and detailed account of the shopkeeper and his business before official leave could be given to Lesley.

"It isn't that I daren't risk her going out to work on her own," Sister Manley explained, with a sort of humility very unusual in her, "I'm sure she can work without too much effort. She has the energy and the intelligence, in a queer restricted way. But she does seem to expose or attract, or in some way bring about unexpected disaster. Well, not exactly disaster — "

71

"Except to herself," Sister Gordon pointed out grimly.

Sister Manley winced.

"We must really get the better of that misfortune," she said.

"I don't attempt to hide it from myself, I dare not."

"You couldn't if you wanted to," Sister Gordon reminded her. "She's wearing a wrist band over the scar now. Got Susan Ford to buy her a strap and buckle at the sports shop. Won't let me see under but Sue says it's quite distinct now. T. Square-cut, straight up and down."

Sister Manley covered her eyes with her hand.

The next morning there was a letter for Lesley among the daily newspapers, addressed to Miss Lesley Rivers, not stamped. It was from Mr Perkins; it invited her to start work at his shop the following morning at 8.30. The shop was opened at 9.00 a.m. sharp. This would be her second duty. The first would be to dust and renovate the window display, to re-fill any bowls needing it, to replace or introduce any fresh foods on offer. Mr Perkins mentioned her wage, (the statutory legal amount) and as an initial concession, he enclosed an order for ten pounds, for which she could sign the receipt in the shop. This would provide any cosmetics and toiletries she liked to choose there after she began her employment.

"I didn't know he sold that kind of thing there," she said to Sue, handing her the letter.

"I suppose he can sell anything he likes if it isn't something you have to be licensed for," Sue answered.

She was surprised that Lesley was not more excited at having found a job at last. But she remembered that the job had been found for Lesley: through the corner shop owner, of course, and she would not, herself, have trusted that beady-eyed little person, but both the Sisters seemed to think it was all right. If they, in turn, were really to be trusted. Sue's doubts were growing, but not her courage. She sighed, gave a weak smile and said, "It's a step in the right direction, anyhow. So good luck and we must be sure to set my alarm clock tonight. You mustn't be late on your first morning."

Early closing day in St Andrews precinct was Wednesday.

Lesley expected to be back at the House by half-past one, when the shop had been tidied and covers drawn over the exposed foods in the window. They would be open again in the morning so she did not expect much clearing up would be needed, though on each of the three days since she began work there had been several customers, each of whom had asked for something different, which she had managed to locate and serve, putting the packet into a take-away thin plastic bag called Mangoes Cuisine in olde-worlde lettering at the top and below Edwin Perkins, herbalist.

Having done what she thought was necessary Lesley went to the cloakroom behind the shop, prepared to take off her overall, put on her coat and leave. She had not seen Mr Perkins since he had closed, locked and bolted the front door of the shop on the stroke of one. She found herself ready to go, wondering which way she was expected to leave.

She had to wait nearly five minutes in the empty shop standing in the middle of the shop floor, until she heard low voices at the back of the building, followed by the sound of a door opening and shutting. She moved towards the sound, which clearly showed her the back way out, but was brought up short by Mr Perkins coming back into his office and surprised to find her nearly running into him.

"Sorry," she said, automatically. "Do I go out that way?"

Mr Perkins flashed an unnaturally angry look at her, but his voice was quite controlled, as he said, "In a great hurry to get back home, aren't you?"

"The Group isn't home. No, not really. But half-day, - I thought I'd be in time for their lunch instead of the sandwich at the pub."

To her surprise Mr Perkins merely said, "Which pub's that?"

"Actually it's the off-licence along the precinct. They've opened a take-away food place next door."

"Run along then."

He waved her towards the shop door; opened half of it and held it while she slipped through. She heard him pushing the bolts fast as she turned to go.

On Saturday Mr Perkins spent the first part of the morning in his office. The precinct outside was crowded, as it always was at weekends. Lesley enjoyed looking at people as much as they enjoyed looking at the health foods. There were now a good many people who enjoyed looking at the pretty girl in the shop even more than at the rice and the beans. When one couple had opened the door and gone in to make enquiries, others followed, from idleness, curiosity, from amusement when they discovered the starchy-looking bespectacled little man in charge.

Most of them bought something. At any rate it was the best Saturday morning Mr Perkins had had since he opened the shop in the precinct and he decided he would keep Lesley as a shop-assistant for the present.

At the end of the morning he told her so.

"The present arrangement satisfies me," he said in a formal voice. "You evidently know the work and how to approach the customer. I hope you find it congenial?"

"Oh yes," Lesley answered, using the casual manner of her generation. She had been flattered at least twice that morning, by a middle-aged husband humouring his wife's fussing over their diet while indulging his sight of Lesley's curves as she bent over the grain bowls, and also by a young man who seemed to know they sold a certain kind of French face powder and thought she must use it herself. Lesley was able to find the identical kind for him, but declared she never used powder, at which the boy's admiration was so marked she nearly laughed aloud.

Mr Perkins was not upset by Lesley's lack of enthusiasm. He did not expect her type, at her age, to behave differently. So he went on "I suggest I now engage you on a permanent basis, with a contract for three months, breakable on either side at a week's notice, or a week's wages in lieu."

"Yes," Lesley said. She was delighted. It was the kind of start she needed. With a reference from Mr Healthfood Eddie, she would get something a darned sight better, move out of the Group in a couple of weeks and find digs, miles away . . . Take Sue with her . . .

74

"Yes — thank you — sir," she said, making a tremendous effort.

"So," said Mr Perkins, who had been watching her very carefully, "we might make a little celebration of the contract at the pub before you go home for the weekend. What d'you say?"

Lesley thought this would be funny, too funny to be much fun. He was so small and thin and old and he wore such enormous glasses. But it was kind and sounded like just a drink —

"I said I'd be in to lunch," she answered sensibly. "I'd better not be too late."

"I think you will be late. Why not ring them up? That lady who came with you the first time?"

"Sister Gordon? Well, I suppose I could."

Sister Gordon was matter of fact. She would not be alarmed if Sister Lesley did not appear until tea-time. Lesley took this as a further loosening of the chains.

Mr Perkins took her to the Swan in the main road near the bottom of Upper Polsen Street. It was not the sort of establishment she would ever have considered going into by herself, nor the sort her foster parents would have used when she was with them.

It was large, brightly lit, a wide expanse of red plush and well-polished brass, crowded on that fine autumn noon, with a blue sky and a brilliant sun low in the sky blinding the drivers of cars, and pedestrians alike. Lesley was grateful for the shining artificial lights in the pub. She had needed the skinny hand of Mr Perkins to guide her blinded steps across the road and she resented it. She recovered quickly as they moved to the bar and she settled on a high stool beside her employer, being soothed as well by the unending, monotonous familiar throb of background music.

It was a super pub, Lesley decided. This was what she had admired, longed for, on the tele. This was natural to her odd little boss, it seemed, for he was recognised and greeted by several men as they looked about them and by one of the barmaids who came directly to them to take their orders.

Mr Perkins ordered for them both, afterwards asking Lesley if that would suit her. As she did not hear what he said, being too much enthralled by the surroundings to pay attention to him, she merely nodded. The glasses, when they arrived, were long tumblers, not of the wine variety, so definitely not champagne, Lesley decided. Silly of her to think they might have been. Little Mr Perkins might speak big, she had already decided, but he would always act mean. Never mind, she'd landed the job, that was the only thing that mattered. She wanted to get back and tell Sue all about it.

Mr Perkins, already regretting the impulse that had brought him to the Swan with his new assistant, began to feel bored. Naturally the girl had no conversation; he might have guessed it. It wasn't shyness, it was sheer ignorance. Not exactly stupidity. No, she wasn't stupid; just green, poor kid. Her parents, if she had ever had any looking after her, must have been the helpless and hopeless kind. So pretty, so dumb, so — very —

It was Mr Perkins's hand that broke the boredom that was settling upon the pair. The crush at the bar grew steadily as they continued to sit on their high stools, side by side. They had to draw closer together, which Lesley resented vaguely, because it disturbed her vision of luxury, of ease, of independence. It made her think, instead, of the crowd waiting for a bus, the crowd waiting to cross a road, traffic signals winking, squeaking cars revving up, honking. And then, with ugly, stupid, rude familiarity, little old Mr Perkins's hand was creeping up her leg under her skirt! Mr *Perkins!* She was affronted, but it was laughable, *Really!*

She brought her own hand down sharply and quite hard, saying nothing, but staring at him with furious eyes in a pale, set face. She saw, with astonishment, his rather silly smile change into a frozen look; she felt the caressing hand fall away. Mr Perkins in a cold voice said, "Well, Miss Rivers, I must be off now. See you on Monday, eight-thirty sharp," and he was gone.

Lesley was startled. She had not responded to that searching hand, or rather she had repelled it very smartly. But his response had not been her doing. Or not that alone. His eyes, as his face changed suddenly, had been directed beyond her, behind her. She turned her head.

Leaning on the bar there was a young man, at that moment paying for a tall glass of lager. As he turned from the bar he lifted the glass to Lesley.

"Congratulations," he said easily. "A very neat brush-off. Pardon, if that's offensive. Only I recognise the coat — uniform, isn't it?"

Lesley, blushing furiously, swallowed the dregs of her drink and choked on it. The whole morning had been too much for her. The shop. The job. Mr Perkins. The contract. The job. 'The Swan'. Mr Perkins.

Another stranger. This one with the sort of appearance, the voice, the manner, she found familiar. So no stranger, really. She could explain. If —

The young man took his glass to a table in a corner near the door of the pub. Lesley pushed her glass across the bar towards the barmaid and got down from her stool. As she passed the young man's table he grinned at her.

It was too much. Lesley turned, dropped into a seat beside him and said, in a challenging voice, "You recognised this overcoat, didn't you? I'm staying at the Holy Group house, but I don't belong there. I'm leaving. At least, unless I've dished . . . "

The young man's eyes, bright and laughing still as she sat down, hardened, but his voice was still low and kind as he said, "Go on."

She told him about getting a job, about the difficulties she had met, about Ma Dill and Cissie, otherwise Sister Gordon, about Sister Manley and Sue Ford. She said nothing whatever about the Ruler or the Great Hall or the ritual or the collecting sprees or the rules.

In the middle of her account of her arrival in London and her meeting with Sister Brook she found a cup of coffee beside her right hand and saw that he had one beside his own hand, too. She noticed then that he had nearly finished his own cup. The tall empty glass that had held his lager had vanished.

77

"Drink up," he said. "They're going to throw us out any minute now."

Before they parted Lesley had agreed to meet him again in a week's time.

"I might have my girl-friend with me," he said in the same pleasant, casual voice he had used all the time. "I'd like you to meet her."

"O.K.," Lesley agreed. "If I've not been thrown out of my job."

"You won't be. But don't think you have to . . . "

"What d'you take me for?"

"I don't."

They left the Swan, Lesley thought, together. But looking round outside she could not see him anywhere.

8

Detective Sergeant George Cole made his report to Detective Inspector Sidney Frost.

"About Perkins, sir. Eddie Perkins. You wanted me . . . "

"To have a dekko at that shop of his in St Andrews Precinct. Well, is it on the level or is it a cover for any of his old games?"

"None of the old customers gone in during patrols in the precinct. That is, of the guys in the prints you told me to look up. Perkins is wearing dark specs outdoors, but clear in the shop. He's not changed at all from our last prints. Not that I could see. I recognised him at once when he came into the Swan with the girl from the shop."

Detective Inspector Frost showed signs of interest, hitherto concealed.

"Girl? How d'you know she was from the shop?"

"I'd seen her serving customers. When I was looking at the window display. Fantastic. Put you off cereals for life."

"You think he employs her in the shop?"

"She said he did."

Detective Inspector Frost threw down the biro he had been playing with.

"Get on with it, George. Make a report if you have anything useful. If you haven't, say so. We've been notified Perkins seems to have settled in our manor. We've watched him set up his health food shop. We've noticed him going into the call girl establishment in Brindley Square. He's been inside for drug-peddling and running girlie specialities. Any luck? Anyone likely been to see him? Want his peculiar gifts and services?"

79

"He was making a pass at the assistant, his shop assistant, in the pub. She gave him a quick brush-off, and he left quickly, sir. He must have seen I'd realised what he must be doing, but he can't have known who I was."

"I wouldn't be too sure. Is that all? Hardly worth making a verbal report, was it, sergeant?"

"It was about the girl, really, sir. She was upset by his behaviour, but more worried her action might have lost her the job as shop assistant."

"What action?"

"Oh, she gave the searching hand quite a chop. He wasn't using it to push open the door as he went out. She was nearly crying."

"Are you going to tell me a long sob-story, George? Because I'm not interested in ordinary shop girls' troubles with their employers. In this day and age they all know . . . "

"This one doesn't know a thing. She's run away from home, in the midlands, I'd guess; she landed herself with the Holy Group and she can't get shot of them. After that alarm we had a few weeks back, I thought I ought to hear what she wanted to tell me."

"You did, did you? Why did you connect her with the Holy Group?"

"She was wearing their uniform visiting coat, sir."

Detective Inspector Frost stared. After a minute he said icily, "Have you been making a study of that crazy so-called religious group?"

"No, sir. But she seems to have been having a raw deal from them. Not getting any help with landing a job, quite the reverse. And she knows exactly what did happen last month when people heard screaming inside the place they call Group House or just Holy Group. I thought as they'd let her take a job with Perkins she might have useful information — "

"O.K. sergeant, you needn't take it any further. We're keeping an eye on Perkins. If you've made yourself obvious to him at The Swan no doubt he'll be careful to avoid you in future, but I don't think he's likely to fire the girl. Too obvious."

"She doesn't know who I am. From the way she spoke I gathered the last thing she wanted was help from the Law."

"Typical," said Detective Inspector Frost, taking his mind away from any further thought of a crackpot called Lesley Rivers.

But George Cole could not so dismiss her image and her problems. He had admired her pretty face; he had admired her well-built body, not only its graceful lines but the well controlled, strong, trained use of her muslces. Though she seemed to need and indeed had almost pleaded for help in her difficult lonely situation, trapped in an organisation of which she had not nor could be expected to have, the least understanding, she was not the familiar weakling, bleating for rescue, but showed every sign of fighting for her freedom and her survival, if only she could be told how to set about it. Inspector Frost had written her off; he only wanted to monitor Perkins, that experienced criminal. He, George Cole, personally wanted to go further. He decided to find out what P.C. Torch had discovered about the Holy Group.

Torch was a middle-aged officer, not far from an honourable well-earned retirement after an old-fashioned routine service, mainly on the beat. He had joined the Force in the mood of straightforward indignation at the goings-on of the early gangs of vandals and hooligans after the war. He was big and strong and law-abiding himself and basically gentle, as big men so often turn out to be. But modern methods and the development of electronic gadgets and equipment were beyond his understanding, so promotion had not come his way and the belated return to foot patrolling had quite recently brought him back into prominence, to the surprise of his superiors, all far younger than he was.

So it was with a certain satisfaction that P.C. Torch found himself accosted by a plain-clothed sergeant not much older than his own eldest son, of a class he would in his own youth have called 'a young gentleman'. And all about that lot of loonies calling themselves Holy Group in the pair of semi's in Upper Polson Street.

"They fetched me up from the precinct, you see. On account

of screams they 'eard from inside the buildings. Quite a crowd 'ad collected, the way they do if they think they'll see something 'orrible. Silly blighters."

"But you didn't hear anything when you got there?" Detective Sergeant Cole asked, hoping to keep the constable down to plain fact.

"Oh no. But they were very positive, so I considered it my duty to go up to the door and make enquiries."

"And?"

"Woman opened it at once. Seeing I was backed by quite a crowd she made as if to shut the door again, but I 'ad my toe in, so she give way, calling for Sister."

"Would that be Sister Gordon?" Cole asked, remembering the name Lesley had mentioned.

"No, sir. She give no name when she called out. But an older woman came and asked me to come inside and said 'er name was Manley, which I wrote down as she spelled it out, with an 'ey'. She told me they'd 'ad a character wot 'ad epileptic fits and two or three that was 'isterical. At one of their services that morning the one with fits threw one in the middle of the service and the other types went into their variety, as I've seen in the street now and then."

"So that was the whole story?"

"According to this Sister Manley, it was. Yes. The whole story."

It sounded feasible enough. Why then, had the shop girl not mentioned it? Loud enough, startling enough, to attract passers-by, to the point of calling for police aid to investigate, but not for the girl to put forward in support of her story of harsh rules, frustration?

"So you had to take this Sister's word for it?"

P.C. Torch drew himself up.

"I insisted on seeing the place where the fit and the screaming occurred," he said. "Sister Manley was perfectly willing to show me."

"And?"

"They've taken over the semi next door and made most of the two ground-floor premises into one long room that they

82

call their Great Hall. Quite a show place it is, too."

"Did you see the inmates involved? The epileptic and the two hysterics?"

P.C. Torch looked astonished, even shocked.

"Oh no, sir. Medical cases. Under treatment, I was given to understand."

"They'd actually already had the doctor in? Or sent them to hospital?"

"No. If it 'ad been an ambulance case they'd not 'ave fetched me to it. The people in the street, I mean. That was what was worrying them, you know."

Cole gave up. The constable had satisfied himself that the loonies of the Holy Group were not too far round the bend on religion not to be in control of their own chronic medical cases. In his day — No wonder — Poor old Torch —

"I see. Yes," he said. "They were taking full responsibility?"

"So they should," growled Torch.

"Quite. No obvious ill-treatment or anything like it?"

"Nothing. Like any of the old Poor Law 'Omes, wot we called the Workus in the old days. Sister showed me their sewing machine room and the laundry and the kitchen. Spick and span, eat off the floor, all that. Cooking, of course. I did remember a distinct smell of burning."

"In the kitchen?"

"Well, no. More in the Great 'All. That's near the kitchen."

"I see. Well, thank you very much, Constable Torch. Sorry to bother you, but I couldn't find any record of your visit to the Group."

"That don't surprise me," said the constable, without rancour. "Thank *you*, sir."

To her great relief Lesley found no trouble at all awaiting her at the shop on Monday morning. She had been prepared for anything from abrupt, instant dismissal, to a vague threat, an indirect warning, even an unwelcome, encouraging greeting.

She got none of these. Mr Perkins, who was in the front of the shop, fixing an inappropriate bunch of violets at the centre of the bowls containing what Lesley called to herself and Sue, 'the dry chews', merely looked up at her and nodded.

She said politely, "Good morning, Mr Perkins," and passed behind him to dispose of her coat and put on the clean overall Sister Gordon had handed out to her after breakfast.

"I suppose he expects me," she had said, taking it and rolling it up.

"Why shouldn't he?"

"I dunno. Except he didn't pay me nothing on Saturday."

Sister Gordon smiled.

"He came round here Saturday evening and paid us. Said you'd made a good start."

Lesley was shocked.

"You never told me! You swiped my pay!"

"You owe us, don't you? A couple of months now, isn't it?"

Lesley's face reddened. She was furious. But she saw she was helpless. The leather wristlet that covered her scar was a constant reminder. She would be in their debt until she had paid back every penny she had taken from the collecting purses or entered against the Group at Ma Dill's. Together with her keep. It would be weeks before she could hope to get her wages direct. Unless she could do a deal with Mr Perkins. Openly, she told herself, shuddering slightly as she left Group House.

Watching her employer's vague fumblings with the window dressing as she walked back into the shop from her tiny cloakroom, Lesley tried to reassure herself. He looked harmless enough. Perhaps he hadn't really been making a pass on Saturday at the pub. She had over reacted; must have. It was him being so old and small and sort of dry; looks like an insect, sort of. She hoped she hadn't hurt the fumbling hand. So she stood quite meekly, waiting to be instructed, and was thankful when a pair of obvious housewives with shopping bags came through the door.

"Shall I?" she asked in a quick low voice.

"Carry on, Miss Rivers, please," said Mr Perkins, and he straightened up and walked away into his office.

So the week passed uneventfully until Saturday came round again. At noon Mr Perkins called Lesley into his office.

"You have done very well, Miss Rivers," he said, not looking at her, but fiddling with an envelope on his desk. "I have your wages here. My agreement with the Holy Group was to engage you, though wages would be paid to them, to settle your account with them, paying their commission for securing the post and . . . "

"They never told me a word!" Lesley interrupted, exasperated by this fresh exposure of the Group's high-handed methods. "Not until I, well, not until this morning, when I wanted to know when I'd be paid for last week."

Mr Perkins gave her a cold smile. There was no sympathy in that quarter she saw plainly.

"And I have now told you," he said. "That is why I propose to give you one fifth of what I owe you in cash and the rest will go to Sister Manley of the Group. You must discuss with her how you discharge your accumulated debt with them. I advise you to get your proper amount from them and have it receipted week by week. When that debt is discharged, if you are still working for me, as I hope you will be, I will pay you the whole sum direct."

Lesley was astonished, but she kept her head, remembering the unusual transactions at the shop at home.

"Didn't I ought to have an insurance card, sir? Or something?" she asked.

"I have dealt with the regulations," Mr Perkins told her, so she left it at that.

It was not until she was out in the precinct that she remembered the young man at The Swan and his invitation to meet him there again this Saturday at the same time. Well, she had a bit of money in her pocket, so she could afford it, if he wasn't there. A cinzano wouldn't set her back too far. Then she'd get some sweets at Ma Dill's and a magazine, too, on her way back to the Group.

George Cole saw Lesley as she came into the pub. He was sitting on one of the wall benches, behind a table.

"That's her," he said, beginning to slide himself along the bench away from his companion.

"Which one?" she asked.

"Blue overcoat. Tallish. Bushy hair. Pretty."

"Making straight for the bar?"

"Was. Standing looking round now. I'm going to wave and get her a drink and bring her over here. I'll introduce you as my girl-friend."

"Pleased I'm sure, Sergeant Cole."

They both laughed. Detective Woman Police Constable Amanda Drew had joined the Police Force as a secretarial assistant two years before, but having shown a marked intelligence, together with a sense of order, also observation above the ordinary, and a wish to make progress in her profession, she was now serving in the plain clothes branch and enjoying it.

"Mandy," Detective Sergeant Cole said. "This is Lesley Rivers."

"Hullo!" Amanda said, pulling her handbag towards her to indicate where Lesley could sit down on the bench beside her.

"Hullo," Lesley answered, thinking this girl was uncomfortably like Fran, the bully, without the latter's face but the same dark brown curls, teased into a thick bush, but a nice, kind smile.

George sat down, facing the girls with his back to the crowded room.

"I hoped you'd look in," he said. "Did you remember you said that last week."

"Yes, I did," Lesley answered. "It went off all right. The job, I mean. Not a word about him going off like he did. Well, you couldn't expect it, could you?"

"Not really."

"He might've fired me. Well, he didn't. Quite the opposite. The job's permanent."

Miss Drew had listened to these cryptic exchanges with some amusement. George had told her he was interested in the girl partly because he knew Perkins was a villain with form and noticed he was making advances, partly because the girl reacted effectively, but chiefly because he guessed she was a Holy Grouper and he wanted to know more about them. So now she decided it was her turn.

"Excuse me asking," she said, very politely, "but have you been in London long? I mean, your voice . . . "

"Everyone says that," Lesley laughed. "All right. Midlands, but not Brum. Must be three months now."

"Why did you come? I mean, did your parents not object?"

"I didn't ask them. I mean, I just came."

All three laughed. The beer George had brought for her was stronger than she expected. It made her feel relaxed. Together with her satisfaction over her job and the pleasure of having, at long last, a few coins of honestly earned money in her pocket, she was inclined to boast.

"I don't mind telling you I just walked out on them," she expounded. "You see they weren't my parents, I was adopted. They had a shop, but the last few years we didn't live over it any more. Sold the upper part as a flat and bought a house in the new private estate built on the old brewery site behind the railway station."

"What station's that?" asked George casually.

"Out of use, too," she answered.

"Do you mean to say you've never told them you've come to London?" Amanda asked.

"That's right," Lesley felt she had been talking too freely, but these new friends were *so* normal, so friendly, it might be a good thing to have them near her. It felt good, as long as she didn't say too much.

"Don't you think you ought to tell them now you're fixed in a job?" George suggested.

"Perhaps. But it would be embarrassing. You see, I just got up early and left. I walked all that day and two days more."

"You *walked!*"

"Why not?" Lesley knew she was talking too much.

"Don't you think you ought to tell them now you're fixed in a job?" George suggested.

"Why not?" Lesley knew she was talking too freely, she blamed the beer, but she did not mind. Those days, before they had grown into a nightmare of hunger and thirst and aching muscles had been wizard: a great enfolding of sunshine, air, woodland, dewy grass, bird song. Why was it strange to walk? Quietly to walk away from people and words she had begun to hate? Until, of course, it had ended with the old woman. Yes, it had all ended, the good part, with the old woman.

She became more aware of her companions' faces of astonishment. She began to button up her coat, preparing to leave.

"You didn't walk all the way to London?" George asked, smiling.

"Of course not. I got the school bus and then a coach."

"A school bus? From a village?"

"After the old woman . . ."

Lesley stopped, horrified now at what she had so very nearly said. She stared at her new friends, who were looking at one another. George got up.

"The other half, Mandy?" he asked, and at her now, to Lesley. "And you, Lesley?"

"No," said Lesley firmly. "I must be going."

But George was on his way to the bar, and Mandy was saying, "You were telling us about an old village woman. Where was that?"

"She gave me a glass of water," Lesley said hurriedly, "and then she fell down. I was terrified. I suppose I ought to have got help? But I didn't want to have to explain my name and everything."

"So you just left?"

"That's right. And got the school bus. It was that early in the morning."

George had come back with the renewed drinks. He had heard the last part of Lesley's story.

"Where did the school bus take you?" he asked.

"To the town, of course."

"Where you got the London coach?"

"That's right."

"Which got to London - when?"

"Late that afternoon, of course."

She was on her feet now, shaking down her skirt and the regulation coat, feeling for the middle button they insisted on the girls doing up, against the universal habit of always wearing cardigans, jackets, coats and mackintoshes flying wide, against any reason of purpose, comfort or common sense.

She gave George Cole a cheerful grin.

"I slept most of the way on that coach," she said. "So I can't tell you any of the places we went through. But we can't have stopped anywhere, or I'd have woken up, wouldn't I?"

"That depends," he said, and they all laughed.

After she had passed through the door of the Swan the two police officers conscientiously got out their note-books and made a few entries which they compared with one another. Amanda entered the episode of the old woman, clearly incomplete.

"Didn't you go into it with her?"

"You got back before I had time to. I think she might have explained, but it would be worth getting more on it as a cause of her not giving her real story."

"It would be if she'd knocked the old girl down on purpose, doing a snatch, if she had any cash lying around. She must have paid her fare on the coach. She can't have had any, or any left, if she got both hungry and thirsty before she found the old woman."

"How did she come to get in with the Holy Group? Straight off, I suppose? Or not?"

"We don't know, do we?"

They sipped their beer in silence. Then Miss Drew said thoughtfully, "I quite see why you wanted to have me with you on this Les Rivers problem. Ties in with Perkins now, good and proper. Monitor his new business with a possible grass on the cheap. She's no idea who we really are, has she?"

"No. And not likely to have unless we think it's safe to tell her. Not put her off telling us, I mean."

"Which she'll never do, unless *she* feels safe over the old woman."

"Most likely an invention. She's scared of the Group. But not enough to come to us."

Amanda shook her head.

89

"I don't think it works like that," she said. "She's one of these kids been brought up wrong from the start. Self-regarding, because no home security, fostered or adopted, innocent — "

"Don't give me the text book, for chrissake! Green yes, bloody ignorant, I'd call it. Vicious, too. I saw her chop old Perkins' hand last week. Put the wind up him, all right."

"I thought it was recognising you had the low-down."

"Well, partly. Anyway, I'll give this place a miss for a week or so. If his lordship Inspector Frost doesn't whip me off to the other end of our division, I want to see if Perkins ties in with the dollies' nests in Brindley Square."

"Then I'll set up some errands in the precinct around shut-shop day. Meet up with Lesley, maybe. I want to know how she managed to land herself with the Group. That outfit has come into a few rather smelly tales over the last six months."

"You do that, if you can wangle it," Cole agreed.

They parted outside the Swan with thanks for assistance on either side. Very formal and professional, Amanda thought, a little ruefully, for Detective Sergeant Cole's manner with Lesley had been nothing if not informal, also kind and amusing; the girl had fallen for it, obviously.

9

George Cole's interest in Lesley did not lessen, but nor did his work load. It was several days before he was able to give his mind to her problem with the Holy Group, and even then he knew that anything he was able to do about her encounters after leaving home must be worked out in his off-duty time, for Detective Inspector Frost saw no reason whatever to involve the police with crackpot religious bodies acting apparently well within the Law.

"Acting on what you told me, George," he said to his subordinate, when the latter made his second report about the health shop, its owner and its staff. "I see no reason to enquire further into the so-called Holy Group. Holy balls, I must say, but it has at least two branches in our manor, one for girls and women in Upper Polson Street and one for boys and men in Playhouse Road. The woman in charge of the girls calls herself Sister Manley. She's well in with old Mrs Trevelyan in Brindley Square, who used to be on the local council, so well in with rate-savers of all kinds. I must say the Groupers do keep about fifty unemployables of one kind and another inside the Law and off the rate-payers, too. Which is largely why the authorities are never keen on bashing their kind of harmless lunacy."

"Which isn't always harmless, by any means — sir," said Cole, stoutly.

"That's enough of that," answered Detective Inspector Frost, dismissing him.

So Detective Sergeant Cole began his own investigations in

his solitary rooms when he was off duty. He was unmarried, and at that time had no particular girl-friend, having fallen out with the last one, now married outside the force, after declaring she could not stand the worry and irregular hours inside it. Cole was totally unwilling to change his employment, which he found more satisfying and even enthralling, with every case he was attached to, even the more humdrum, such as watching the old villain Perkins in his new enterprise. So George had his off-duty hours to himself and he began to employ them in research into the whereabouts of Lesley Rivers's home and the detail of her journey to London. Also the reason for her present connection with that doubtful haven, the Holy Group.

He had one locality, Victoria Coach Station, and one inexact date, late summer, which might mean towards the end of August, but could be, in the recent strange vagaries of climate, September or even early October. He guessed the earlier time because they were still in November and much seemed to have happened to her since she reached London.

On the day she arrived at Victoria she had, it seemed, joined her coach around noon or early afternoon. Assuming from her accent, this had been somewhere in the midlands, and from the fact that she had slept through a rapid, non-stop journey to the capital, the coach probably travelled on one of the motorways.

George had maps, collections from early days of old-fashioned Ordnance Survey, that had belonged to his father; also the latest Book of the Road type. He discovered, with little effort, that motorways from the midlands to the capital were roughly the M1, M4 or M3. Of these only the M1 provided a route without a stop before the terminus, except for the statutory twenty minutes halt at a service station.

From Swindon, to where the girl might have walked from a West Midland town, the coaches stopped at Newbury, Basing-stoke, and Farnham. From Basingstoke passengers could change on to other London coaches. This was not a likely route for her to have taken.

The M3 was a fairly new south-western motorway. Lesley was not likely to have walked in her three days to any point from which she would have used this route.

But the east midlands were well served by the M1. It passed near to a great many towns, even cities such as Sheffield and Nottingham, with connecting links to Coventry and Birmingham, with towns of medium size and a great many villages.

From his maps George decided the next thing he needed was time tables of coaches serving this main route. He would be able to get all the information he needed at his own police station, but he wanted to avoid using it for work he was doing entirely in his own time, so he went to the Victoria coach station in his own car, hoping to extend his research if his first conclusion about Lesley's route proved to be possible.

In this he was successful. The M1 was not only possible, but very likely. Coaches *did* run non-stop from Northampton to Victoria. There was a daily one in the afternoon. In fact, several, not all non-stop.

The next question that called for an answer, if he could get any nearer to solving his problem, was did Lesley in fact travel on one of these coaches? If he could find any direct evidence that she did, he could begin his search for the village near Northampton from which she had taken the school bus into the town.

He went out of the enquiry and booking office into the noisy, bustling concourse. No wonder the midlands lass had been confused, even terrified. He found the area where the notice overhead indicated East Midlands. He had the numbers of the buses that used the bays there and went up to a uniformed inspector who was trying vainly to keep intending passengers behind the barriers instead of wandering with their luggage, their children in prams, their dogs on leads, their cats in baskets, among the lines of empty buses, locked up while they waited for fresh drivers to take them out.

The coach inspectors for the most part were young, inclined to be rough with the customers, not very adept at wielding authority, never having learned to respect it in their own childhood. George was of the same generation, of course, and understood this, which he did not find an obstacle. Being in plain clothes was nearly always an advantage. He used that now: he could not do otherwise, since this self-appointed search had no official backing.

He began briskly, but respectfully.

"Excuse me, I wonder if you can help me?"

"Yes?" the inspector said, paying the minimum of attention.

"I really want to find the driver of a coach from Northampton in late August, who took on a girl travelling to London. She hadn't booked but paid on the nail."

"Expect me to know all that?"

"Not really." Not bloody half, George thought. But he fought to keep his cool, only saying, "Well, no, of course not. Can you tell me who to go to?"

This unexpected humility roused the inspector's suspicions. His crowd of passengers was under control at the moment, so he gave George another look.

"Why d'you want to know?"

"Because the girl's gone off from home without saying, and her folk are worried. I'm acting for them on the off-chance she's made for London."

The inspector had another look at his questioner.

"Not the bloody fuzz, are you?"

"They're not in this at all," George declared forcefully.

The inspector relented.

"Better ask at the staff office. I can't help you."

Detective Sergeant Cole, now short of time, did no more that day than locate the staff office and state the nature of his enquiry. A reluctant young woman took down a garbled account of it, said she didn't know if she was allowed to put him in touch with their drivers, didn't know if they still had those who had been working for them in August, wanted to know the exact date the girl had travelled on, and a description of her and her luggage.

George gave as much as he knew and said if she could find any information for him he would call again and anyway was grateful for help given so far.

The young woman gave no promise, but a vague suggestion of payment seemed to stimulate her interest to a mild degree.

94

Especially his declaration, that had gone down well with the coach inspector, that the police were not in this emergency and would not be called in by the family.

It was nearly a week before George was able to visit Victoria again. It was not the same young woman at the enquiry desk he had been told to see before, but his business was known there and seemed to have aroused interest, either because, as he had presented it, the former assistant had found it a worthy human life story, or the veiled hint of a bonus had kept it going at a lower level.

"Oh," the new girl said. "Yes, I think I've got something for you. Taken your time coming in again, haven't you? Maisie thought you'd be back in a day or two."

"I'm asking for a friend," George said. "Didn't have time before. I happen to work for my living."

"You don't say. Well, anyway, Maisie looked out the names on her own. Thought if she went to the boss with your enquiry he'd be sure to hand it on to the police, which was what you seemed anxious to avoid."

"That's right," George said, meaning it. "So you have names for me, have you?"

"I'll get it in a minute." She leaned over the counter, pushing a timetable sheet towards him. "Take a look at this while I attend to the lady behind you. I've got your info in my bag here."

When the girl was free again she produced an envelope, unsealed, pulling out a short list and showing it to George, still holding it.

The price was not named, but payment was clearly indicated. After all, he had hinted at it before. So he took out the five pound note he had prepared for the occasion and slipping it into the envelope drew out the list to stow in his own wallet. There were three names on it and two addresses.

The girl gave him a warm smile.

"Maisie said you were genuine," she told him. "A real winner. The first name there has retired early, but was driving for us up until the end of September. So he may not be at that address now. The other two are quite young. Maisie said go for the old boy, he'd be more likely to remember a case, as he'd call it, where the boys wouldn't notice anything out of the ordinary in a scruffy appearance, they'd be too used to it. Just careful to charge the right money and enter it up the right way."

"I see. Thanks a lot," George said, leaving at once and rapidly, for a queue of enquirers was forming behind him.

Maisie had been right. One of the names on the list, a thin young man with a face of a weasel, gave him a sharp look from small black eyes and said, "Don't make me laugh, mate. My passengers has tickets or they goes get them. They don't board, else."

The other driver lived within walking distance of Victoria but was on holiday, his next door neighbour said, when George called at his door on his way home.

But the retired driver was pottering in a small suburban garden near Bromley. The interview began over the garden gate and ended inside the greenhouse. It began as a discussion on the waywardness of the English weather and the difficulties of cultivating a small plot when you wanted vegetables yourself and your wife wanted flowers. After that Mr Gray was silent, looked steadily at his visitor and then said, "Did you stop at my gate to pass the time of day, or did you have a purpose in calling?"

"I hoped to find you in," George told him. "Because I was told you had retired from the coach business."

"That's right. Forty-two years driving motors, vans, cabs and coaches. Retired last September, sixty-five. May I ask how you come to know my address and what may be your business?"

George told him. This produced another silence, rather longer than the first. Then Mr Gray said, "Would you by any chance, sir, be from the police?"

George Cole hesitated. This was not the sort of person to whom you told lies. They would not succeed and you would be humiliated by a closed memory and a respectful contempt.

"I am a policeman," he said quietly, "in the investigation branch. But my enquiry is my own personal affair. My inspector has turned it down as of no importance, but I feel interested in it. The girl comes from the north — the midlands, she sounds like, but not Birmingham. She ran away from home and walked for a couple of days. Then she got a morning school bus into a town, found there were London coaches and bought a ticket, she says, from the driver. She gave him a fiver and got change, but not much. He let her have a ticket to Victoria. She says she slept all the way there."

Mr Gray listened carefully and when George finished his story, remained thoughtful. But it was clear that his manner would be helpful.

"I'd like to know what this interest of yours is based on," he said at last.

"I've seen her with an old lag we're keeping an eye on," George answered. "She was brushing him off, actually. And getting away with it on her own, I think. But he recognised me. It was in a pub. At least, I think he knew me — maybe not. Anyway, I spoke to the girl and she must have been a bit upset because she talked rather freely and told me she'd left home, but wouldn't go back. She doesn't know my job. I saw her again with one of our women officers, same branch; she thinks Mandy's my girl-friend. That's not so. But we'd like to help this kid, because she's got mixed up with a crazy religious sect. Group, they call themselves. Holy Group."

Mr Gray nodded.

"I've heard of them," he said. "Brain washers, the papers call them." He paused for another few seconds, then said, "Can you describe this girl, officer?"

"I'd rather you didn't call me that, Mr Gray. I'm not on duty, as well as not in uniform. I'm just George Cole. Yes, I can describe her. Tall, like so many of them, but not the six foot kind. Strong build, country style, pretty face, wavy hair, mid-brown, clear complexion, grey-green eyes. Nervous manner or else aggressive. Same thing, really. Out of place in London, entirely. Not stupid, not really ignorant, but green — that strikes you at once."

Mr Gray nodded solemnly. "That struck me at once," he said. "But I wouldn't call it green. I'd call it innocent. Which

97

was why I *did* take her money and give her a ticket for the ride to Victoria. It looked like a genuine fiver, but I must say I wondered where it come from."

He smiled as he spoke and George smiled back. He had often wondered where Lesley had got hold of that note; he had always assumed she had stolen it, either from her home or during the first part of her journey. Now he was a step nearer to discovering that part of the story; perhaps he would know if she was a thief as well as a truant. Innocent, indeed!

It took Amanda Drew over two weeks to run into Lesley again, at the beginning of the lunch hour closing of the health food shop. They greeted one another shyly, for the shop girl's face was sad and the young detective was unsure how to accost her. But Lesley smiled first in recognition, so Amanda stopped, smiling too.

"Time for a quick coffee?" she asked.

"My turn," Lesley said. "There's a restaurant just round the corner opposite the pub where I met you before."

"I know. It won't be crowded today, either, as it's early closing."

The two girls settled at a table near a window. Lesley had added a lavishly decorated cream cake to her coffee, but Mandy refused a confection, so obviously weight promoting.

"All right for you," she said. "You've got the right figure. Thin as a bean stalk."

Lesley laughed.

"No chance to be anything else. The Holy Group don't go in for rich meals. I've done nothing but lose weight since I went there."

"Is that how you want it? I mean, you could leave now, couldn't you? If you wanted to?"

"And find lodgings? Not so easy, I'm told."

Mandy sipped her coffee, telling herself to go slowly, go carefully. First things, first.

"Were you recommended to this Group place?" she asked, casually. "I mean, before you decided to come to London?"

"I was *not*!" All Lesley's sense of betrayal, anger, fear,

outrage, rose to meet the other girl's quiet, sympathetic support. In a rapid, eloquent rush of words she told the story of her arrival at Victoria, her encounter with Group's scout, Sister Brook, and the old woman's young partner, Reg Bridge.

The way her abduction had succeeded both shocked and enthralled Amanda Drew.

"Gosh!" she breathed as Lesley returned to her cake, demolishing its cream-filled base with vicious stabs. "You were conned, good and proper!"

"That's right. Once in, you have a hell of a time getting out again too, you know."

"How come?"

"Personally, I'd just walk off if I had the mon. And somewhere to go. But the ones that go there to find religion and don't find the sort they want, they've got their claws in those and they hang on to them."

"Why?"

"God knows! There's a friend of mine there, — poor little thing, gentle, weak but obstinate as they come, if you know what I mean."

"I do indeed. Go on."

"Well, she was disappointed in the Holy Group. She'd insisted on trying it out and her parents had given in to her. She gets a monthly allowance from them, so she could if she wanted. But can she? Not on your nelly. She says she's written to them, but she never gets a letter back. I don't believe they get her letters and I do believe the Group keeps back any letters her parents write to her. She's very miserable and getting worse."

"But that's dreadful!" Detective W.P.C. Drew felt inclined to pull out her notebook and start taking down the details of this story, but she controlled herself. After a suitable pause, since they both had finished their coffee and had no reason to linger there, she gathered together her bag and the parcel of her supposed shopping and said, "Well I must get on. Thanks for the coffee. If I was you, I'd get that girl's home address from her and write a letter to her folk yourself, putting what you've just told me. Write it in the post office up the road

99

here and post it there on the spot. Then it's sure to get there."

She was on her feet now, seeing and half fearing the look of suspicion in Lesley's eyes.

"Be seeing you," she said quickly and was gone.

Lesley followed more slowly. She was surprised by her own willingness to confide in someone she hardly knew. But less pleasantly surprised by the way the other girl had lapped up Sue's story and the way she had suggested action to help her. Of course she had tried to get Sue to write to her mother and had told her she would post the letter at the main, not Ma Dill's now suspect sub-post office. Well, she would try again.

But was Mandy any safer than Sister Gordon, Cissie, who knew the girls in the flats in Brindley Square? She was on both sides, Cissie was, the Group with Sister Manley and that monster, the Ruler, and poor girls like Sue, who relied on Mrs Trevelyan, retired councillor: and those tarts in the flats, perhaps one of them when she was younger, the loud-mouthed Cissie. Well, she herself belonged to none of them. But she knew better than to take advice from comparative strangers. It might be good advice or it might get poor Sue into worse trouble. Not to mention herself.

She had, since her wrist no longer needed a bandage, taken first to an elastic strapping over a pad of gauze and then, when she had tired of answering questions about her sprained wrist, to a leather supporting wristlet. Underneath it the scar had contracted and lost its red colour, so that now a neat little T, pale and slightly puckered, reminded her of her time-fixed fault, her totally untrained, uncontrolled proclivity. But now, in a nearly fatal lesson, a constantly forbidden habit constantly remembered, a hidden shame. She might sample the goods in Mr Perkins's health store, but she shrank from the till and he had no complaint to make.

Sister Manley was pleased with Lesley's progress. As she said to Sister Gordon, "Sister Lesley is doing well. I have had a satisfactory report from Mr Perkins."

"Marvel, marvel!" said Sister Gordon. "And *he's* no angel to give out honesty bonuses."

100

"We taught her a lesson and she has profited," Sister Manley pronounced.

"We damn nearly killed her."

"Hush. It was a late lesson. But if well-learned, then we cannot regret it."

"*She* regrets it," said Sister Gordon. "Like hell she does!"

"I do *wish*," Sister Manley answered, "You would modify your language. You can be emphatic without using these ugly swear words so often."

"Shit!" said Sister Gordon.

10

Amanda considered that Lesley's account of Susan Ford's plight, in the grip of the Holy Group, was sufficiently serious to call for some real action. At least for recognition under the Law. It was a recognised problem and though she had not handled it at all in her limited experience, it had appeared as high drama in the newspapers and as a solemnly discussed subject with clerical, ecumenical, scientific, political, psychological and social science experts giving their separate thoroughly confusing views on all aspects of religion, authority, brainwashing, indulgence and so forth.

Since George Cole had engaged her help with Lesley for his second meeting with the girl, she decided to put the matter to him. But as none of it was official, this was not easy to manage. However, W.P.C. Drew was a determined young woman and she had found Cole quite easy to work with, contrary to the opinion of other police women in her division.

"He doesn't like women any more," she was told, "he had a nasty brush-off from the last girl-friend. After they'd got engaged too, official and all. Set him back for good, I wouldn't wonder."

Others had told her George Cole was dead keen on his job, very ambitious. Yet here he was, going out of his way, only not far out, because the old villain, Perkins, was a prime object. Well, it was worth trying.

So when George seemed quite pleased to raise the subject of Lesley and her worries again and even found a meeting time for them quite soon, she felt a certain glow of personal interest and pleasure of success quite in addition to her primary purpose.

"You handled that right," he said, after hearing about Sue's apparent captivity. "Shows Lesley's capable of giving help to others besides herself. Carry on keeping an eye open for her. I know a bit more about our Les myself."

He told her the details of his off-duty research at Victoria and the visit to the retired driver, Gray.

"Sounds possible enough to fix where she got the London coach," he went on. "Now we have to find the school bus that took her from a village near enough to work a regular service to a school the kids would be likely to go to."

"Complicated," said Amanda, doubtfully.

"You've said it. Have to get a list of schools in the town and environs. Education Authority and all that. Not so easy in another county, but could be done."

"And then what?"

"My guess is there must be a school not far off the general bus station where the London coaches call. It would serve a number of villages near enough to one another and to the town. It would be typical to have a big comprehensive serving a wide area and do away with a lot of village schools, now they've cut these down to primary only and done away with the eleven-plus."

"Are you hoping to find a school bus driver who remembers her as well as Mr Gray does?"

"Not really."

Though he spoke pleasantly, as always, George's eyes had hardened. A clear warning, which she knew she was anxious to obey.

"Look," she said, frowning a little to imply deep thought, "Suppose I do the Educational part of the exercise? It was a bus for ordinary morning school on a weekday, wasn't it?"

"So she said, or rather implied. Not very exact. Didn't want to be."

"No. She isn't very clear how long she's been in London at the Group, is she?"

"It must have been in school term time, anyway. So late

July, or early September. I can check on that too, if you like."

George was smiling now, as he looked at her. Quite keen and quick in the uptake, wasn't she? Why not give her a hand in his private enquiries?

"O.K." he said. "You do that. Schools in walking distance of a main bus station, taking some kids from villages up to short trips, say fifteen to twenty minutes, from their home, for arrival at school assembly nine o'clock or thereabouts."

Amanda wrote these details in her personal diary. Not that she did not know them already, but it looked more business-like.

"Shall I tell Lesley what I'm doing? She might come up with the name of the village and save a lot of trouble."

"Christ, no! She'd probably start her judo on you. She gave Perkins quite a professional chop."

Amanda grinned.

"I've got my own belt," she told him.

"That so? Well, I'd be sorry to have you two laying each other out. No, Mandy, you do my home work and I'll . . . " He paused, frowning, pulling himself back from a familiarity he had no wish to pursue.

"I'll let you know," he said and walked away from her, only turning to say, "Seeing you," before he disappeared.

Amanda was surprised, but she remembered George Cole's reputation and its cause, all at least two years old. Surely he should have got over it by now or was his vanity too stubborn. It was nearly two years since she had joined Inspector Frost's squad. Cole's enemies, or rather those whose lack of over-whelming keenness had delayed their promotion, food for malicious gossip. Since she did not belong to any faction with regard to him, she decided to ignore or perhaps overlook any curtness in his manner as unintentional. In any case it held no significance for her. She was as interested in Lesley Rivers as he was. She would do the homework he suggested. It would be a a useful exercise in the sort of detailed painstaking research she must expect to work on.

Her progress, where it depended upon written requests, was slow, because answers came only after painfully long intervals, and were not always the real answers to her questions; which meant another letter with the same question, differently phrased. Telephone enquiries were useless. They never reached the official or assistant to whom they were directed, for this one was out or away, in conference or in bed, ill; quite often, even though it was now November, on holiday.

But Detective W.P.C. Drew was intelligent and keen, so after a couple of weeks, presenting herself throughout as a private person with a vaguely social, educational motive, she located not only the likely comprehensive school served by three country buses from villages within a ten mile range, but also that most of the villages were visited at a shelter beside their centre point or their cricket field or their church, while the pupils from two straggling villages were obliged to meet the bus at the end of the lane that linked them with the B road to their destination.

"There!" Amanda pointed to a spot on the map she showed to George Cole. "Littleham. Those little black dots, all here and there beside that black line joining the yellow one that merges with the next roundabout in the A road."

George peered, read the names, agreed.

"I've got it. Gayton, Blissworth, Rothersthorpe. Yes, Littleham. That's the most likely. Good. So now we go up to Littleham and see if we can find an isolated cottage with an old woman in it. Unless our Les did her more damage than she confesses to."

"Or was never there, but Les found a few bank notes in an empty house."

"She wouldn't have a conscience about that. No, she's scared she did the old thing a mischief."

"In that case why hasn't it been known about?"

"I'm certain she doesn't know how much damage she did. She's scared proper, though not sure it hasn't been hushed up while the search for her goes on."

"Could be. So do we ask them up there or what?"

"It's still not official. Frost has the Chief's backing in not taking on scatty organisations such as this Group, unless they openly act unlawfully."

"What about the local press?"

"Good idea. Have you time to go into that?"

"O.K. Entirely unofficial, as before. A bit of period do-gooding or social research on geriatrics, material for a book or just an article for the county paper. Letter to local editor."

Amanda laughed.

"What a ghastly character you make yourself out to be," George told her. "Any self-respecting journalist would put the letter in the bin straight off. No, I'll write for info on a reported assault on a pensioner in the area. Ask for any knowledge, research, police action if known, hospital admission etc. etc."

"If you'd rather," Amanda said briefly.

George Cole had not been difficult, sour, unwilling to share the search. But an idea had come to her. She remembered that her mother had a cousin living in Rugby, not very far away from the cluster of villages they were hoping to pin on to Lesley's walk. Surely the cousin, Madge Small, who lived in Rugby, might take the Northampton paper, perhaps know something anyhow.

She did not suggest getting in touch with this person, who might have left Rugby or even this world altogether. It was years since she had given the distant relation a thought. Did she even have her address? Possibly, in that tattered little suede-covered gold-edged treasure of an early childhood Christmas present that she still cherished and used, where the B's, C's and D's overflowed their allotted pages, while the I's O's and X to Z were quite unused.

She made no further suggestions, just repeated her promise to try to find any mention of injury or medical emergency relating to an old woman living in a cottage on the outskirts of a village near Northampton.

She was near the door on her way out of the room where they had been talking when George said, still in the same slightly resentful, cold voice and manner, "Of course, if you get a completely negative result it doesn't prove the old woman is non-existent and Lesley's story untrue from start to finish."

Mandy answered, without looking round or stopping, "Of

course not," and shut the door softly behind her.

George gathered together the papers, maps, coach and bus time-tables and pushed them all into a large envelope which he locked away in a personal drawer in his desk. He had two separate reports to assemble and he turned, with a sense of relief, to this, his real work. He expected to present these reports to Sidney Frost the next time he was sent for, when they would discuss further action in a new case of fatal child battering, followed by the disappearance of the mother. There had never been a father in this shamefully called 'one parent family'. Such a thing did not exist. It was a contradiction in terms. Good thing the poor little brat had not suffered long.

George Cole forced himself to lay aside personal disgust and moral judgment and instead assembled the reports he had gathered from the delinquent's neighbours, who had full knowledge of what had been going on, including descriptions of the man who had recently been visiting the ill-tempered mother. Also the names of the social worker and the health visitor, who were never able to find her at home.

This case and other official work prevented Detective Sergeant Cole from following up his interest in Lesley for several weeks. But he had a two week period of leave coming to him, so when it became due within a few days, he found Detective W.P.C. Drew to suggest some action in the field.

"I'd like to give a day to it and go out to those villages we thought were likely. See if we can find the old woman Les stole the money from and hit or pushed over."

"I've not been able to find that story in any of the local papers fed from those villages and others in the area. Nor at the hospitals that serve them. I did it all as a so-called friend of her family, not official."

"Quite. I don't propose to go to the local force unless we have some real news for them or a real problem."

"Such as?"

He shrugged.

"If Les did use violence and hurt the old dame she could have got the victim's own doctor in and got help as if she'd hurt herself by just falling down. These geriatrics have their pride."

"They're easily scared, too. Afraid to accuse anyone for fear of gang revenge. Sounds scatty, but it's like that now."

"Too right. I'll be driving down. Like to come too?"

"Yes," Mandy said. "Very much. When would that be?"

Though she spoke calmly, in her natural, quiet, pleasant voice, Mandy felt a wave of amused surprise at this offer. George Cole's reputation for cynical distrust of women in general and a special dislike, very old-fashioned of course, of women in the police force, were well-known. So she felt she had been favoured especially and must be very careful not to let him know she realised this. There was no danger of her taking advantage of the situation. For her it was definitely an official enterprise, part of her normal work, though not yet backed officially. All experience was valuable, she told herself. Even a day with Detective Sergeant Cole, whose small talk was very far from entertaining though it compared favourably with that of the several more or less ardent boy-friends in the student world she had left when she was accepted for police training.

They set out on a Saturday morning, crossing the Thames at Blackfriars Bridge to drive northwards through Swiss Cottage to reach the extension of the M1 where it branches off the North Circular. They left the motorway at exit 15 to drive south for a few miles, until at the small town of Roade they found a narrow country lane where a signpost directed them to Blissworth, one of the names on their maps.

It was a bright, late autumn morning. After a very wet summer, in London and the south, with little sun until the latter part of August, the trees in the countryside were still a surprising red-gold with still unfallen leaves against a brilliant blue sky, while the low sun threw long shadows across ploughed earth of many changing colours as they sped north-west again.

After they left the main roads behind, the country lanes brought the colour and the golden carpet under the trees nearer to the car, while wide lakes of recent rain on the winding

108

surfaces reflected the sky in pools startlingly blue.

Sergeant Cole maintained an official attitude throughout the early part of the drive. He certainly had no intention of starting any kind of chatty exchange apart from the job in hand. It might be taking place as a purely personal exercise in their free time; he on the first day of a fortnight's leave, Mandy on a weekend off duty and on her way to a relation in Rugby, at that. There was nothing to discuss in their planned investigation. He was determined not to talk about anything.else.

Mandy understood his absurdly starchy attitude and behaviour. She found it laughable, but was not really inclined to laugh. Instead she was grateful that she was spared any need for small talk so that she could allow herself to drift into a mood of quiet enjoyment of the smooth skilful drive through a landscape wiped clean of piled brick and concrete, as uniformly grey and depressing as the crowds moving endlessly through it: a rapidly changing scene now of sweeping country-side lit by this late blaze of colour.

At a cross roads of lanes George drew in to the verge and stopped.

"Have you got this village coming up?" he asked.

"Yes — sir," Mandy answered, taking a quick look at the solemn face beside her. It did not change, only stared ahead. "Blissworth. We ought to get a signpost on to Gayton and to Littleham. It could be either of those."

"Right," George said, beginning to move off again.

He drove slowly through Blissworth and turned when directed to Gayton. Almost at once Mandy said, "Littleham. Next right! Sorry, the signpost's been knocked over. Have we passed it?"

"How should I know? What about this?"

He flung the car to the left, round a double farm gate leading into a field and beyond this into a side road rather wider than the lane they had just left.

"Littleham to the left, not the right," he said with controlled scorn.

"The signpost had fallen the wrong way," Mandy felt it fair to answer. "I do know my right from my left."

"Congratulations." He drove on until they reached an untidy little village square with a post office store, a newsagent and sweet shop combined and a straggle of small houses, some very old, on both sides of the road.

George drew up. Mandy handed him the maps.

"We need to find out if there's a cottage on the outskirts on beyond here, I think," she said with more assurance than she felt, for she still smarted from his assumption of her incapacity over right and left.

"That's right," he agreed. "Come on, then."

They got out, met at a grass verge on the near side and began to stroll along the road, leaving the two shops with their adjacent neighbouring houses, passing the end of the untidy 'green' and continuing along the lane beyond.

People passed them from time to time. It was just after noon, so the locals would be expected to be in their houses going about the business of a Saturday midday meal. The few inhabitants who did pass them made no acknowledgement of their appearance. Not a friendly village, Mandy thought, but she did not bother to say so aloud. A rather scruffy, uninviting place; dull, not curious about the probably frequent passers-by in cars. Or perhaps they seldom had any that stopped.

As the houses thinned to a widely spaced line, with small front gardens and a view of hills beyond, they passed one more carefully maintained as an old-fashioned cottage. It had stacked metal garden chairs and little tables in front and a notice, rain-sodden and fallen to one side announcing 'Cream Teas'.

"Could this be it?" Mandy said, frowning. Lesley Rivers had not said anything about a tea shop or place selling teas, but this cottage was on its own and they had come about half a mile from the square.

"Shouldn't think so," George answered, seeming to bring his mind back to the object of their search from some considerable distance.

"Might see if they know who lives further out. If anyone does. Godforsaken place altogether. Shouldn't think anyone takes a penny-worth of interest outside their own front door."

It took some ringing and two loud knocks to get a response.

The man who opened the door at last was in his shirtsleeves, frayed jeans and bare feet.

"Hello," he said ungraciously.

George asked how far the village stretched and if there were any more wayside cottages. They were doing a bit of research on rural England, the origin of villages, agricultural, industrial, railway, home crafts and so on.

The man listened with a bored expression. Then he said "Too many of your lot about. Waste of time. Left a car up in the green? Thought so. Season's over, you know."

"I guessed that," George said, pointing to the stacked tables and chairs. "You're the last house this end, then?"

"Never said so. There's old Mrs Tavern half a mile further on. Not really in our parish as they used to call it. Comes in to the Post Office for her pension once a week. Never see her 'cept the once. Keeps herself to 'erself. Don't speak if she can help it. Got an old sick husband, so they say. Mrs Tavern."

George moved to go.

"Well, thanks very much, Mr — "

But the man did not offer his name, nor take leave. He had the front door locked and bolted before they had passed the garden gate.

"I wonder what sort of cream teas they serve to the summer visitors," Mandy said thoughtfully, as they walked on up the lane.

"Sour," George said. "Bloody yoghurt."

The outlying cottage had a less tumbledown appearance than they expected. The front garden was certainly grossly over-grown and the path from the gate to the door hardly passable for nettles and brambles but it was in use. Also the cottage windows were clean and the curtains hanging inside were clean too and not frayed. They knocked and waited.

Lesley had told Mandy of a face peering out, so, standing just behind George, she watched after he had knocked several times and saw an old yellow, lined face staring at them.

"She's in, sarge," she whispered. "Just looked out."

"She's coming," he answered and added fiercely, "Don't you dare call me that when we go in."

111

"Sorry, sir," she said meekly.

When the door opened George gave the old woman a respectful smile and said, "Am I speaking to Mrs — Tavern?"

"That's me name," the old woman answered. "Wot d'you want?"

"I want to ask you about a girl we know." He drew Mandy into the conversation, "whom we think may have called at your house in August last, very early in the morning."

Mrs Tavern's face grew hard.

"That bitch!" she said. "I knew I'd not 'eard the last of 'er." She broke off, sudden fear in her old eyes. "You're not the police?"

"We have no official standing whatever in these enquiries," Mandy said, speaking for the first time. "I know the girl and I want to help her. She called here, I believe, when she had just run away from home. You helped her and she rewarded your kindness with very bad behaviour."

"I should just say she did, wicked hussy she was. Putting on 'er act, going to die of thirst, starving!"

"Tell us exactly what happened," George suggested.

"You'd better come in. You're not the welfare, neether?" Mrs Tavern persisted.

They reassured her, so she led the way into the small sitting-room to which the door gave entrance and seating herself beside the table while they remained standing just inside the door, she gave them a highly dramatised version of that early morning scene when Lesley had persuaded her to offer help and then when she had gone out to her kitchen to get a mug of water, had stolen from her handbag which had lain on the table, she having only just before got back with her shopping and the pension she had just drawn.

"Have you any idea where she'd come from?" Mandy asked when Mrs Tavern had described how she had stayed lying on the floor, partly recovering from the fall, partly listening for Lesley to latch the gate and walk away.

"No, I 'aven't!" Mrs Tavern was indignant. "Never asked meself. Glad to see the last of 'er. Scared me proper, an I don't scare easy, never did, but these kids now with their good food

112

all the way up and do as you like ways. Strong!" Mrs Tavern was too indignant and too breathless to continue.

Her visitors had heard enough. They were convinced that Lesley's story was true and that they had found its true source.

"You two's may not be the welfare nor yet the law," Mrs Tavern finished with a certain unholy glee in her voice, "but that young devil 'as met 'er proper match this time, I reckon."

"Not quite," George said. "We are genuinely concerned to find her family and her real home, and she is really sorry for the way she treated you, and so," he went on, pulling out his wallet, "she wants to make amends as far as she can by giving back what she took. How much was it, exactly?"

George and Mandy watched the old woman reckoning her chances of asking for a good round sum, then becoming afraid of open lying, of starting that dreaded search, that ever-feared exposure.

"I was missing a five-pound note and three ones," she said at last.

George produced a small sheet of writing paper on which he wrote down a formal statement about the nature of the money he was about to hand over. It was a receipt for this sum, given by Miss Lesley Rivers to Mrs Maud Tavern and it was signed by the old woman in the presence of two witnesses, George Cole and Amanda Drew.

George left a blank space for the old woman to fill in with her own signature. She managed to produce a new looking biro and did so with unexpected ease.

"She asked us to give you the money," Mandy said. "She must have been in a very confused state not to remember exactly how much she had taken."

Mrs Tavern paid no attention to this. She was by now shaking with excitement, chuckling with glee, while tears filled her eyes and she swept them away with the back of her twisted hand.

Later, as they were walking back to the car on the village green George said, "Did you manage to get a look at that pension book of hers, when she was unloading her handbag to find her note case?"

"Yes. Mr Tavern and wife, retired farm labourer."

"Not much sign of the old boy in that cottage, was there?"

"None at all. I took it for granted she was a widow."

"I think she is."

11

"So that's that," George said as they climbed back into the car. "And now?"

"Well, we're not official, so we'll have to be very careful. But we can't be more than thirty to forty miles from Les's home town. Give us the road books."

Mandy handed them to him and opened the Ordnance Survey map on her own lap.

"We want a smallish town or the outer suburb of a big one. Les says she went to the local grammar. Somewhere likely to have several secondary type schools or a big fairly new comprehensive."

"It wasn't a comprehensive," Mandy insisted. "She's told me that more than once."

"Well then, I'd put my money on Rugby."

Mandy laughed.

"Which is where you're going to drive me to my mother's cousin, who said she'd put me up any time, if I wanted to stay the night. She's a dear; she's my godmother, actually. Not married. Runs a dress shop. Marguerite Small. We call her Madge."

George looked at his companion in some astonishment.

"Blimey!" he said slowly. "You sound like an Edwardian fairytale. Godmother. Spinster. Boutique." He drew a deep breath. "Look," he went on. "I suggest we drive out of this place before the word goes round, which it surely will, that we asked for the Tavern cottage at the mouldering tea garden; that we called there, prospecting and — "

115

"I'm certain old Tavern won't breathe a word of anyone giving her back money nicked from her. I don't expect she ever breathed a word of the Lesley episode. The teashop man didn't seem to know anything at all about her, did he?"

"That's right. Which supports my theory that the old hag is fiddling her dead husband's pension, at least until the present book runs out."

"That's right. So better not hang about Littleham any longer. I agree."

They followed his plan. George continued to drive along lanes and country roads. They ate their sandwiches and sausage rolls and munched their Cox's orange pippins and drank their real coffee supplied in a large thermos by Mandy. Then they moved on to a pleasant small pub, where they discussed the weather and the year's harvest and the local elderly population with the landlord. A casual reference to a pair called Tavern drew no response.

"Not surprising," George said as they re-embarked. "We're quite a way from Littleham now and the Taverns may have lived there too long to be noticeable now. He may still be in that house, or lying in the garden, some place."

Mandy shook her head.

"House, possibly. The old girl's not capable of digging in a canary, let alone a whole man, however old."

"Even in suitably small portions?"

"Ugh! Don't!"

So they drove on, reaching Rugby after a ridiculously slow drive spent trying to work out a route Lesley might have used to occupy her two whole days walking from village to village without declaring herself at all, until hunger and thirst and general exhaustion forced her to knock at Mrs Tavern's door.

Miss Small lived over her shop, her house door being in an alley way beside the building. George put Mandy down with her bag, but refused to stay until Miss Small appeared. He was going to spend his leave in the west country, he explained, and wanted to get south again before dark, which gave him less than an hour.

Mandy made no effort to keep him. Before he drove off he said, "I'll deal with the Tavern end of the story. You get your Madge to help you sort out if the local coppers have got Lesley on their missing-persons list. That sort of thing. O.K.?"

"Right — sir," said Mandy, with a grin, which sent George off almost before she had taken her hand from the open window of the car.

Miss Small was misnamed, being of rather more than average height for her generation, born between the two wars. She was calm, capable, well-groomed, dressed quietly in the clothes she stocked so successfully for women of her own age and the older generation.

She welcomed Mandy with a kiss, looking round behind her to discover her means of arrival.

"Car," Mandy said. "Colleague of superior rank at the start of two weeks' leave. In a hurry to get away south before dark."

"Then why . . . ? No, come in first and I'll get us some tea."

"Can you leave the shop?"

"I close at weekends. My clientele doesn't buy dresses on a Saturday afternoon. They show their menfolk what they bought in the week."

She turned and led the way in, leaving Mandy to collect her luggage and follow.

Later, after two welcome cups of tea and a slice of home-made cake, the girl described her contacts with the runaway Lesley Rivers and with Detective Sergeant Cole, who had engaged her to help him to keep in touch with the girl as part of his current problem.

"He's really doing a proper job that I can't tell you about," Mandy went on. "What we're doing about Lesley is unofficial, but we know *how* and roughly *when* she got to London, so we've been working backwards, so to speak; I mean, from the things she's told me we know she got to London in a coach on the M1 and where she joined it and how she got there. Then today we confirmed the next part of her story, going backwards, so to speak, and we came to the conclusion her home town might be Rugby."

"But you wrote to me last week to invite yourself for today."

117

Mandy laughed.

"Yes. On a guess it looked like working out as it has. I did say I'd phone to confirm."

"Yesterday. But you weren't sure even then, were you?"

"I'd have rung again if I wasn't coming."

Miss Small tightened her thin lips and poured Mandy another cup.

"So what happens now?" she asked.

"Perhaps you could help me over the next obstacle, Madge," Mandy said humbly. "You see this girl calls herself Lesley Rivers, but I'm pretty sure that isn't her right name. In fact, poor kid, she probably hasn't got a name at all, really. I think she has foster parents or adoptive ones, but I don't know which. The so-called Dad keeps a shop and has been training her as his assistant since she left school, not a comprehensive. Perhaps grant-aided; I don't know. She says she passed some O levels."

"How old is she now?"

"She says she's nineteen. She could be anything from fifteen to twenty."

Miss Small sat back, considering.

"So how can I help you?" she asked. "I do happen to know the headmistress of our one and only girls' grammar school in this part of town. Shall I ask her in for a drink this evening? Short notice for that. Or tomorrow? Can you stay over?"

"Oh Madge, that'd be super! She must know — "

But Miss Small had already reached her telephone. The headmistress was in, but expecting two friends for drinks within the hour. Could she come round for coffee after supper? Come for coffee *and* supper she was told.

Mandy recited her story again, or rather an expanded version, including some facts about the Holy Group which made Madge Small exclaim in horror and the headmistress whose name was Anne, look both fierce and sad.

"So really, though it's not a police matter, you feel you want to establish the real home of this girl, if she has one, and a caring one, before the Holy Group gets her permanently under its thumb?"

118

"They won't be able to do that. She's tough in a queer way, but defenceless, too. I'm not putting it clearly, I know. But she has told me a bit about this odd sect and she has a poor little friend there who wants to get out and can't or is too scared to try hard enough."

"Surely you can do something about *that* without bothering so much over this Lesley — Rivers, didn't you say?"

"Yes, but I'm pretty sure it's not her real name. Don't you see I must have a few real, correct details about Lesley before I can put it to my Inspector it's our job to take steps to take the other girl out of the Group."

"I see what you mean," Anne said thoughtfully. "You want to know if any of our schools here in Rugby have had an adopted girl, who did reasonably well, left with some O-levels and has since vanished."

"And it must be a school likely to be near a fairly new housing estate for respectable shop-keeping parents, no longer living over the shop, like me, but pushing up the social ladder," Madge put in.

"I could check on their list of missing persons at your police station here," Mandy added, "only I don't want to, until I've told them in London what I've done so far."

And told George too, she thought, but did not want to bring him into the matter just yet.

The two older women continued to discuss possible schools in probable neighbourhoods, but without reaching any conclusion firm enough to warrant an expanded search. Until the headmistress said, "Must it be Rugby?"

"Oh no!" Mandy was emphatic. "No, I hope I didn't suggest it *had* to be here. Anywhere about the same distance from that village, Littleham."

"Because," Anne went on, "one of my staff left me for a better post at Brockton. That's about fifteen miles further west, but still well south of Birmingham. Actually she's been there four years now so she may have known this Lesley Rivers before the girl left. She would be sure to know her if she was taking public examinations."

"Have you got her address?" Madge asked.

"I keep in touch; I know her phone number, too."

"Then please may I have it?" Mandy asked, amused that the others seemed to have forgotten her own part in the search.

"Why not ring her now, — from here?" Madge persisted.

But the call was not answered and as by now it was getting late and the headmistress declared she was going to the early service at her church in the morning, she wished the others luck and went away. But not before she had made Mandy promise to tell Madge the outcome of her search, so that she might know how it finished.

When she had come back from seeing Anne go, Madge said, "Well, we've got an address and a phone number so I suggest we go over to Brockton tomorrow morning in my car and find the school and this friend of Anne's."

"Super. Look first for a possible home and school to fit and find the teacher later if it seems at all likely to be right. Do we know her name?"

"It's with the address. Mrs Home. No first name. School mistresses are often married these days. Anne was married years ago. Lost her husband early and went back to teaching."

"I know all that sort of thing. I'm just surprised she is down as Mrs Home. Never mind. We'll soon find her full name if it works out."

But it did not do so. They drove round the outskirts of Brockton and discovered two sets of possible sites for Lesley's home; sets of private villas of modern size, three or four bedrooms, two or three ground floor rooms, 'lounges' with 'patios', close-shaved lawns, late roses hanging brown and withered, rain-sodden or frozen, a sprinkling of fallen leaves from small flowering cherries, but no large trees of any kind.

There were two obvious schools within walking or at least cycling distance on safe side roads from the residential areas. They were named but Anne had not given the name of the girls' school to which her assistant mistress had transferred.

"It doesn't matter," Mandy said. "Let's find Mrs Home's house."

"I rang her number again before we left this morning," Madge said. "No answer. She must be away."

"Never mind. We can do some asking about the schools at the same time."

But here again they were baffled. The school mistress lived some distance from each of the possible schools, in a block of flats with garages near the centre of a small town. Mrs Home clearly drove to school and preferred to live well away from it.

"Typical," said Miss Small. "She likes to be in what was a pleasant ordinary country town, until industry pushed in with all those factories we passed on the way here."

"It doesn't matter," Mandy told her. "I've got enough solid fact to take to Inspector Frost. I'll write to Mrs Home tonight."

So Madge drove her back to Rugby, where Mandy gave her cousin lunch at a surprisingly good small restaurant within an easy walk from the dress shop. It made a point of cooking, in the old-fashioned teashop manner, a Sunday roast with two vegetables followed by a fruit tart and cream.

"They can still keep it up." Madge told her. "I don't know how long. The commercial hotel up the road has gone over to buffet meals. Tired commercial travellers prefer this if they're held here over Sunday."

Back in London on an afternoon train, Mandy called at her police-station. Her short leave was up, but there was nothing for her to do and Det. Inspector Frost was not on duty. So she went home and wrote a long non-official letter to Mrs Home. She explained fully who she was, why she did not want to put Lesley's case into official hands at Brockton until she had some solid confirmation of her guess that the girl's home was really there and if so what her real name was and how much of her story was true.

When she had finished she took her letter to the nearest pillarbox to catch the first post in the morning. On reaching her flat again the phone was ringing. It was George Cole.

"I've been trying to get you since early today," he said, in the determined, energetic, professional voice she found irritating but forgivable.

"I stayed with Madge overnight. I've only been home an hour and just dashed out to post a letter."

"Any luck at Rugby?"

"Nothing definite, except it can't be Rugby but could well be Brockton."

"I don't get you."

"Sorry. Brockton is fifteen miles from Rugby and has a fairly up-stage housing area, convenient for two possible schools. My cousin knows a local teacher in Rugby and she came to supper yesterday and was helpful about Rugby being no good, and she gave me the address of someone who teaches in Brockton. That's where I've written to and just posted."

"Fair enough. You've not been along to the station yet then?"

"Well, no. I'm not due till tomorrow morning. I've not got anything urgent to report, have I?"

"I'm not sure. I have, though. I've been recalled. Can't tell you on the blower. Be seeing you. Tomorrow morning."

He rang off, leaving Mandy with an unexpectedly keen sympathy for Detective Sergeant Cole. Just when the late autumn seemed set for a spell of dry warm weather, even in the west country. Fate really did seem to have it in for the detective sergeant, she thought. So he was to be back on duty tomorrow. She had to agree that she looked forward to that with considerable curiosity. What a pity her own line of inquiry had come to a dead end, — almost. Well, she couldn't expect to have an answer to her letter until the day after tomorrow at the very earliest.

As matters were developing, the question of Lesley's real name and home address seemed likely to be taken right out of her hands. For on clocking in at the station next morning she found she was to appear at once in Det. Inspector Frost's office. On arriving there she found George Cole already seated opposite the Inspector, with an open file lying on the table before each man.

"Come and sit down, Miss Drew," said Frost, "and give me an account of your dealings with and knowledge of a young woman who calls herself Lesley Rivers and works as assistant at a so-called health store called Mangoes in St Andrew's place, owned by a man called Perkins."

George added, before she could begin, "Miss Drew came with me in both our off-duty hours, to encourage Lesley to join us in a beer and talk about herself."

"Miss Drew is quite capable of explaining all that herself, I hope," Frost said, coldly.

Mandy, ignoring both men, began a recital she had been preparing from the start and had sorted out in her mind on the train journey from Rugby to London the day before.

When she finished Frost said, "You must be aware our int⸱est in this girl lies solely in the fact the man Perkins employs her in his shop and Perkins is an old lag who may be setting up a new business on old lines."

"Yes, sir."

"What is *your* interest in her, Miss Drew?"

Without hesitation Mandy answered, "The fact that she's been fostered or adopted, has run away from home, got into the hands of the Holy Group, who have been ill-treating and frustrating her. But she won't say how and now has managed to get this job as shop assistant with Group help and wants to free another girl they're holding against her will."

"Sending her to us?"

"Do you mean Lesley or this other girl, Susan Ford? You see, Lesley is dead against us, calls us the Law, the fuzz; not pigs, not anything stronger. Strange girl really, very ignorant, but not stupid. Healthy, strong physically . . ."

Frost interrupted to say, with a smile, "We are not a social service unit, Miss Drew, nor health visitors, nor probation officers. Our job is crime. George here is after Perkins and as this girl Rivers works for him at his new shop we ought to know as much as we can get about her, too."

"Yes. I'm sorry. I expect Detective Sergeant Cole has told you we found the old woman, Mrs Tavern, in Littleham, so that rather fixed our guess over Rugby."

"But you haven't got much further than concluding the Rivers' home town isn't Rugby but might be Brockton?"

"That's right, sir."

Det. Inspector Frost pushed open the file towards Mandy.

"Take a look at Perkins, Miss Drew. Intelligent boy, passed

123

the 11 plus, grammar school, red brick university, qualified dispensing chemist. Fell for the drugs racket and from there the other forms of vice. Been inside twice. You'd think he wouldn't stay in this country; he's not all that widely known abroad. We'd be glad to see him go, I should think."

Geoge put in, "Nor stick to London, which he always has."

Having looked briefly at the files Mandy pushed them away and said, "If I get an answer from this school mistress in Brockton, shall I bring it to you, sir?"

"Of course. The questions about Lesley Rivers are now part of the official monitoring of Perkins and the Mangoes shop, which is now on my plate."

George said, "So now I can get the people up there, I mean in the Northampton area, to go into old Mrs Tavern's reason for not reporting Lesley's assault on her and therefore hiding up the theft she alleges from her pension, her hubby's pension, that is. Also what Mrs Tavern has done with the old man. We saw no sight or smell of him in that cottage, did we?" he asked, swinging round towards Mandy. She nodded agreement, but said nothing. She was thinking about Lesley's friend, the poor little brain-washed or just scared girl, trapped in the Holy Group. Is she now no part of my continued contact with Lesley herself? Admittedly Sue had nothing whatever to do with Perkins. She accepted that: she understood that she was not criticised for starting an unofficial search for Lesley's origin, but this was because the girl had become part of a much more serious preventive operation. Det. Inspector Frost clearly assumed that the experienced villain, Perkins, was at his old game, that it was unbelievable that he could be running straight. Was that always true? Mandy was prepared to be shown that this gloomy view was correct, while keeping a small part of her mind and a larger slice of her emotions ready to accept proof, but real proof, of a miracle.

In the meantime when she could fit it in, she determined to run across Lesley in the precinct quite accidentally, when shopping, and persuade her to have another coffee and chat at the small place near the Swan in the main road.

But it also occurred to her, as she left the inspector's room that she still did not know why and for what active purpose George Cole had had his leave savaged. Was Perkins already suspected of something definite? If so, what? She had not had time to read the gen on him in the files. Only identify the pictures and read the summaries of his former crimes. Would George tell her, if she asked him? Almost certainly not.

12

Unaware of the interest she now held with the local police, Lesley Rivers continued to work peacefully at Mangoes, the health food shop. Her main thoughts now lay in her work there, for Sue had not provided that home address she needed in order to write to the girl's parents. In fact Sue had been as near to anger at the idea as her timid nature allowed. When persuasion failed, even an unaccustomed pleading, Lesley fell back on the Group's only sane ally, in her opinion, old Mrs Trevelyan.

"If you have to go on being a poor bloody sap, Susan Ford," she stormed at her friend, "why not get Mrs Trevelyan to write to your mother. Give *her* your home address. Let her write to say you want to go home for Christmas. That ought to do the trick."

"No, it wouldn't," Sue said. "She'd only speak to Sister Manley and you know what that means."

"Not half! So why not give me the address or put your phone number on a bit of paper for me. Then I could find out if your early letters ever reached her and if she writes to you at all."

"No, no!" Sue said, shrinking into tearful despair.

So Lesley herself retreated, baffled by an attitude she could not understand, an incapacity for self-defence that had played no part at any stage of her own upbringing. True, she had been passed to one or other of her several keepers, at hospital, institution or private home, an infant or small child, a parcel to be fed and guarded from harm. But these were surroundings to be accepted or fought, but on the whole without rancour,

126

occasionally with a certain glee in battle. Since she became old enough to think about her real parents she had always written off the young, lonely, stupid mother as worthless, while keeping a vaguely romantic admiration for the equally young, irresponsible father. He had known how to look after himself.

So she would always do likewise. Fight when she had to, take what she wanted by any means available; owe nothing, give nothing, for she began life with nothing.

At school she had got on well with her class, making no enemies, nor any friends. All the time she was planning to leave home she never discussed her intention nor her plans. Poor little Susan Ford was the very first individual she had genuinely pitied, not for what she suffered, but for her failure to stop it. Sue had a good home that she had left in a fit of religious mania, according to Lesley. Not to be able to throw it off was inexplicable.

However, she was not to be persuaded and before long Lesley had a new problem, a fresh acquaintance, a much more promising relationship.

This was a young man not altogether unknown to her, for she had seen him at all the combined gatherings or so-called services, of the Holy Group, during the weeks before the Christmas holiday. He came in a party of six or seven from the nearest of the men's and boys' houses, where the Ruler had his office, but did not live. This did nothing to recommend the young man, or his pals, and Lesley had made a point of avoiding them when the combined members were given coffee and biscuits together after their curious devotions. But Lesley did not fail to recognise him when he pushed his way into Mangoes one morning and asked to see Mr Perkins.

"He's in his office," she said, waving an arm towards the back of the shop.

"Could you ask him if he'll see me?" the young man said awkwardly.

There was no other customer, so Lesley just said, "What name?" and waited.

"Ben Shaw."

"Wait here."

She took the message to her employer, who gave her a keen look but simply said, "Show him in," sitting back in his swivel chair and following her with his small cold eyes as she went back into the shop.

"He'll see you," she said. "That door on the left. Go straight in. He doesn't like customers knocking."

The young man was absent for about fifteen minutes, during which time a pair of Asian women came in to buy the kind of rice they favoured. After that a couple of vegetarian students, both men, came in to ask if Mangoes kept a special kind of soya product they had been told to get, but had so far not been able to find.

Lesley was used to this sort of thing. She had not got it in stock, she told them, but could order it and in the meantime could she offer them — ?

They declined, hesitated, left the shop, came back after a discussion outside in St Andrew's Place and gave an order, but bought nothing.

"Bet they won't be back," a voice said behind her. It was the young man who called himself Ben Shaw.

"Got what you wanted from Mr Perkins?" she asked.

Ben nodded, hesitating as he moved towards the door of the shop. "You belong to the Holy Group, don't you?" he asked.

"Yes. So do you, don't you?"

"Thought I recognised you. The get-up really. Have you left them?"

"Not really. Still have a pad there and breakfast. Supper sometimes."

"But they let you come to work here?"

As another customer came in before she could answer, she turned away and Ben left at once.

He came again a few weeks later and again saw Mr Perkins, but he went straight to the office, and spent nearly half an hour there, leaving with only a nod and a muttered "Seeing you," as he crossed the shop.

However, on the following Saturday he came just before noon, when Mr Perkins was in the shop with Lesley, putting away or covering up the goods in the window.

128

Mr Perkins took him to the office at once; the visit lasted no more than five minutes. When the office door opened both Perkins and Ben came out, still talking; perhaps arguing, Lesley thought, turning her back on them. She heard Perkins say, as he saw Ben out of the door, "Playhouse Road, not here again. You understand?" Then the door shut and she heard Perkins turn the key in the lock and fasten the bolts.

"Have you finished, Miss Rivers?" the boss said, quite calmly, as if he had said and done nothing at all unusual.

"Yes, Mr Perkins."

"Come to the office, then. I have your money ready."

In the office she accepted the usual envelope and waited. As a rule Mr Perkins paid her and then let her out in the precinct, locking up after she had left. She always found him in the open shop on Monday morning. Today she waited.

"You are wondering why I have shut up already," he said, smiling his small cold smile. "I did not want that boy pushing in again. Also I want you to open the shop next Monday. The front door key is in the lock on the inside, as you have seen."

He paused, waiting for Lesley to nod, which she did quite automatically. Then he said, "I will let you out at the back and give you the key to that door. So get your things and come back here to the office."

So what? Lesley asked herself as she pulled on her overcoat. Was he going away for the weekend? Would he walk in on Monday after she arrived? Or was he doing a flit? Was the business cracking up? She remembered the order to Ben. Playhouse Road. Another branch of Mangoes? Or what? Finished? It might well be so, with the scatty nature of their business. Though the takings here had been improving steadily week by week and they had re-ordered several items in bulk, which she had been told to store in the cellar when the main storeroom on the ground floor was full.

She had been surprised to find a cellar on the premises. It was the first indication she had that the row of shops lining that side of the precinct had been developed from a group of small dwellings of the type of workmen's homes put up all over the south side of the river in late Victorian times to house the growing industrial invasion of the capital.

As she climbed back into the shop after storing the bulk parcels Lesley had wondered if Mr Perkins had living room, bedroom, a bathroom, lounge, kitchen, on the floors above the shop. There were obviously two floors above, but perhaps only two rooms on each.

Mr Perkins was waiting for her in his small hall, holding two keys on a ring.

"I shall be away until the middle of Monday morning," he told her.

"My rooms upstairs will be locked — against burglars," he added slowly and deliberately. Lesley felt herself growing red, but with a great effort kept her temper until her cheeks cooled.

She accepted the keys, thanked her boss, said she understood her orders but made no further answer, only a curt nod when he wished her goodbye.

In St Andrew's Place she found Ben waiting. In fact she was walking past him, very deep in thought about Mr Perkins's strange holiday when Ben Shaw stepped out of the crowd to join her.

They said "Hullo", still moving on and it was not until they had passed the end of St Andrew's Place that either of them spoke again. Then Ben said, "Where are you going?"

"Back to the House."

"Do you have to?"

"No. Not really."

"It's fine for once. Let's get something at Smollets and go along to Battersea Park."

"I've never been there. Is it far?"

"Not really. Couple of buses."

"O.K. Don't mind if I do."

Smollet's was new to Lesley. It was a large buffet-style food shop, on two floors: an upper storey served half a dozen hot dishes, with an alternative cold meal of varied salads, the same fresh lettuce, tomato and cucumber made up with ham, hard-boiled egg, spam or cheese. On the ground floor of the place a wide variety of sandwiches could be augmented by sausage rolls, veal and ham pies, or pâté.

They took separate trays and filled them on the ground floor. Lesley added an orange drink and Ben a can of beer. Both also added cups of coffee before they reached the pay desk.

Lesley had often passed this eating place, but had been put off by its size. However, the prices compared very favourably with the Swan Inn, which she had entered by herself only once when she wanted to find George. After that she considered it a waste of money. The little shop where she had talked to Mandy only did coffee, tea and sweet things, pastries, cream buns or biscuits.

The sun was still shining when they reached Battersea Park, that afternoon. The low beams sent long shafts across the grass, dazzling the pair as they strolled westwards, making the shadows of the tall trees run twice their standing height to cut the brilliant rain-splashed green of the grass into a flickering, changing pattern.

It was the first time Lesley had seen such things since she arrived in London. She was delighted, excited, astonished to find such scenes in a city she had begun to hate and had always regarded with doubt and growing fear.

"Come and look at the river," Ben said, taking her hand in his to guide her.

She let it rest there: it seemed the natural thing to do. Boys usually wanted to hold you after a bit. She felt quite easy with Ben, quite natural. This was something she had missed for far too long.

They stood and admired the river. Ben told her all he knew about it, which was not much.

"Have you always lived in London?" she asked.

"I think I was born in Devon," he answered.

"Don't you know?"

He dropped her hand abruptly.

"No, I don't. And I'm not going to talk about it. I joined the Group to find a home, with a friend at school, who felt the same. That's it, and you can pass up your bloody curiosity."

Lesley swept into anger and as rapidly out of it. Ben was walking away; she daren't be left, she'd be lost. She ran after him, caught him up, fastened on his arm in a grip he found surprisingly firm.

"Don't be a gormless idiot!" she stormed at him. "I'm the same. No family. No real home. Ditched them to get to London."

That surprised him into stopping to look at her.

"Honest?" he asked, unwilling to believe.

She nodded. She was not sure of her voice. She felt tears behind her eyes.

They walked on side by side. As the sun died the air grew very cold. Ben turned towards the distant gate through which they had come in.

"They close after dark here," he said. "We'd better not get shut in."

"There are more parks the other side of the river, aren't there?" Lesley asked, to avoid discussing the closing rules.

"Plenty. Hyde Park. Kensington Gardens. The Zoo. This side we've got Wandsworth Common, Clapham Common, Greenwich Park . . . "

"I've never heard of any of those."

"You haven't heard of much anywhere, have you?"

They reached the gate in good time and Ben led the way to the right bus stops, explaining the route as they made their way back to Upper Polson Road. He left her three doors away from Group House. Lesley thanked him shyly for showing her Battersea Park. It did not occur to her to ask for his address. He knew hers and she assumed he would continue to visit Mangoes for whatever business it was he performed with Mr Perkins.

That evening her mind was full of Battersea Park so she gave very little thought to Sue's problem and was both surprised and pleased when the girl came to her after supper with real news at last.

"I've been to see Mrs Trevelyan," she said. "You were right to persuade me to see her. She says she'll write to my mother."

"That's marvellous!" Lesley cried, taking Sue by the shoulders and kissing her. "Best thing you could do. When your mother knows how you've been deceived, she'll come and take you away."

132

"I do hope so," poor Sue answered. "Without any fuss, don't you think?" She tried to laugh, but did not quite manage it. "This *is* a free country, isn't it?"

Lesley assured her that it was, but knew, or thought she knew, that freedom took many forms. The freedom to bully and ill-treat children, the freedom to do criminal acts all too easily, to tell lies, to shut people up, not only in prisons, but in Homes, too. Yes, it was free enough for all that: you had to watch out for yourself, at all times, in all places.

Sister Manley rang the bell at Mrs Trevelyan's front door and waited. The delay that followed increased her growing anxiety, but her most recent interview with the Ruler offered no alternative to her present purpose. Mrs Trevelyan's letter had been a very serious threat to the smooth progress of the Group's real being: very serious indeed.

Mrs Trevelyan opened the door herself, apologised for her delay in welcoming her visitor, but gave no explanation of it.

"Come in, Helen, my dear. What can I do for you?"

Sister Manley said nothing until she was sitting near the log fire in Mrs Trevelyan's large drawing room, furnished amply as it had been in former days when Mr Trevelyan had been alive. He was a successful merchant between the wars, later a benevolent landlord watching at close quarters his surrounding district decline into latter day slums. But being of a strict puritan mind and heart he had clung to his bleak religion until he died. This meant holding on to and living in a property quite out of place, bereft of value, which continued to decline until his widow had to choose between small comfort in a flimsy box in suburbia or no real comfort at all among outworn, but long familiar surroundings.

"You are troubled, my dear," Mrs Trevelyan said as she sat down in her usual armchair opposite her visitor. "You look cold, too. What is the matter?"

"It's about one of our girls. I think you know her. Susan Ford."

"Of course I know her. Dear little person. Gentle, rather timid, I think. Not always happy."

"That's the trouble." Sister Manley leaned forward. "I am in constant touch with her mother. Sister Susan has a heart and mind that longs for true religion, true worship and service to others. But she is very emotional with it. At times we have been anxious about her. She has crises of doubt — She becomes confused — "

"I don't think I understand you," Mrs Trevelyan said slowly. "I have always found her a very sensible girl. In fact, far the most normal and sensible of any of your little party of charity collectors."

"She tends to make unwise friendships," Sister Manley said, moving the argument to a more intimately domestic line.

"You mean, of course, Lesley Rivers."

Mrs Trevelyan nodded her head as she spoke, considering Lesley, whom she could not help admiring, for her marked independence. The late Mr Trevelyan would have been delighted with Lesley, as a flourishing ewe lamb snatched into religion most unexpectedly. "Surely they hardly ever see one another these days? Lesley seems to be doing very well at that funny little shop in the precinct."

"Not so funny," Sister Manley said stiffly. "I'm afraid Sister Lesley is not at all good for Susan Ford. The Ruler himself is becoming anxious. He could consider moving Sue to another of our houses, where she would be away from Lesley's influence."

Sister Manley was astonished at her own disclosure. It was the last thing she had intended. Why had old Mrs T. talked about Lesley? She might have known it would upset her visitor. Better cut short the gen about Sue and go away before she had to explain —

Mrs Trevelyan stared at the fire while Sister Manley regained her usual composure; then she said, still not looking round, "What do Sue's parents think of it all? What do they write to her about it?"

"We have advised them not to write directly. We feared it might confuse the poor girl further. I write to them and they to me."

134

"They take this? They don't suggest coming to see her?"

"God forbid!" said Sister Manley fervently.

Mrs Trevelyan, looking straight at Sister Manley now and speaking very sternly for such a mild old lady said, "I think God is more likely to encourage a visit than otherwise. Or at any rate a letter. But the girl must make up her own mind about her beliefs and her actions. My sympathies, I don't mind telling you are with Sue in her uncertainties. I know all about rigidity in religious beliefs, Helen. My husband suffered from it; in his childhood from his father and in our marriage with his own children and mine, when we differed. So I know what I'm talking about."

Cunning old woman Sister Manley thought, smothering up what she's guessed about Sue's parents, their endless questions and nagging over Susan. All that twaddle about old Trevelyan. Been dead twenty years at least. She felt more not less desperate. She had nothing new to tell Mervyn. Better have that special service for Sue. Confession. Renewal of the oath. Forgiveness. Blessing. Get Mervyn to agree to sending Lesley away. Perhaps to the Y.W. If they'd have her?

When Sister Manley had gone Mrs Trevelyan went to her desk and found the piece of paper Sue had given her on which she had written her home address. Mrs Trevelyan then asked the telephone inquiry department to find her the number of that name and address. But when she dialled it there was no answer, either then or several times later that day and the next, and again later in the week.

"They are probably away for Christmas," Sue told her sadly, the next time the girl called on her.

"I suppose they may be," answered Mrs Trevelyan. "We must be patient, dear. You have waited a very long time for news of them, and they, as I see it, for real news of you. We must just go on trying at intervals."

"They want me to dedicate myself all over again," Sue complained.

"Well, that is something Christians do constantly, without a special service, isn't it? There is no harm in that."

"But I won't promise not to see Lesley or talk to her. They

can't make me do that. Les still wants me to let her ring up my mother and explain."

Mrs Trevelyan said firmly, "Tell Lesley that I have promised to get in touch with your mother as soon as I can. Tell her that is the safest, I mean, the best way for us all."

At the police station Detective Sergeant Cole made a point of running across Detective W.P.C. Drew.

He had not seen her since his urgent recall from his leave. He had been too busy and too fed up by the loss of a much needed holiday.

"Hullo!" he greeted her as his well managed path crossed hers.

"How did it go?" she asked. She did not seem at all surprised to see him, which was disappointing.

"Zero. Damn all. The bird hadn't flown; there wasn't the faintest whiff of a clue where he'd been except to visit his old ma."

"Just away for the weekend, as he told Lesley Rivers. Back on Monday, as expected."

"She told you that."

"Didn't she tell you?"

"I was away at the other end of the scene. Sussex."

"And then?"

"We wait for the next move. If there is one."

"So they need not have pulled you in. Big mistake. Frost, I suppose?"

"Maybe. He doesn't like me."

George laughed without mirth, turned to go but stopped.

"That girl, Lesley, still meets you occasionally?" he asked, and without waiting for an answer went on, "because if Perkins takes another weekend, leaving Les to lock up on the Saturday and leave by the back door, taking the keys with her and *if* he's given her notice a day or two before that he's going to do this, I'd like to know."

"I expect you would," Mandy told him, not particularly pleased by his manner of approach.

"You know what I mean?"

136

"Oh yes. But will it fit in with what Inspector Frost would like me to be doing?"

"Bugger Inspector Frost!"

"Hardly possible."

They glared at one another, each struggling to keep cool, to avoid cursing in language the more ridiculous, the more violently coarse it became. Mandy gave way first. Poor old George had lost his holiday, after all. And to no purpose.

"O.K. I'll report to you first, if anything about Perkins and the Mangoes shop comes my way. Is it likely to, or what, if anything?"

"Up to his old tricks, the word goes," Cole told her, but did not explain further.

It was her own fault, she told herself, for not reading quickly enough those bloody files.

13

Christmas came to Group House much as it did to the rest of
London, of England, of the northern European protestant
parts of practising Christendom. Not for most, the wider, extra-
vagant pagan season of mid-winter feasting and jollification
built up over the centuries rightly and understandably to break
into two unpleasant, icy parts, the bleak dark months of the
year, but for some people to add to the godless festivities an
infant Hope, a Divine Gift of continuing happiness, the better
life grown from continuing, if stern, effort. The Holy Group
extolled the aim, the goal, while, in withering insistence,
promoting the effort.

Feasting did occur, to a very moderate degree. The sisters
and brothers gave one another small presents at carefully
organised parties in the Great Hall in Upper Polson Street.
Sister Gordon played old-fashioned tunes on the little-used
grand piano there; dance tunes of the early jazz days and
popular songs of the three wars, the Boer, the First World, and
the Second World, War. Cissie herself had been on the stage
just after the Second World War; she knew that period best.
Surprisingly she had a clear, ringing soprano, well in tune,
which she produced, without lessons, in the style of Gracie
Fields, who was at the height of her fame when Cissie was a
small girl living in a bombed back street in the East End.

Lesley had the usual three days holiday over Christmas and
spent it almost entirely at Group House. It was difficult for her
to do anything else. Ben was equally caught up at his own
living house and though they met when the two groups came

138

to the Great Hall for the main services and for a community dance and a film show, also a rather unpleasant lecture from the Ruler on the subject of Service, they had long ago decided to keep their growing friendship and affection carefully hidden from Group House. Lesley was pretty sure it was known, since the ruling Sisters and Brothers and especially the Ruler himself, made it a chief part of their system to watch everyone closely. Particularly those whom they judged to be capable of living by the Rule, such as Susan Ford, or of destroying it, such as Lesley Rivers.

However, Ben and Lesley, comparing notes at fairly frequent intervals, were able to congratulate themselves on a genuine freedom from observation, or at any rate from comment, far less criticism.

Christmas over, work began again smoothly. Mr Perkins had another weekend away in a particularly cold spell of snow and ice in February. It followed exactly the same routine as on other occasions. It was in no way notable at Mangoes. It was the source of renewed bafflement for Det. Inspector Frost and his men.

Susan Ford, warned by Mrs Trevelyan, went about her work and her devotions at Group House calmly and in much better general health.

"Sister Susan has gained much benefit from her service of renewal," Sister Manley said to Sister Gordon at the conclusion of one of the former's audit of the kitchen accounts.

"She's better in health, that's for sure," Cissie answered, "I wouldn't like to say how it came about."

But she had a shrewd idea, for Ma Dill had told her that Miss Manley was upset she got no letters from that Mrs Ford now; not had a line since Christmas in spite of two of her own, gone unanswered.

Cissie had nothing to tell Ma Dill, nor was she in the habit of ever telling the old fraud the naked truth about the Group's doings: she would be too genuinely shocked, it was so far outside her cheerful petty wickedness.

Sister Gordon had, of course, guessed the real truth. Sue was again in touch with her parents and the means of her doing so were in the highly respectable, venerable, unassailable hands of their prime benefactress, Mrs Trevelyan. Whether Lesley Rivers had had any hand in it Cissie very much doubted. The girl was well established at her shop and her case had lost interest for Sister Manley. But not, of course, with Mervyn Grant, Ruler and Mind Twister. Cissie could not prevent herself giving and feeling a quick shudder every time he came within touching distance of her. Not that he ever made the slightest advance. His tastes she was sure, lay quite away from the straightforward whore she had been in her youth, on and off the stage.

"Meet me next Tuesday, Les," Sue whispered, as they left the Great Hall one evening.

They occupied single bedrooms now on different floors of the building. Sue was in charge of a larger dormitory on her floor, housing three newcomers of very different ages. Her gentle ways, effective now with her increased confidence, was just what was needed to dissolve the bitter tone of their incessant bickering.

"Same old coffee shop?" Lesley whispered back. "Quarter after twelve? O.K. Time you gave me all the latest, isn't it?"

This was, of course, the whole reason for Sue's marked improvement, Les knew. That approach to Mrs Trevelyan had done the trick. Sue must be in touch with her mother again.

It had been at Mrs Trevelyan's insistence, of course. The old lady had waited until a week after the New Year's Day was over and had then repeated her telephone calls until she got in touch with Mrs Ford.

This was followed by a call from Mr Ford, asking for an interview. He and his wife were completely surprised and indignant at the apparent deception. At any rate by the failure of their early letters to reach Susan and hers to reach them. Taking Mrs Trevelyan's advice he would not begin an attack upon the Group officially until he had spoken with her and been put in the correct picture, not the vague landscape offered by Miss Helen Manley.

"An arid desert, I begin to fear, my dear," Mrs Trevelyan

said, when Sue had read this letter and handed it back to her friend.

"I suppose so," the girl answered. She was still smarting from her new knowledge of the strange, dangerous methods used by the cult to secure its acolytes. "I was mistaken in its methods because its aims seemed beautiful to me in their writings."

"Which were made by the original founder, Susan. Not this Mr Grant, who took over, very persuasively, I must say."

"Definitely *not* Mr Grant," Sue agreed.

"I have asked your mother to write to you and send the letter to me. So you will collect it here the next time you call. I will arrange to meet your father in the City when he next comes up on business. Do you agree to that?"

"Agree! Oh, of course! And bless you, bless you — "

Sue was half-laughing, half-crying, and the tears of thankfulness and gratitude won, so Mrs Trevelyan went away to make a pot of tea to calm them both before the girl went back to her strange duties.

It was not surprising then that Sue had a lot to tell Lesley as they sipped their coffee and ate some very tasteless but hygienically wrapped sandwiches at the shop in the main road.

"You'd better not let them know at Group House," Lesley said.

"No fear! I may be wet, but not quite nuts."

"Far from it. But I honestly think the Ruler *is* cracked. He must be. I don't forget." She patted her wrist strap.

"I don't blame you."

They were silent for a few seconds. Then, to change the subject Susan said, "Are you still going out with Ben Shaw?"

"As a matter of fact, I am. He's a bit rough, but he means well, I think. He's lonely. He didn't choose to leave home. It broke up. Neither of his parents wanted him, so it was a kid's home, the public kind, like me."

Susan nodded and sighed her sympathy. It was so ordinary and so sad. She felt guilty over deserting her own home, leaving them, not the other way round. Her fault. Never again if it worked out the way Mrs Trevelyan wanted. And the way she herself wanted now, most fervently. Father, more than silly little mother, with her painted nails and her blue-circled eyes and her hair dyed to hide the white bits, not the punk colours, thank goodness, but a hard dark brown that had never been its real shade.

As the spring advanced Ben grew more and more restless on his outings with Lesley. The evenings were too light, the sun stayed higher in the sky, more inviting. In the country it would be staying up even longer, the sunset would not drive it below the embracing, imprisoning, tower blocks. It was not yet warm enough to suggest camping out for a weekend, even if he could have got leave at his House to do so, except possibly with others of his Group there. But a shorter outing must surely be possible, if they could stay out all the evening.

"Yes, I'd like that," Lesley told him when he suggested this way of spending a Sunday afternoon. "Where could we go? Old Perks is working up to another round again, isn't it, for whatever they send you in for?"

"Two weeks from now," Ben told her.

So when Mr Perkins announced his intention of leaving her to lock up on Saturday and open again the following Monday morning, and when Ben, as expected, made his usual discreet entrance, moving quietly past several customers she was serving in turn, to pass without knocking into the office at the back of the shop before Lesley took the first of them to the pay-desk, she was not surprised. It confirmed their plans, already made. Three more days. She would leave the detail to him.

She went on dealing with the work in the shop. Ben did not come through the front again, but that was not unusual. Old Perks always let him out at the back. So she had no inclination and indeed no time to look out into the precinct. Nor, if she had done so, would she, most probably, have noticed George Cole move away from staring at the goods in a photographic store on the opposite side of St Andrew's Place.

But the next day she did run into Mandy Drew again, passing through with a bag of food from the multiple chain store at the end of the precinct. They had not seen one another for several weeks, so Mandy insisted upon sharing news over a cup of coffee, though she had very little to say for herself when they did sit down and were served.

"Well I've not done anything much myself," Lesley said. "Ben Shaw turns up very regularly, I must say. Gets a bit edgy these days."

"What way? Making passes?"

"That? Oh well, at the pictures it's the usual, of course. But never goes far."

Mandy laughed.

"Proper old hand, are you? With your face, I suppose — "

Lesley flushed. She knew her own feelings about Ben well enough. Progressive. Only with him it wasn't holding him off or knocking him off. It was trying sometimes to bring him on. Only she wasn't going to let Mandy in on that sort of thing. So she changed the subject, or rather moved it sideways.

"Actually he's been in at Mangoes this morning. He brings a message of some sort to Perkins from the Ruler. That's the bloke that runs the Group houses. Ben gets a parcel to take back to this Ruler. Or so he says. Might be for himself for all I know."

"Really? What do you think it is? I mean, you do sell odd things, don't you? Could it be — ?"

"Drugs? I don't know. Of course that's what you're bound to think of, isn't it?"

"Is it?"

Mandy was looking very bright-eyed and inquisitive, Lesley thought, so she changed the subject again and began to talk about bus and coach trips into the country now that summer was coming on. Mandy listened with interest but showed no more curiosity about the boy friend.

Meanwhile Ben's plans went ahead, so that when the free weekend came along he had tickets for Sunday that would take them to Box Hill in the morning and back to south London by nine o'clock that evening. Saturday would not give them enough time for the round trip, only starting in the afternoon.

All went well. At 12 p.m. exactly on Saturday Mr Perkins put the 'Closed' notice on the door, locked and bolted it, called

Lesley into the office, paid her the week's wages, minus as usual her board and lodging fee for the Group, gave her the shop key and a key to the back door and sent her off with his usual bleak, half-smile.

"See you Monday, Miss Rivers. Goodbye."

"Yes, Mr Perkins. Goodbye."

She hurried back to Group House to make ready for her outing with Ben on Sunday. They were to start mid-morning on a coach into Kent and leave it near Sevenoaks. A picnic lunch which she would provide. Not to doll up, he had said. As if she would. She knew why they were going to Box Hill. To get away from the crowds, to find country solitude in some spot where the sun shone clearly, where there were trees and bushes and soft grass to lie on; where Ben would make love to her if she was willing. And she had known at the cinema ever since Christmas he would not need much persuading. He turned her on all right now. He'd just been waiting for a real chance.

She was right. They did not have to say anything. Words had never been their mode of communication, nor much used in any place where they had passed their childhood, nor even at their schools. But words had no part in their progress from friendship to affection, to passion.

Ben led the way: for once, Lesley was content to follow. They climbed a wooded slope by a well-used track, left it by a ragged patch, half blocked by bramble and nettles and came out on the sunny side of the hill, where the ground fell away sharply towards the edge of chalk cliffs. Here they had to turn back towards the trees, but moving along parallel with the steep edge they reached the end of the thick undergrowth and found just what they had wished for, a patch of sunlit grass with bushes, at the foot of short trees, and with a wide view across the valley.

Here Ben threw down the haversack with their lunch packets and beer cans. They ate, drank, and lay back, resting in the sun, happy, not tired by the longish walk, for both were strongly built and always active. They were not sleepy, but equally expectant.

144

Ben had discarded his jacket when they boarded the coach and his T-shirt when they began their walk. His belt went now and he rolled close to Lesley to undo the fastenings of her jeans and unbutton her blouse. She had taken off her cardigan for the climb up the hill and tied the arms round her waist. She had rolled up the sleeves of her shirt blouse. Ben unfastened the buttons, felt behind her back for the fastening of her bra and began to pull it away too.

Lesley began to laugh.

"You're tickling!"

"Do it yourself, then."

She sat up, still laughing, pulling off blouse and bra, then flopped back, arms spread for him.

He began to kiss and fondle her until he felt the fastening of the leather strap she always wore on her right wrist scrape his neck as she closed her arms about him. He pulled away, took hold of her arm, quickly undid the fastening, pulled the offending leather away.

Lesley, dazed by her growing passion, had not understood his complaint, nor what he was doing. In fact she had shut her eyes when he began to kiss her, but now she opened them.

She saw him gazing at her wrist, turning it over and back, his eyes puzzled, then understanding, with such a face of horrified astonishment that she cried out, "The mark! What *He* did to me, the devil! The bloody - "

"T," he whispered. "The mark! T for *Thief*!"

"Because I nicked a few things from Ma Dill's and that."

Understanding grew in both of them.

"You must of been there with the rest! You were, weren't you? Saw me held down, that pad over my mouth, suffocating, the pain! Nearly killed me, it did, honest, the wicked devil! Nuts! Must be to do a thing like that! Nearly *killed* me!"

"It was *me*," he told her, in the same hoarse whisper. "Oh, my darling! Oh my love, my poor love! He made me - I saw nothing but that wrist, strapped down, not a movement. Automatic. Worked up. Couple of pills, too."

He broke off, rolled away and covering his face with his hands, began to shake with slow, painful sobs.

145

Lesley heaved herself upright. Was Ben telling her it was he who had assaulted her, wounded her, disfigured her! No lover, Ben! Just another parcel of deceit! Another enemy! No breakaway, no reward for good behaviour. Only another crippling blow from the ever hostile world!

She launched a well-directed kick at the long sun-tanned back on the ground beside her, yelling abuse the stronger for the real grief behind it.

This brought Ben instantly out of his shocked remorse into self-defence. He sprang up to face her.

"I tell you I didn't know it was you! I was acting under orders. He does that. You know he does. Bloody devil! I'll kill him! I swear I will!"

"You did it and nothing can take it away? You're as guilty as him! I hate you! I hate you!"

She rushed at him, seized his hand and tried to throw him. But Ben too had learned self-defence in early boyhood. He was a good deal stronger and heavier than she was. She had the knack, the method, but she was very much out of practice during her months at Group House. He was prepared by her kick and met her attack with equal skill but more than equal effectiveness. They fell together, rolled in wild combat until Lesley lay inert under his weight.

He could have taken her then; he was ready to do so, with a great surge of male desire, male lust for triumph as well as possession. But the inner weakness that had made him the prey, the messenger, the servant of the Ruler, came to his help now to save him from destroying a real love for both Lesley and himself. He saw the look of fury, misery and despair in the white face below him. A closed face, turned inwards. Closed to him, perhaps for ever.

He rolled away, dragged himself to his feet, gathered up his clothes and the haversack and dashed away into the wood, knocking into tree trunks until he nearly winded himself and was forced into a walk and at last to a standstill in a small clearing. Here, in utter silence, in slowly darkening shade, he sat, recovering, until at last he pulled on his shirt and jacket and began slowly to find his way back to the road.

Lesley stayed as Ben had left her. She did not question her attempted revenge upon him for the Ruler's atrocious injury, but as her fury melted away it was replaced by an overwhelming sense of loss, more considerable than the cynical affirmation of her general outlook on the world of mankind, the universal, deliberate giving of pain, frustration, the universal hypocrisy.

She ought to have understood that Ben was the Ruler's hitman, his messenger, his slave. Of course, Ben could not have recognised her in the darkened Great Hall. They had never met or spoken until he came to Mangoes on the Ruler's errand. But he had held the branding iron; he had pressed it down on her wrist; he had done that, watched her struck into unconsciousness, heart-stopping, no mere faint they told her; or rather Sue told her, weeks later. He had not known her from any other girl in the Group, but he had been willing to burn another human being, and think nothing much of doing so. With unusual honesty she told herself she did not really mind that. What she did not forgive was that it was done to herself.

Having at last understood this, recognised a familiar pattern, however bitter, Lesley sat up, groaning a little because she had suffered bruises in her fight with Ben. More than he had, she realised, remembering how he had rushed away, as vigorous as ever, not a muscle suffering, as hers were, with the bruises stiffening rapidly.

She got back into her clothes, found a comb in her handbag and also the return tickets for their coach from Sevenoaks. Both tickets.

She looked at her watch. Time to get down off this damned hill and back to the bus stop. Would he turn up there, knowing as he must by now, that she had the tickets? Or find some other way?

It took her longer to get back, without him to guide her. But she managed it. She could not be defeated twice on the same day. And Ben was not at the stop, nor did he arrive before the coach left. She travelled alone, had no heart to buy herself a lonely meal and having got back to Group House a little before dark, went to bed hungry, but exhausted and slept at once the night through, soundly, without dreams.

On Monday, another sunny morning mocked both Lesley and Ben in their respective bleak homesteads with memories of their ruined Sunday outing. Each of them felt guilty pangs on waking, then self-justification took over. Ben knew he had been callous to behave in real life with the same disregard for inflicting physical pain that he was well used to viewing with indifference on television or at the cinema.

But, after all, the bint was a proved petty thief, so she deserved it.

Lesley, still feeling an occasional twinge from her many bruises, knew that she had begun the fight that she had lost, also that Ben could not possibly have known her in the darkened hall, nor recognised her at Mangoes. But he was a sap to confess his part in maiming her and a brute in taking advantage of his male strength in crushing her attack. Also when he had her where he wanted her, underneath him, helpless and still, inevitably willing, he had not taken this advantage but run off like a bloody little schoolboy.

In this saddened but defiant mood Lesley went along to the shop punctually at eight o'clock on Monday morning. She let herself in at the back door, leaving the key in the inside hole in the lock and the door unfastened. She did not expect Mr Perkins to show up until nine o'clock, and he would have his own key, but the door must be open for him, according to his rule.

It was when she had the shop in running order, everything looking fresh and tidy and the notice 'Open' hanging on the door, that the non-appearance of the boss began to bother her.

She had served three customers, all West Indian and regular users of several special grains, that Lesley decided it was time she discovered if Mr Perkins was still absent or was he staying in his flat on purpose, leaving her to run the shop on her own? Surely unlikely? Then was he ill? If so he must be *very* ill, too ill to have put out a written message for her, even rung up

Group House with a warning not to come, even called out, thumped on the floor, even —

There were more customers in the shop now, none she recognised. Monday was always slack. She must do something when she had seen them off. That meant she must go upstairs to find out.

Find out. To stop panicking. Stop making a fool of herself by running out into St Andrew's Place calling out — what? Lost the boss? Lost the little twit with the nasty smile and wrinkly hands!

She tried to laugh at herself: told herself not to be a scatty idiot; still upset by yesterday, of course. With great resolution she went first to the office. There was nothing alarming there. All tidiness and locked drawers.

Next into the tiny hall inside the back door and the stairs to Mr Perkins's flat. She called his name several times, heard nothing, except the arrival of a pair of customers in the shop behind her. With relief she went back to the job.

Later, she knew she must try again. There was nothing to be afraid of, since there had been no response whatever to her calls. She had only to go up to make sure he was not back. Probably the three doors on the landing would be locked, too. That would prove he was still away. She must just make sure, then she could go back to the shop and wait.

The three doors were not locked. The first opened on a bathroom: everything in order there. The second was evidently Mr Perkins's small lounge, also tidy, lifeless in appearance, Lesley thought, leaving it without going in, closing the door again softly.

The third door led to Mr Perkins's bedroom. He was there all right.

He was half sitting, half lying, fully dressed, on his bed, reclining stiffly against piled-up pillows. His face, swollen, distorted, a mottled purplish red colour, the mouth half-open, the tongue thrust forward behind the upper denture, that hung grotesquely from it. He glared at Lesley from inside the large plastic bag that covered his head and was fastened tightly about his neck.

149

Lesley screamed and ran. She stumbled, almost fell, down the steep, narrow stairs. As she reached the foot of them the back door opened and in stepped a familiar figure.

"George!"

"What's up? You screamed!"

He caught hold of her as she lurched forward.

"Perkins! Up there! Horrible! Horrible!"

He let go, pushing her towards a new figure that appeared from the shop.

Mandy said to her, "Something awful, Les?"

"Perkins! Done himself in! Horrible!" She leaned on the banisters, vomiting, sobbing, feeling Mandy's arms supporting her, hearing Mandy's voice asking, "Is it him, George?"

"Yes. Stiff. Murder by the look of it. Go out front and clear the shop. Our team'll be here in five minutes. I'll see to Lesley. Leave her to me."

Lesley looked up, fighting her misery, the shock, the terror.

"So you two really *are* the fucking fuzz, George," she said.

14

By the time George and Mandy had persuaded Lesley to walk to the former's car, parked in the road that led from the alley behind Mangoes to Brindley Square, the uniformed police had arrived in the precinct to complete the closure of the shop and disperse the crowd still eagerly hoping for some drama to justify the awful scream that had thrilled those nearest to its source.

The more intelligent soon realised that they would see no ambulance, no interesting stretcher, bearing an inert bundle hidden under blankets, no handcuffed villain rushed to a waiting police car. For no vehicles of any kind were allowed on to the sacred pavement of the precinct, at any time, except a necessary fire engine perhaps. There was clearly not a fire.

In fact, before the reluctant crowd gave up all hope of an actual thrill, a police unit had arrived at the back of the shop, to be shown the incident by Constable Torch and settle down to exercise their various skills of photography, finger printing and so on, while a police doctor, arriving separately, dealt with the corpse, together with Detective Superintendent Walsh, who had been directing the whole matter of Perkins's recent activities and was now to investigate the old lag's murder.

They stared at the corpse for a few seconds, then the doctor said, "Phoney suicide. Obviously strangled. Can we have the bag off?"

"Of course."

The prints men got busy, the bag was removed. There was no deeper ligature round the victim's neck. It had been a manual strangulation stopping the air from reaching the lungs and the blood from passing to and also from, the face, head and brain.

"Strong grip," the doctor said. "But this is a small man, getting on, too. Never had much of a life, I'd guess."

"Spent a fair amount of it in the nick," remarked the superintendent.

"Ready for the ambulance, doc?"

"Oh yes. Mortuary P.M. as soon as possible. I'd say he's been dead for at least thirty hours. Perhaps longer; the weather's been reasonably cool over the whole weekend, of course."

The black police ambulance picked up the shrouded remains of Mr Perkins from the road behind St Andrew's Place and nobody noticed it go.

Meanwhile George, in the passenger seat of the police car that had brought him and Mandy to the shop that morning, with Lesley sitting beside Mandy in the back, were driven to the local police station. George spoke a few words to his driver, but the girls did not speak at all.

In fact it soon became clear that Lesley had no intention of saying anything again, at least until she was out of police hands. She moved when she was told to do so, she left the car, she took Mandy's hand, or rather she did not pull her own away when the policewoman helped her from the car. She stood waiting in the small bare room she was taken to, and sat on one of the small upright chairs beside a mica-topped central table. But she did not speak and when George began to ask her about her discovery of Perkins's body she did not even move her head in his direction.

He very soon gave up his attempt to get a statement and after a whispered consultation with Mandy he left the room to return almost at once with another woman police officer, in uniform, with a pleasant unremarkable face, who was introduced as Constable Janet, after which the two detectives went out again together.

Lesley still stared ahead, saying nothing.

"Well," Constable Janet said pleasantly. "You've had a particularly nasty shock, dear, I can see that. Has Sergeant Cole ordered some tea for you, Miss — I didn't catch the name?"

"Rivers," Lesley said, looking at her questioner for the first time. "Lesley Rivers, as I bet you know quite well already."

"You've had a very nasty shock, Miss Rivers," the constable went on, repeating herself, "and I'm sure you need a good strong cuppa. If Sergeant Cole didn't order — "

"I need the *loo*!" said Lesley. "Pretty soon, too, or else — "

"Come along then!" said Constable Janet smartly, dropping the soft-toned voice in favour of a ringing tone of command, to which Lesley, whose need was desperate, responded at once.

On getting back to the small room, she found another policeman in charge, an older man, who said crisply, "This is — "

"Miss Lesley Rivers, sir," said the constable and turning to Lesley said, "This is Detective Inspector Frost, Miss Rivers. He will need to hear your account of what happened at the shop this morning."

"Why?" asked Lesley, still defiant. "George knows what happened. He was just coming in, a couple of minutes after I screamed out, seeing that poor little bugger's face inside his suicide bag."

"Why do you say suicide, Miss Rivers?" Frost asked.

"Stands to reason. The bag. They take the pills and then fasten the bag on — "

She put both hands to her face and swayed forward. Constable Janet eased her into a chair opposite Frost, who pushed a steaming cup across the table towards her.

"Drink some of this, dear," the constable said. The soothing voice had returned; this time Lesley accepted the help offered.

She realised that she must give an account of her discovery: for the inquest of course. She had been the first to discover Perkins's death. She need not fight the coppers over her misfortune, the publicity and all that — not their fault — sort of job they had to do.

She sipped the hot tea and felt a good deal better. She heard Inspector Frost saying, "But it was not suicide, Miss Rivers.

We have clear evidence that suggests it was murder. In which case your description of what you found will be most important in our finding the murderer and the motive and in fact resolving the whole case."

"Not suicide! That's crazy! Who'd want to rub out that little runt!"

"You'd be surprised," said Frost. "That little runt, as you call him, was not as harmless as you imagine. Or are you putting that on?"

Lesley stared. She finished the tea, then said slowly, "I don't know what you mean."

But a light was beginning to shine in her brain, her memory. George and Mandy, the betrayers — Perkins at the Swan — George, the first time she'd met him — Perkins fumbling — Her cut at him — Not that, so much as George, that he'd recognised . . . Well, what d'you —

"A very bad hat," Inspector Frost told her. "You may hear some details of his past at the inquest. But I'm not concerned at this moment with your connection as his assistant. We'll be having a very close look at the health food angle and the books of the business and all that, later on. What I want from you now is a clear, detailed account of your movements this morning from the time you opened the shop to the discovery of the body and the arrival of Detective Sergeant Cole and Woman Detective Constable Drew."

Lesley had listened carefully to this long explanation, but she was not going to accept it. Not yet.

"I feel cold," she complained. "That bloody pair rushed me out without my things."

"You mean your outdoor coat?"

"I mean my cardigan and my handbag." She pulled off the flowered overall she always wore in the shop, bundled it up and pushed it across the table towards the inspector. Constable Janet intercepted it and at a signal from Frost left the room.

"I'm sure your belongings will have been brought away safely," he said, frowning. "Didn't Sergeant Cole or Constable Drew mention having them?"

"I'm not talking to *them*," Lesley said angrily. "Not ever

again, the way they've conned me, with them pretending they were just boy and girl-friends and sorry I was a bit lost in London on account of running away from home."

"But what you told them was true, Miss Rivers?"

"If they reported it truly, yes."

Frost could have told her that George had recorded some of his conversations with her, but he had no intention of feeding her obvious grievance. It had been an idea of George's, quite unofficial, which might or might not prove ultimately useful. In the meantime he did not seem to have got very far with this reluctant witness's statement.

However, after Lesley was again in possession of her handbag and cardigan, which she put on, taking her own time to do so and attending to her hair and face as well, Detective Inspector Frost did persuade her to describe the morning's shocking discovery and did convince her of the doctor's decision that Perkins had been murdered. He led her into making a coherent account of the morning's events, which he recorded, together with his promptings, and then sent away to be turned into a typed statement for her to sign.

At this point Lesley got up to go. She saw no point in waiting any longer in this dreary room.

"Sit down," said Frost, with authority. "You still have to sign your statement."

Cursing inwardly, Lesley sat.

"Tell me more about those weekends when Perkins left you in charge," the Inspector said. "Do you remember the first time?"

"Of course. It was last autumn. I remember because it was a Saturday, when Ben was . . . " She stopped, for it had flashed into her mind that her boy-friend or no — never again, damn him . . .

"Yes?" Frost said carefully. "Would that be a fellow — er — Grouper?"

"Of course. Ben Shaw. Met at the Great Hall. Before he started coming to Mangoes."

"What did he come there for?"

"How do I know? To see Mr Perkins. Never stayed long."

155

"I see. That was on a Saturday, too, then?"

"Yes. Not the first time. I don't remember."

She began to wonder if these visits for the Ruler could have anything to do with Perkins's death. The bloody Ruler. If Perks was a baddy, mixed up with some gang in which the Ruler operated; if Ben was acting as the Ruler's hit-man and the boss had indeed been murdered — ? No way! Impossible! Not Ben, not her first real boy-friend! Never! Never!

"The first time you were given the backdoor key and asked to open the shop the following Monday morning was on a Saturday when Ben Shaw had visited Perkins?"

"Sent by the Ruler with a message. Not for himself."

"How do you know that?"

"Ben told me."

"You are real friends then?"

"Sort of. Same Group. I live at the Holy Group House. He lives at the Ruler's house, wherever that is."

"You don't know? You have not been there?"

"Of course not. I told you, we'd met at the Great Hall, for so-called parties. Only they weren't real parties. No band. Not much fun."

Detective Inspector Frost nodded.

"I can believe that," he said. "Now, let us go back to that first time you were given the back-door key. This was a Saturday, I think you said?"

"You damn well know I did. Yes. Ben always came on a Saturday."

"You left that day by the back door?"

"I always left by the back door."

"Did Mr Perkins show you his flat at any time?"

Lesley flushed.

"I'll say he didn't! Not that I'd have gone up there. Catch me!" She gave one of her unexpectedly raucous laughs. "He said the doors were locked. Said that on purpose — putting ideas! I took no notice."

"No. So when did you see Ben Shaw again?"

"Don't remember."

She saw the unbelief in the detective's eyes, which increased

156

her anxiety. Were they trying to put something on Ben, the bloody snoopers? Pick on the first name going. But it was no good just shutting up; have to do better than that to satisfy them. And no lies, either. This thin one with the thin nose; far too sharp, carve up poor weak Ben, poor rough lout, poor *love*!

"When did he come again on Mr Grant's business?"

"Who's that?"

"You call him the Ruler. His name, which you must really know is Grant, Mervyn Grant. When did Ben come to Mangoes again?"

"He didn't. At least — "

Now the copper was really getting at Ben and she remembered hearing Perks say to him not to call at the precinct shop but at a place called ... called — Play boy — no — Play-house Road — "

"Go on, Miss Rivers."

"Mr Perkins said to call at some place else — called Play-something. I don't remember." She was exasperated. They were trying to get her to sneak on Ben. She wasn't having that, damn them.

"Look!" she cried, and there was an hysterical note in her voice, "Ben Shaw's been my boy-friend ever since then. We've been out weekends to the Park — "

"Battersea?" asked Frost, calmly.

"That and the ones over the river, too."

"And this last weekend? Were you out with Ben Shaw then, too?"

"Yes. Sunday. To Box Hill, by coach."

"There and back?"

"Yes."

Detective Inspector Frost stared at her before he asked the next question, then said, "And what about Saturday? Another time you were given the keys, wasn't it? At noon on the Saturday. What did you and Shaw do on Saturday, Miss Rivers?"

She stared back. This was serious. She had not seen Ben at all. No, that was wrong. She had met him in the precinct, just to confirm times and the meeting place for the next day's

157

outing to Box Hill. So Ben had the whole afternoon and evening to himself. Perkins had died that day, the cop had told her, quoting the police doctor. So had Ben? They'd put it on him if they could. Had Ben? Her Ben?

All the feelings of anger, of revenge for her branding, of shame, of resentment for George and Mandy's deception, all this vanished in her urgent need to protect the only person she had ever seriously cared for in her whole life.

She said, quite calmly, after a short pause, "Met up same as usual. Too hot for the Parks. Too many sods lying everywhere on the grass. Couldn't afford much with the coach ride coming up next day. Had lunch and got things for the Sunday picnic. Oh yes, sat on the river front near the National. Went to the pictures."

"Can you tell me where?"

"The Phoenix," Lesley said, because she had been there during the week and remembered the main programme.

"What did you see?"

"Meaning the film? Oh yes, *The Dark Tide*."

There was a knock on the door. Frost said "Come" and a young uniformed officer appeared with Lesley's statement, neatly typed. She looked round for a pen, but Detective Inspector Frost said, "Read it first, Miss Rivers. If there is anything you dispute I'd like to know."

In another room at the Police Station Ben had given a reluctant but quite clear account of his dealings with Mr Perkins. His interviewer was George Cole, who seemed to him to be more interested in the Holy Group than in the late Mr Eddie Perkins.

The news of the shopkeeper's death had been a shock to Ben, particularly unwelcome because he had recognised his questioner among the people in St Andrew's Place that morning as someone he had often seen there before when he had carried messages to Perkins from the Ruler. As with Lesley he had not connected the plain clothes man with the police, but unlike her he felt no particular resentment when the uniformed copper drove him with others from the door of the shop after it was locked by a girl, not Lesley, who appeared behind the glass to hang up the notice 'CLOSED' when she had expelled the last of the customers.

"Why were you in the precinct this morning?"

No answer.

"Were you there with another of those messages?"

"I told you. He said never again at the shop."

"Where then?"

George looked down at a slip of paper that had been brought to him.

"Was it an address in Playhouse Road?"

"If you know it, why ask?"

"What is the exact address in Playhouse Road? Why did you refuse to give it if you were acting only as a messenger, not knowing the nature of the message?"

"It's the Group House; hasn't a number, nor a name except Holy Group like the one in Upper Polson Street. As if you didn't know."

"Actually, I did *not* know."

"Don't give me — "

"Don't be cheeky, Ben. I'm only asking these questions for your own good."

Ben stared. His face wore the blank look he always put on before authority of any kind, when physical resistance could not be used because the odds were impossibly high. As now, he had already failed: again as now, with this chap, so bloody smooth you'd skid for sure which ever way you took off.

George knew the look and was worried. He'd got no further at present on the lad's relations with Perkins or with the so-called Ruler. He changed the subject.

"Why were you in St Andrew's Place this morning?"

The different tone of voice encouraged Ben's reluctant respect for his interviewer.

"To see my girl. That's Lesley Rivers."

"Yes. She has been telling us how she found Mr Perkins."

Ben jumped up. Cole raised a hand. The looker-on beside the door was on his feet in a second.

"Sit down," Sergeant Cole ordered. "She is being well and

159

kindly treated. Her story must be recorded for the inquest as well as in the investigation of the murder."

Ben subsided. No point in going into all that about her reaction to sudden shock, the branding, her illness. No, by God, he'd not tell the fuzz a damned thing.

"I think you and Miss Rivers have become friends," George patiently began again. "You will appreciate that this last weekend is critical to the case. Has Les — has Miss Rivers told you Perkins left her to shut shop, which she did? We think we know now that his death probably took place on Saturday afternoon or evening, at any rate before Sunday morning, more than thirty hours before discovery, the doctor says. Not proved, of course, but you will realise we have to know of anyone who called to see him during the weekend, at any time after Miss Rivers left the shop by the back door, locking it with the key Mr Perkins gave her."

This last bit of information gave Ben a clue to the detective's purpose. He had to know exactly how the couple, so closely connected, even if ignorant, or more important, innocent, of any criminal act, had passed their time at the weekend in possession of direct means of entering Mr Perkin's premises. Well, he'd tell him, tell him proper, tell him . . .

Christ! That Saturday. They'd only had a word when she finished at the shop. He'd waited for that in the road at the back and not seen her again till they met at the bus stop on the way to the coach. Could she? No, nor he himself. They'd both said too often they'd like to kill the Ruler, but little old Perks. Why should they?

"No," he said loudly, after a pause that George Cole knew was longer than it should have been. "I don't know anything about Perkins except the Ruler sent me for his medicine parcel or whatever it was."

This told George rather more about the Shaw visits than he already knew, but he was intent upon finishing the account of the pair's doings over the whole weekend, so he simply said, "You waited to join Miss Rivers after the shop closed that Saturday?"

"How many more times — "

160

"Did you stay together that Saturday afternoon?"

"Course we did. Battersea Park in the sun. Went to the flicks later," Ben lied.

"Do you remember which cinema?"

"Regal. Local one."

"What did you see? Can you remember that, too?"

"Forget the name, Air fighting, car, America, noisy stunts, like they always do have. All right, if you go for that kind of thing."

George looked at him, a grin he did not try to hide showing plainly his unbelief in young Shaw's lame account of a film he certainly had not seen, but perhaps had noticed its advertised delights outside the cinema. He got up.

"Wait here a few minutes," he said, moving away.

"What the hell?" Ben was on his feet too, prepared to leap for the door himself.

"No, you don't," the silent watcher told him, instantly in his way.

When Lesley had signed her name at the bottom of the statement she laid down the pen she had accepted for that purpose and rose to her feet. Surely now?

"I know you are anxious to get away from here," Detective Inspector Frost said quietly, "and so you shall. But my superior officer, who is now in charge of the murder case, has ordered me to take you to meet him. He is Detective Superintendent Walsh. He is impressed by the clear detail in your statement."

"Seen it, has he?" Lesley said, her impatience fading at the praise implied by these words. "Clear detail — all put in by you, Mr — er,"

"Detective Inspector Frost," murmured Constable Janet.

"Mr Frost," said Lesley, defiantly. But she made no objection to leaving the interview room and following the detective inspector to a door at the end of another corridor, on which Frost knocked and hearing a loud 'Come', opened and ushered in Lesley and her escorting policewoman.

Lesley saw a keen-faced, tall man with grey hair and a short,

161

nearly white moustache, who rose from his chair behind a dark wooden desk and held out a hand towards her over a row of telephones.

"How d'you do, Miss Colbert," he said clearly, pronouncing the name in two syllables, equally and distinctly pronounced.

Lesley stood frozen, two paces from the intervening desk, staring, terror choking her, the room whirling, while the detective superintendent's voice boomed from the growing darkness, "That is your real name, isn't it, Miss Colbert? Marion Colbert. — Marion — COLBERT — "

Lesley fell on to the desk, scattering the telephones, a limp figure, white-faced, open-mouthed, without breath or pulse.

15

By the evening of that eventful Monday Lesley had recovered full consciousness, though she did not yet choose to open her eyes, far less attempt to move her body. She lay flat on her back now, the foot of the bed slightly raised to encourage her restored circulation to feed her brain as well as possible after the dangerous lack during the time her heart had stopped beating.

The shock this time had been purely mental, and treatment rapid and effective. Mandy was in Detective Superintendent Walsh's room: she had tried to warn him of Lesley's account of her previous shock, much against the sharp order of Detective Inspector Frost, but the two men had decided against 'soft soap'. You got the truth from liars by jumping a surprise on them. The bigger the surprise the better.

The bigger the result. All that unofficial work by Detective W.P.C. Drew proved correct, the operation was a total success, but the patient very nearly died.

However, Lesley did survive, in a hospital bed in a single room, in the nearest hospital to which she was rushed from the police station with two ambulance men and a young doctor giving her heart massage and oxygen and an injection, so that she arrived with feebly responding lungs and an irregular pulse and a definite hope that the brain damage would not be severe.

Lesley lay with her eyes closed and her brain continuing to clear. At first her return to consciousness was a mixed vision of childhood scenes, school friends, school teachers, Marion do this, Marion don't do that, the shop, Uncle C, as she called her adoptive father, the grocer, for she never would call him Pa or Dad at home. She never called either of them anything if she could help it. She never called herself Marion to herself. But that was her name at school. While the clouds surged back and forth in her brain the name she hated, spoken by her sometime friends, spoken by that couple she disliked and despised, and had at last deserted, came back again and again. It was a bloody shame! It wasn't fair! It was those two, damn them, damn them!

The constable sitting at the bedside watched the slow changes in the patient's facial expressions and crooked a finger at Mandy, who sat behind him out of sight of the bed. She came forward and together they saw tears roll slowly from under the closed lids and down the smooth pale cheeks.

"Les," Mandy whispered. "You're all right now, Les!"

It was the right name, her own name, her real name, but the voice — surely not! —

She opened her eyes so suddenly that Mandy had no time to retreat. She appeared to Lesley to look bright, eager, inquisitive, as she remembered her at the café on one of those coffee breaks —

"*You!*" she said. "Get the hell out!"

The young policeman grinned.

"Feeling better, miss? I'll be off then."

The girls knew he was just obeying orders. Report when she came round. Job over. Thank God. Get some air for a change.

Lesley tried to drag up some farewell insult to hurl at him but failed to find it before a junior nurse came in, carrying a cup and saucer on a small tray.

"Feeling better, Miss Colbert?"

"The name's Lesley Rivers. Don't you dare . . . "

It was too much. She heard the feeble whine where she had intended a full blast. She shut her eyes again and would not open them until Mandy, most concerned for her special care, witness, friend, had persuaded the junior nurse to bring someone more experienced, more knowledgeable, someone who understood real nursing skills, not only the routines of administration and a mass of book learning.

This one, better briefed, called Lesley Miss Rivers, persuaded her to drink the hot soup which was no longer hot but quite acceptable, and to swallow two pills and then settle down to a normal quiet sleep.

They kept Lesley in hospital for two days; she was an interesting and unusual case. Because she was connected with the affair of the murdered ex-chemist, ex-criminal shop keeper, Eddie Perkins — had, in fact, been the first to discover his dead body — she held a very special interest for the public as well as the police. The doctor who had made the first examination of the corpse found it astonishing that the revolting sight in the polythene bag had not thrown the girl into her attack of Heart Stoppage, narrowly over-come by good first aid and heart massage. So why did the exposure of her real name cause such an extreme result?

The question raised by this doctor was echoed by those consultants at the hospital interested in neurological diseases and also the psychiatrists, together with the senior general physician who was quite ready to believe that the girl's long history of deception, carefully and skilfully maintained, then destroyed at a single blow, totally unexpected, by Detective Superintendent Walsh's stern, incisive tenor voice, was quite enough to produce fainting, and in her particular case, sudden death. The senior physician had dealt with similar cases, all at inquests, and with two other survivors, where compensation for injury was the chief subject of argument. In this girl's history a former attack appeared: he wanted to hear about this.

Lesley would not tell him. She had found, when she recovered enough to check her possessions, that both her wrists were bare. Her watch and her leather wrist strap were produced from the drawer in the locker at her bedside. She put them on, without comment. But the nurse was curious, the word sent to Sister, also young and without much worldly wisdom, so back to the police, round to George Cole and from him to Ben Shaw, who spent long hours at the hospital waiting for news of his girl-friend, Lesley Rivers, as he insisted upon calling her.

Ben's first interview with George had come to an abrupt end with the emergency over Lesley. His account of his friendship with her must clearly wait for her recovery, so he had been told he could go back to the Group and wait until asked to visit them again. Detective Inspector Frost thought this was a mistake, but Detective Sergeant Cole was sure the lad was genuinely attached to Lesley and would be more concerned by her dangerous collapse than by any threat to himself over his connection with the dead Perkins.

With Lesley's recovery assured, George arranged another meeting with Ben. The result astonished him.

"It was worse the first time," Ben said. "She told me she'd been very ill after that punishment service we had last year: not so long after she joined the Group. They let that Asian girl, Sister Nana, look after her. Nice kid, but what did she know of such things? No doctor, Les says."

George said, slowly, "Is that when she was given the scar on her right wrist?"

Ben looked down. His horror and remorse at what he had been ordered to do to an unknown person to whom he was totally indifferent at the time, but who now was more important to him than anyone else in his world, was genuine enough at Box Hill, when he had first heard of it. Since then his sense of guilt and shame had grown. So now they knew: she'd told them! There was more grief than fear in his present collapse. It was right he ought to be punished. When he had given this detective johnny a full account of the ceremony, the branding, Lesley's spectacular 'faint', the screams and confusion in the Great Hall, he said with misery in his voice, "I deserve all I'll get."

Cole said, "That so-called Ruler seems to have been the prime mover; a right bastard. You say you were given pills before this so-called service began? What were they? D'you know?"

"No. I don't. But I think those parcels I had to fetch from Mangoes may have been pills. But I never saw the inside of them."

"Does this man, Grant . . . "

166

"Brother Mervyn Grant, M.A."

"That's the full name, is it?"

"What he calls himself."

"Yes. Now tell me again exactly what you did over this last weekend."

Ben, whose memory had never been trained to any sort of accuracy, struggled to remember what he had said before. Battersea Park, yes, that was right. The Regal cinema, a film about war-time flying. Again it sounded the same as the first time. George simply nodded at Ben's confession of a definite outrage, a deliberate wounding, grievous bodily harm, by God it was and they couldn't possibly pass it up. But neither could they lay a charge on Ben Shaw at this stage in the murder case. Inquiries, more inquiries. Lesley still in hospital.

"Look," he said, "I'm afraid I must hand in a full account of this interview to my superior officer, Detective Inspector Frost and now also the superintendent in charge of the Perkins murder, Walsh. I can't let you just walk off and possibly disappear. It'll mean waiting for hours, I expect. I can't . . . "

"Lock me up without charging me, I suppose," Ben said morosely. "Lock me up if you like. I couldn't care less until I know Les is all right. She'll never want to see me again now she knows what I did to her arm. I'd as soon be in the nick as anywhere. No fear I'll run out on you."

"Good lad," murmured Detective Sergeant Cole, not quite knowing what he meant.

Lesley's Tuesday of that week being occupied by the visits and examinations of the several eminent physicians who were interested in her case, it was not until Wednesday morning that Detective W.P.C. Drew came to her private ward again.

Lesley's confidence had grown with the successive compliments and encouragements of the consultant physicians. She was a valuable specimen. She had displayed a fairly rare type of heart action, or rather lack of action, due to an exaggeration of human gland chemistry acting through the nerves governing the heart. This attempt to explain what had happened to her she failed to understand at all, but it sounded most important nevertheless. What she did understand was the

167

gratifying fact that several high-up medics, far from thinking her a useless, ailing, unhealthy creature was, in their opinion, an extremely valuable person, a help to research, because she had survived twice, where like sufferers had invariably died.

She welcomed Mandy with one of her fishwives's laughs. "Put me in a museum if they could," she said. "Would have done if I'd kicked the bucket, which I didn't."

"Thank heaven for that," said Mandy. "Can I sit down? I want to tell you how we came to find out your real name."

"Oh, that!" Lesley flushed. "Bloody snoopers, you and George, both! Liars too: said you weren't the law . . ."

"We started it in our off-duty time. Honest," Mandy insisted. "Because George knew Perkins was a villain, an old lag too, a real criminal. We were anxious about you working for him. And you did start it all yourself, you know, telling George you had run away from home."

"I was a fool there: I agree to that," Lesley told her. "But go on. How did you two pull it off?"

Mandy gave her a short account of how they discovered Mrs Tavern which led on from finding the coach driver, Mr Gray, now retired and that fixed the area to be searched and her personal visit to Madge Small in Rugby.

"Dress shop," Lesley said. "Aunt Colbert went there once with me. Thought the dresses very dull and far too pricey. Liked flashy colours after we moved house."

"Madge had friends at the grammar school." Mandy went on to describe the next steps she took, ending with the arrival of a letter from Brockton giving two possibilities, a girl called Frances, who had left in mid-term to elope with her boy-friend, not warning her parents, and Marion Colbert, who had disappeared one late summer day, but some time after she had finished with school. The school mistress was not in touch with the Colberts, so she had not heard when or even if, Marion had come home, or written to say where she was. She knew that Marion had left school to help in the shop, perhaps against her will.

"Too right," said Lesley.

"Nor if the Colberts had appealed for help to the police."

168

"They'd never."

"Why d'you say that?"

"Old Uncle Colbert's books might surprise them. I know that. I worked in the shop."

"How d'you know?"

Lesley laughed again. Her spirits were very high.

"Doing my own kind of fiddle, of course."

Mandy sighed. Would they ever reach bottom where Lesley was concerned? She changed the subject.

"Do you know your real age?"

Lesley stared.

"Of course I do. Left school at seventeen, two and a half years ago. My birthday is November 15th. I didn't let anyone know at the Group, not even Sue. I'm twenty now, I suppose?"

"That's right. For two and a half years you could have left the Colberts any time you chose. Did no one ever tell you? You came of age at eighteen, with full independence and voting rights and everything."

"Oh, my God!" Lesley groaned. "D'you mean to say I could just have told them to go to hell and walked out quite openly?"

"That's right. But they would naturally have made a fuss and refused to give you any money to take with you."

"Instead of me nicking a few notes from the till," Lesley said with a reckless grin on her excited face.

"That's right," Mandy repeated, "but you'd better not tell me any more in that line. This visit is supposed to be official."

"What do you really want then?"

"I want you to understand that you need have no feelings of obligation to the Colberts, though I do think you should try to be grateful for the early years . . . "

"Not so early! I was over five, going to be moved anyhow, to start school."

"They say they don't want you back."

"Good of them! Wipe them off the screen. I'll never use their bloody name."

Mandy said, carefully, "You don't have to, you know. Or didn't you know?"

How many more things, quite ordinary things, did this girl, over twenty, *not* know? She explained 'deed poll' and how to go about using it.

"You'll be leaving here soon," she finished. "I'll give you the address of a good local solicitor who'll tell you exactly how to go about it. What would you call yourself?"

"My name, of course. Lesley Rivers. Won't it cost money?"

"Some, but there are ways of raising it. Not yours!" she added, seeing a gleam in the other's eyes.

Lesley was encouraged to get up and dress that afternoon. Though she had been in the hospital for only four days, undergoing the full investigation of her collapse, she still tottered on to the balcony of her private room and was happy to have a nurse beside her to lower her into a wicker armchair. But the open air, the pleasant sun, the distant view over surrounding roofs soon raised her spirits and turned her thought to Box Hill and Ben Shaw. How was he? Where was he? Those visits to Perks, a messenger for the Ruler? A menace, a danger? Was he another innocent victim as she had been? How was she to get back into touch with him. An incomplete answer came with her next visitor, who was Detective Sergeant Cole.

Anger swept over her as he was shown on to the balcony by the nurse. She heard the latter say, "You're not to upset her, officer."

"I'll say you're not," Lesley greeted him and laughed. "Mandy came this morning. I needn't have kept the real name from you earlier, because I'm over age. They never really were a menace. Anyway, I'm changing it. Mandy told me how. So it's Lesley Rivers as before. Or will be in a day or two."

George sighed, mostly from relief, a little from irritation. All that work, waste of effort. Well, not really. Never mind, it disposed of half his brief. Frost would have to swallow it. Now for Ben Shaw.

Lesley listened to Ben's account of the Saturday afternoon before the Sunday on Box Hill. Sensible story, except for the cinema bit. Like enough to her own except for that. She listened and made no comment, only nodded from time to time.

"He's very upset over this — er — heart attack of yours," George said. "He told me about the last time and how it was his fault."

"Not his, poor sap, the damned Ruler!" Lesley cried.

"Would you like to tell me your account of what was done to you and why?" George asked, very gently, very quietly. "We think it constitutes an assault, a deliberate infliction of grievous bodily harm."

"Too right," Lesley said and added, "but it wasn't deliberate from Ben, only from that devil, Grant."

"Would you mind, could I possibly, would it upset you, to show me the scar?" George suggested, praying he had not launched a grenade that would prove lethal.

Lesley's face paled and set into her usual expression of obstinate rejection, but without a word she undid the strap of her leather wristband and held out her right arm to George, palm down. He took it in his and she heard him draw in his breath in shock and anger.

"Christ!" He looked up. "T! Why T?"

"For 'Thief'," said Lesley, surprised at her own lack of emotion. "They had it in for me, because I was keeping back some of the collections and other things."

George dropped her hand to write busily in his notebook for a few minutes. Then he got up to go.

"I hope you'll lay a charge for this," he said, "when the Perkins business is cleared up. You'll be able to appear at the inquest, won't you? Next Monday. You'll be notified." He paused, with a hand on the back of her chair. "I should think the surgeons could do a good operation on that wrist. I've seen very good results on old burns."

He did not explain that they had been treated in prison hospitals from time to time on old lags and young ones whose general health, outlook and behaviour had altered markedly after skin grafts for old injuries and for new ones in younger men.

Another problem for the medics, Lesley thought, fastening her wristband on again when George Cole had gone. The surgeons this time.

171

She lay back, staring contentedly at the roofs stretching away below her balcony. More consultations with more men highly skilled in their particular crafts. God, she'd be as good as new by the time they'd done with her.

But what about Ben? For that matter, what about herself? Were they safe? Could they ever be completely safe?

Her temperature was up a little that evening, but her pulse remained perfectly steady and normal. She was allowed to leave the hospital the next day, in the early part of the afternoon. Sister Gordon came to escort her to Group House. Sister Manley greeted her in her office, calling her Sister Marion. Lesley explained, quite calmly, that her name was still Lesley Rivers and that the Law would shortly confirm this.

"We shall see," said Sister Manley, with firm lips.

"That's right," Lesley answered, mechanically.

16

The Perkins murder was given very little publicity in the media. The manner of it was horrifying, sordid, disgusting, but not particularly dramatic, since it first appeared to the general public as the suicide of a shopkeeper, taking place at a weekend and discovered by his assistant, a member of a religious sect, known locally as Groupers.

This young woman, after making a statement to the police at the local police station, suffered from a prolonged fit of delayed shock or hysteria and was removed to hospital.

The Press, discouraged by the hospital authorities, then lost interest. The very brief inquest was adjourned after a short session, when police and medical evidence established how and when the body was discovered and also the fact that death was *not* by suicide but by manual strangulation with a faked attempt to suggest suicide. So with these few, dry, unappetising facts about a totally unimportant citizen and his markedly frail assistant, the Press, including the other media, decided to wait for more tasty news to evolve from police action, which surely was necessary.

Detective Inspector Frost was particularly gloomy. Both he and Detective Sergeant Cole had done their best to watch Perkins's movements. They had expected him to get into trouble of the kind for which he had suffered several times, with gradually increasing stints in the nick. But they had not anticipated *violence* against him.

"Who the devil would want to snuff out the little runt?" Frost asked indignantly when he joined Detective Superintendent Walsh and Detective Sergeant Cole for a conference on the third day after the discovery. They met in the Incident Room at the local station, to which all relevant reports were now directed.

"He seems to have been running that shop, Mangoes, quite openly and honestly, and reasonably profitably too, as far as the accountants have got at present," Frost declared.

"What about that young pair? Girl assistant and her boyfriend, Shaw and Colbert?" the superintendent asked.

Inspector Frost nodded towards George.

"I interviewed the lad, Ben Shaw, sir," Cole began, while Frost handed a file to Walsh. "He swears he never knew what those messages were, except that they came from the chap who runs this Group. They call him the Ruler. Ben used to bring a sealed letter to Perkins who left him in the office while he went into his flat, shutting the shop door behind him. Perkins came back with a parcel, about nine inches square, by two to three inches high. It made no noise if you shook it."

"Did he volunteer that?"

"Yes, sir, he did. Quite open about it. Thought it must be drugs of some sort."

"For this Ruler? Does Shaw take drugs of any sort himself?"

"No obvious signs of any hard drugs, sir. But I haven't much — "

"Yes, yes." The senior man had been turning over the pages of Perkins's file. "It doesn't seem very likely this young chap, Shaw, is part of this curious connection. The most likely thing is a gang-killing. Perkins never gave his partners in crime away, did he?" Walsh was turning pages in the file. "Trafficked in spreading sales, hiding bulk and distributing — What's this? — Three years ago — no, discharge three years ago — Six year sentence, full remission — offence, manufacturing — He was a full-blown chemist, was he?"

"Yes, sir." Frost had done his homework more thoroughly than George Cole. "Respectable parents, bright boy at school, grant to Polytechnic for physics and chemistry. Military service last two years of the War, ambulance corps. But he stuck to chemistry on release and qualified as a dispensing chemist."

"Then why the hell did he go off the rails?"

"Why do any of the clever ones? Ambition? Conceit?"

"Sorry for the junkies," George suggested.

Frost, looking annoyed, ignored this. Detective Superintendent Walsh closed the file, sat back and said, "What about the assistant, this girl, Marion Colbert?"

Frost drew in a breath and repeated the story as it had emerged over the last few days, ending with Detective W.P.C. Drew's final success in locating the Colbert adoptive parents, but not Mandy's final report of her interview in the hospital.

"An enterprising young woman," the superintendent remarked when the inspector had finished. He had fully understood the latter's bitterness at failing to unravel Lesley's past earlier. He foresaw further trouble from that source, but all he said was "She's a friend of this Ben Shaw, is she? Have either of them any kind of motive for getting rid of Perkins?"

"Quite the opposite so far as I know." Frost's tone was still sour.

"Have they alibis for that weekend?"

"Sergeant Cole interviewed the man Shaw, sir, and Constable Drew Miss Colbert, or Rivers, as she insists upon calling herself."

"Well, Cole?"

"May I speak for both, sir, as Mandy — as Miss Drew and I went over the reports together?" George was eager in spite of Frost's unconcealed anger.

"Go ahead."

"Well, sir, Lesley Rivers was told by Perkins he was going off for the weekend, she was to lock up at twelve noon and open the shop again on Monday. The usual routine. She met Ben in the road at the back, they had lunch together and sat in the Park, Battersea Park, and they say, they each say, they

175

went to the pictures later. Only they don't say the same cinema."

"Do you mean they went to separate cinemas?"

"No sir, the same cinema. I mean, they say they went to the pictures together, but they each give different cinemas and different film shows."

Frost made an impatient noise, but the Superintendent said, smiling "In fact, parts of their accounts are probably true and in the evening they were *not* together?"

"Yes, sir."

"So you need an alibi for Ben and also one for this Lesley or whatever her real name is." He turned to Frost, "Perhaps Miss Drew could check this out, inspector?"

"Yes, sir. She's here in the station." He left the room, his irritation with himself growing rapidly.

Walsh said, "I'll be seeing the religious fellow, Grant, Mervyn Grant, God help us! I'll check Ben's alibi with the lad himself. His relationship with his Ruler doesn't sound very healthy to me. But it's fairly obvious the two youngsters are keen to shield one another and not 100% sure of one another, either. What do *you* think, sergeant?"

"I think they have a fairly close relationship, sir, but they always have, most probably always have had, only one answer to authority and that is 'I never!'"

"You may be right, Cole," agreed the superintendent, playing with his ball-point pen as he waited for Frost to come back with Detective W.P.C. Drew.

Mandy repeated, in a skilfully condensed form, the whole saga of Lesley's escape from Brockton, her connection with the Holy Group, her success in finding the job at Mangoes, which was how she and Sergeant Cole had become interested in her.

"It was when she and Ben Shaw seemed to be going together and she let out how much she hated this Group and especially the Ruler, as they all call him, I tried to find out why that was. But it was the boy-friend, Ben, who gave that away?"

"Go on. What was it?"

Mandy repeated the story of the branding: Detective Superintendent Walsh expressed surprise and disgust, Detective Inspector Frost said the Group ought to be brought to court, Detective Sergeant Cole nodded agreement and murmured something about Les and Ben having no motive to kill Perkins, unless his packets for the Ruler held illegal drugs for Grant's personal use, making him part of the same conspiracy to defeat the law.

"Which was always Perkins's type of crime," said Walsh. "They don't change, in my book: not in late middle-age, like old Perkins."

"May I say, sir," Mandy asked the superintendent, "I am sure, dead sure, Lesley had nothing to do with the murder. She let me see the scar on her wrist. She agreed, without any sign of shame, only anger, that it was T for Thief. When I told her she could have surgery to alter it anyway, with a graft or something, she was very surprised and over-joyed. She's such an innocent, poor kid."

Walsh gave a short laugh.

"For an innocent girl she's not done too badly in exposing crime, don't you think, Miss Drew? The old woman, Mrs Tavern, whose husband died in Paignton where they were on holiday at a private charitable Holiday Home, which buried him and sent her home with a letter to her local Social Security that she never gave them, but carried on collecting her husband's pension. After that, we have strange criminal doings at the Group Houses in Upper Polson Street, an old lag turns up in St Andrew's Place and gets killed there. We discover her former home and a successful shopkeeper who may have been working various frauds for years in his trading."

"She may be some sort of jinx," Frost said stiffly, "but we still don't know where she was or what she was doing on Saturday afternoon, and we do know that the only sign of any other person in Perkins's flat is some hand prints, in a plastic glove probably, of a size exactly matching Miss Colbert's."

"Better go on calling her Rivers, don't you think, Inspector," Walsh said. "Confusing enough as it is. Besides, she's insisted she's going to change her name, which was only invented for her — Marion in the Home she was in as a baby,

177

and Colbert when the grocer adopted her. Apparently she invented Lesley Rivers on her complicated journey to London and she'll make that legal by deed poll. We can't charge her on the hand print alone, can we? And you've always stood for a gang killing, haven't you? So what about possible villains in your manor, Frost?"

"Nothing doing, sir, nor anyone likely, according to the best of the regular paid-up grasses."

In the little room behind Ma Dill's shop Sister Manley was trying to compose a convincing letter to explain her conduct with regard to Sister Susan Ford.

It was not an easy task. How far must she go in humble apology for those manifest lies in her correspondence with the fond, but shallow parents of the girl. White lies, of course. She would call them that. Her intention was always pure, but perhaps her methods laid her open to this unfortunate mis-understanding. Surely Mrs Trevelyan was one of the Group's most faithful supporters, a distant relative, actually, of the originator of the Group in the last years of Queen Victoria, she had been told.

Sister Manley paused at this point, wondering who, if she was asked, she could say had told her this interesting fact. No one, of course, because she had only just thought of it. So she crossed out 'been told' and wrote instead 'always understood'.

She began again. Got back to her main theme, to counter-acting these appalling moves by the old woman in the decayed mansion on the corner of Brindley Square, introduce her own distress at the intolerable interference of a newcomer, Lesley Rivers, she called herself, but that was not her real name. She had been rescued from the streets one autumn evening the year before, an absconding girl from her respectable home in the provinces, asking for shelter, without vocation, without morals, a liar and petty thief, as it turned out. This undesirable had wormed herself into Susan's confidence, though she had not been able to deceive Mrs Trevelyan fully, but only to the extent of condoning her friendship with dear, forgiving, Sister Susan.

After a good many words in this vein Sister Manley, making no comment on the Fords' expressed intention of visiting their daughter in the near future, continued her letter by declaring that everything necessary would be done to remove Sister Lesley's influence as soon as possible. She ended with the pious hope that the police might help in this, since the girl was now mixed up with a particularly sordid crime in the near neighbourhood.

Sister Gordon had come into the shop while Sister Manley was at work on this attempt to confuse the Ford parents and delay their intended visit. The Group caterer, housekeeper, and dining room supervisor, kept herself up to date at a conveniently low level with the help of Ma Dill. She also kept herself in stock with sweets and cigarettes, two means of overcoming the rigours of life at Group House.

Sister Gordon began by asking for the usual, which meant two packets of cigarettes and two of small cheroots. She accepted on this occasion a boiled sweet from a new jar at Ma Dill's elbow, one that the latter had only just opened and therefore had not been seriously contaminated by the shopkeeper's moistened finger.

"Any news?" Cissie asked. "Les isn't back yet, but the police guard is off, the hospital told me."

Ma Dill jerked her head towards the back of the shop at the same time as swallowing a sucked mixture of saliva and acid drop. This made her choke alarmingly, so Sister Gordon leaned over the counter to thump her stout back and Ma Dill was able to whisper, between gasps and coughs, "She's in there! Another letter to them Fords!"

"Could be. And much good that'd do us!" Cissie answered, but not wanting to meet her employer in the shop, she gathered up her purchases and left.

Sister Gordon felt distinctly upset. The Group was in a bad way, chiefly over the struggle to keep Susan Ford. No good, the way they were trying. Only be shown up as liars and hypocrites. Helen Manley thought she was doing good and serving God. Queer sort of god who let you do cruel, wicked things in his name. All bunkum really, of course. The people

179

who did the most good in that district were the girls in Brindley Square. There'd been some changes there recently, she'd heard. What if they needed someone, too old to be in active competition, who could act as secretary or something of that sort. Thinking on these lines, Cissie decided to pay them a visit. Her young friend, Mame, would know the general feeling at the house in Brindley Square. Mame wouldn't be working in the morning, and she might be still asleep, but it was worth trying. Cissie had a feeling in her bones that things were going to crack up in the Group. Half Helen's obstinate persistence over Sue came from her silly feeling for that cold-hearted, self-lover, bloody little devil, that called himself the Ruler.

Sister Gordon shivered, remembering several so-called services in the Great Hall and the trouble afterwards with certain of the more sensitive of the Brothers and Sisters. She fumbled for one of her new boiled sweets and sucking steadily, turned her steps towards Brindley Square.

Detective Superintendent Walsh went with Detective Sergeant Cole to the Group building in Playhouse Road, where Ben Shaw lived and where the Ruler, who had an office there, conducted the affairs of the sect, but did not stay at night, though he usually took lunch on the premises.

The two detectives, very neat and correct in dark suits, found Mr Mervyn Grant in well-furnished office rooms on the first floor of the building. Like the rest of the area the house was a mid-Victorian villa of the kind very plentiful when London suburbs had begun to grow rapidly south of the Thames. Unlike Brindley Square and Upper Polson Street, Playhouse Road had not declined into near slum. In fact it seemed to be developing into student occupation, so the Group was not entirely out of place there.

A heavily-bearded man opened the front door and without asking the visitors to identify themselves, said in a deep voice, "Come this way, Mr Walsh," and walked off towards a wide staircase, clearly expecting them to follow.

"Better shut the door, sergeant," the superintendent

muttered. Cole turned back to do so, then joined the others, now climbing the stairs.

If they expected further eccentricity in the office, they were disappointed. The Ruler, also dressed in a plain dark suit, but with a narrow gold cross and chain about his neck, rose to greet them.

"Mr Walsh?" he asked, but without making any other gesture of welcome. He ignored George. "Do sit down. Can I offer you — er — tea or coffee."

"Neither, thanks. Yes, I am Detective Superintendent Walsh, sir, and this is Detective Sergeant Cole, my assistant."

He displayed his card, George did likewise. Mr Grant, nodding in a distant, rather haughty manner, sat down again at his desk and waited. The other two found seats and the superintendent began to explain their presence there.

"You may be surprised that we want to ask you for information, Mr Grant, but it is in connection with this unfortunate death in St Andrew's Place."

The Ruler, turning a calmly interested face, said, "How can I help you, superintendent?"

"Mr Perkins, who kept a health shop in the precinct, was in the habit of sending one of your — your — "

"Acolytes?"

"A member of your followers, of the sect, if that is what you call it — "

"Of the Holy Group, Mr Walsh."

"A young man called Benjamin Shaw. You were in the habit of sending Shaw to Mr Perkins with a written message, which he gave him in his office at the back of the shop and Shaw received in exchange a package, which Perkins fetched from the flat behind the shop. This package young Shaw brought back to you here. Will you tell me what the package held and what was the object of these visits, repeated fairly regularly?"

"Willingly," the Ruler said, opening a side drawer in his broad desk and taking out a number of papers, clipped together. They were National Health Service prescriptions, made out to two different names at the Playhouse Road

181

address. The drugs prescribed had a trade name, were ordered in large quantities, 100 tablets for each, the dose given to be 2 tablets taken once daily. The doctor's signature was illegible, but was given, with his address, in a rubber-stamped version underneath the signature.

Walsh passed them over to Cole, who looked at them, took down the full details, before giving them back to his senior, who handed them to Grant.

"They seem to be medicine for two of your inmates," he said. "Are they still resident here?"

"Oh yes. Actually I'm sure they wouldn't object to my telling you that they are mild epileptics. These pills are a special brand, the doctor tells me. My usual chemist does not stock them. Mr Perkins was a qualified dispensing chemist, until he retired, so he knew how to get them for me."

"What did the epileptics' doctor think of that arrangement?"

Mr Grant frowned.

"I'm afraid I don't quite understand you."

"He must know that Perkins lost his licence some eight years ago, surely? The doctor must know that."

An unexpected gleam behind his spectacles gave the Ruler's face an altogether different aspect and the conversation faded out altogether for a few minutes.

Then Walsh said, "You will know, of course, Mr Grant, it has been in all the papers and on radio and television, that the inquest on Perkins has been adjourned and why?"

"His suicide — lamentable."

"His murder, Mr Grant. Manual strangulation, arranged after death, to simulate suicide."

Mr Grant shook his head slowly from side to side, then said, "That unhappy girl! His assistant in the shop. One of our failures in the Group, Mr Walsh. Alas, alas!"

"It was indeed unfortunate for Miss Rivers to find the corpse," the superintendent went on. "She has had over a week in hospital suffering from delayed shock. She was unnaturally calm and helpful at the time of her discovery."

"She would be!"

The words broke from the Ruler, loud, full of spiteful fury. He was as shocked as his hearers: he clasped his hands together, leaned forward over his desk, and began to gabble a prayer. That finished, he sat back again, eyes open, but watchful now.

Detective Superintendent Walsh got up; George followed. Mr Grant also got to his feet: he even walked quite steadily to the door to see the detectives out, even to watch them pass into the hall, see them pass the doorkeeper, to whom he gave a friendly nod.

Walsh and Cole got back into the police car in silence and remained so until they reached the Incident Room, where Detective Inspector Frost was waiting for them.

Then Walsh said, speaking directly to Frost, "Two things. Perhaps three. First Cole here has the detail. Who is the doctor whose name is on the prescription? Partner, or solo practice? Age? Standing? Nature of drug ordered? Contact with patients etc.? Second. Lesley River's wrist. I'll go into that myself. I haven't seen the photographs, before and after the graft or whatever they did. This is important if there is to be a charge of assault against Grant. Third. Keep in touch with Ben Shaw. There's more in that messenger's job than caring for epileptics' medicine, however much Grant may want us to think. It might rebound on Ben and he's not overbright, I gather."

"He's all right, sir," George defended. "Scared of the Law, sulky when he doesn't understand something. But quite quick when he does."

"Warn him to watch his step, then. The so-called Ruler gives me the grues. 'Zero at the bone.' "

"Sir?"

"Poem about a snake. Forget it."

"He's nuts, sir, isn't he?" asked Frost, in his precise voice. Poetry at a working conference seemed to him to smack of real lunacy, however much the man Grant was afflicted.

"Undoubtedly," Walsh sighed. "Murderers come in four main categories now: perhaps they always did. Domestic. Nut cases. Fanatics. Professional. They all overlap, of course. And we have only one piece of real evidence. Those gloved palm prints, size suggesting a woman."

"Miss Colbert — Rivers, I mean. A strong girl. We know that," said Frost. "But I still think it's a gang killing."

"I'll see Lesley Rivers myself," Walsh assured him.

17

Lesley waited for Detective Superintendent Walsh in a small room near the porter's office just inside the wide front doors of the hospital. She had agreed to the interview provided it took place neither at Group House nor the police station. The hospital seemed very suitable to them both, the girl because she was still attending every day for her wrist dressings to be changed, which process she enjoyed because so many surgeons came to look at the cosmetic surgeon's work, to praise him, to admire the job he had done and her courage and stamina all along.

Lesley had never felt so important; she flowered like a rose recovering from a dangerous late frost. She did not know, would not have believed, that she had this time been as near to death as before, when she had survived by her own courage, helped by Sister Nana's far eastern skills.

Detective Superintendent Walsh welcomed his visit to the hospital because he was due there in any case to see the photographs of Lesley's injury, before operation and afterwards, though the series was not yet complete, as it would be only when the restored area was fully healed. The surgeon was to meet the detective to give his views of the whole case. He might be called upon to express these views in court, he was told.

"Of course," the surgeon agreed. He saw a good, quite legal and ethical advertisement of his skill resting behind the glamorous, compassionate restoration of a young woman's delicate beauty, so savagely outraged.

The detective joined Lesley in a very good mood: the photographs were excellent. He told her so.

"And now, Miss Rivers — "

"They all call me Les, don't they, nurse?" she said, interrupting.

"Lesley, then." He smiled and went on. "I'm going into rather personal details, so can we ask nurse to wait — er — outside?"

"I expect so. O.K. nurse?"

"Staff said — "

"That's all right. We won't tell her." She lifted an eyebrow at Walsh, who decided this was going a bit far, but said nothing.

Lesley went on, in a harsher tone, "If I throw another fit I'll be sure to yell first. I always do, they tell me. So out, nursie, out!"

The nurse, deeply offended and disappointed of some hopes for juicy details she could sell to the B.B.C., left the room, banging the door.

"Rash, wasn't it, Miss — Lesley?" Walsh said. "Won't they all walk out?"

"Not the nurses. They aren't N.U.P.E."

So the superintendent settled to his interview. He had heard a full account of Ben Shaw's actions during the Group ceremony when Lesley was assaulted. Genuine bodily harm all right. Ben's overall responsibility was in question, but partial guilt was unquestionable. He had confessed to that, with maximum remorse.

Walsh heard what sounded like a muffled, "Poor love!" from Lesley, but ignored it.

He told her Ben's account of his visits to Mangoes. "How many altogether?" he asked. "According to you? We know what he says."

"Not many. About once a month, then they stopped."

"Yes? How d'you know that? Just that they didn't happen at the shop?"

"Not exactly. I heard Perkins tell him at the door not to come to St Andrew's Place again but . . . "

"Well?"

"I didn't hear if he said he'd go himself. Ben was to go to

Playhouse Road. I didn't know then it was where the Ruler and Ben both live."

"The Ruler, as you call him, Mr Mervyn Grant, doesn't live in Playhouse Road but he has an office there."

Lesley gave one of her music hall laughs.

"Mervyn! That's a scream! La-di-da!"

"Now," Walsh said in a severe voice that recalled Lesley to the nature of this conversation. "Now, I want to hear your version of the weekend before the Monday, when you found Perkins dead."

Lesley did so: she described her quarrel with Ben, his view of her wrist and immediate collapse and flight. She gave no hint of their fight. She had not seen him since nor even heard from him.

Walsh made a note or two and seemed to have come to an end of his questions.

"I've said all this to Mandy," Lesley prompted him. "I mean the girl detective. There isn't any more."

"No?"

"Well no. Except — "

"Yes?"

"I wish I could take on the shop. Mangoes. You see," she said, warming to a proposal she had thought out over her stay in hospital, "you see, it's all those customers, a lot of them foreigners, black or Asian, living round here: they depend on getting their special foods at Mangoes. They can get it nearly everywhere now, of course, but not always just what they like. They've told me and Perkins used to order one or two items in bulk with the other bulk orders. There'll be some in the shop store now, going to waste if it isn't used. I don't know if you've seen it, or any of the stock."

"We have lists," said Walsh slowly. He had left the full search of the shop itself to Frost and his local man. He doubted if Frost had inspected the goods that Lesley had described.

"Where are the bulk stores kept?" he asked. "You know all this and have seen them?"

"Of course I have. In the cellar. That door beside my

187

cloakroom, as Perks called the place where I hung my coat up in. Beside the loo."

"Yes."

"Always locked that door. Perks kept the key for it in his desk. That was always locked, too. Great little one for locking things up, our old Perks."

"Yes."

Detective Superintendent Walsh found Lesley's request intriguing. The girl was no do-gooder; quite the opposite. But she sounded sincere and her wish was in character as far as he knew, on very slender evidence. Certainly the police could not keep the shop and its business locked up much longer, stagnating, losing value, wasting good if eccentric food. The premises belonged to Perkins, who had bought them outright, with a mortgage, his bank had disclosed. His payments on this had been regular and up to date. He had no known relatives. He had never made a will. His account was in reasonable credit. If the business could be started again, the shop opened and served, was there any reason why Lesley Rivers should not run it?

"I can't advise you about taking over the shop," he said, "but a solicitor could. You had better find one. A good one, too. He'd want to see over the premises before giving you his opinion. And for that you'll need the keys, so you will have to have one of our officers with you."

Lesley flushed.

"Don't trust me, do you? That bloody scar . . . "

Walsh did not bother to answer the charge. After all, their only good bit of evidence in the murder case was a print that might be Lesley's. He said in his most official voice, getting to his feet, "Well, Miss Rivers, thank you for answering my questions. I appreciate your wish to take over the shop. When you have found and engaged a solicitor I shall be interested to hear from you again and arrange to provide the keys for you and the lawyer to go over the premises together. Right?"

"I suppose so." She did not get up. He could go to hell! He'd insulted her, she hated him.

Her nurse came back to her directly after the detective left.

She too, was still feeling insulted. Together, in silence, they went back to the ward.

At the police station Walsh found Detective Inspector Frost and together they discussed the interview with Lesley Rivers.

"Interesting, don't you think?" Walsh said.

"Very. She's not worried over the wogs and the spades, but she wants to get back into the health food business. Begins to look as if she might be further into Perkins's under-cover line than we thought."

"Gang warfare? You still have your money on that?"

"I do."

"I'd like to go over the shop's contents and lists and that with you again. And the question of the keys."

This last was the most potentially rewarding. For it appeared that three bunches of keys, on separate rings, had been found, examined and labelled. One related to the front door and back door of the building, including the back door of the shop, leading to the small hall, stairs and flat, and also of the door to the cellar. Another held the keys to the various rooms of the flat itself. This ring also held the key of the office desk, which also unlocked the drawers on each side of the desk. The third ring held a mixed bunch of replicas of some of the shop door keys and included another copy of the cellar key.

Together Walsh and Frost lost no time in checking the contents of the shop's goods, using the listed keys to the various parts of it. In the cellar they found the bulk packages of special kinds of rice and other more exotic products.

"The girl Rivers described these quite accurately," the superintendent said, pulling a softly pliable sack off a pile of similar objects.

"Hang on!" cried Frost. He was too late. The whole pile slid forward out of control, making the two men jump aside as the soft sacks spread themselves across the floor.

"My God!" said Walsh, staring.

But Frost sprang forward, for behind the pile they had displaced another door appeared, a door very skilfully disguised, a door the police had not hitherto discovered, a door for which they had not found a key.

Working from the back of the shop the police, under the superintendent, had the hidden door opened. It revealed a neatly arranged laboratory, where the experts later confirmed that Perkins had not only renewed his former manufactures of illegal pills, but had produced a recent type of heroin made from new material supplied from an eastern, very new source.

"Up to date, all right," Frost said as he and Walsh studied the report of the forensic chemical expert.

"Back to supplying the drug trade," Walsh agreed. "You were right, Frost. But why kill their supplier?"

"Why openly? Why brutally?" the latter said. "Suggests a novice, doesn't it? Nearly all the chemicals cleared off the shelves and cupboards; the key to that hidden door vanished. Perkins would have kept it always on him, surely?"

"Where his murderer must have found it and did this tidying up." Palm prints, again seemingly in gloves, were found in the laboratory after a further intensive search. Reluctantly Walsh compared these with Lesley's prints, taken as soon as she was well enough to give her first detailed interview to the police after her collapse.

"Better repeat them," the superintendent suggested to Frost. "If that girl joined some gang Perkins has been working for, she doesn't know what she's supposed to be doing for them now," Walsh said. He was reluctant to come to any firm conclusion about her.

"Perhaps they just want to keep her at the shop until they've moved all that stuff, which is why she wants to take over."

"Could be. Too easy. Not very clever."

"They often go off the lines if they get rattled, and if they're a mixed lot, Middle Eastern often."

"That's right."

"We'll keep a close watch on Mangoes," Walsh said. "They've got means of access to the cellar lab, that's pretty certain, so we'll have to put that back for them, the lock, I mean, when we've got a key cut for ourselves. It's dark down here, they may not realise we've rumbled them. If Rivers is in this with a criminal purpose, and goes on trying to take over the shop, I'll show her over and see what happens in the cellar."

"You'd better look out, then. She's a wizard at throwing her special kind of fit," Frost said, crossly.

But Walsh shook his head.

"It's genuine all right. And dangerous. But to her, only."

Frost did not believe him.

Lesley went back to Group House two days after her interview with Detective Superintendent Walsh. But she did not at once begin to follow up her wish to take over Mangoes, though she did go to Mrs Trevelyan's house to ask the kind old lady to recommend her to an honest lawyer in the neighbourhood.

"I can't afford a posh one," she said. "But I don't know if the sort that would want to work in this part of London would be — er — reliable."

It was a word she had heard used a good deal at Group House: it seemed to have a good many different meanings, vague ones at that, but Sue had said Mrs T would know of someone reliable, so that was how she put her request.

Mrs Trevelyan was very interested in Lesley now. The girl had shown courage and loyalty and a real wish to improve herself. This new idea to help the coloured citizens in the neighbourhood was excellent. She recommended a youngish man who came down from a firm in the City to give law sessions at a local methodist mission. She also confided to Lesley that she was in touch with Sue's parents, who had had a strange, excited sort of letter from Sister Manley, which had made Mr Ford decide finally to take his daughter home the following week.

"Oh yes," Sue said, when Lesley reported her conversation with their benefactor. "Don't let Sister Manley know, will you?"

"Don't *you* give it away," Lesley said, laughing.

Perhaps Susan's happy face, her jaunty air as she joked in their dormitory with the three subdued girls in her care there, did alert the ever-watchful eye of Sister Manley; perhaps it was just Mervyn Grant's fury when he came to know that Lesley, far from having her prospects at the shop brought to an abrupt end by the death of her boss, was trying to take on the business herself; whichever lay behind the move, the Ruler did decide to separate Lesley from her friend and by the same act secure the meek and highly useful little Sue Ford from her parents, for good, for ever, as in his shaky, now dangerously unsound mind, he saw the case.

The day came when a car drew up outside Holy Group House. Sister Manley sent Sister Gordon to find Sister Susan.

"Tell her we think it is her parents," Sister Manley ordered.

"You lying old bitch!" Cissie cried. "I'll do nothing of the sort!"

"Well, you need not bother," Sister Manley said, rushing to the foot of the stairs. "Here she comes!"

Sue ran across the hall, followed closely by Sister Manley, behind whom Lesley dodged, and pushed, trying to keep near Sue. Sister Gordon stopped on the top step outside, waiting, as she later told Ma Dill, to see which way the cat jumped. My God, cat wasn't in it! Tiger, more like!

Susan's joyful impetus was brought to a sickening halt at the edge of the pavement. The car was like the family British model, but the occupants were not Mummy and Dad. In front a young man driving, beside him a stout, elderly person in the regulation Group dress, whom she recognised as a non-resident, Sister Brook. And behind, climbing out of the rear passenger seat, Les's former boy-friend, weak-kneed servant of the Ruler, Ben Shaw!

Susan turned to run back into the house, too horrified to cry for help. Lesley tried to get past Sister Manley, who called out to Ben to get the girl into the car and go, GO! Susan began to scream.

On the top step of the house, Sister Gordon put two fingers in her mouth and gave a piercing whistle that at once attracted the attention of Constable Torch at the far end of Upper Polson Street. He began to run.

Ben called, "Les, get Sue away! Up to Mrs T! Go on! Get her away! Now!"

He caught hold of Sister Manley's arm and wrenched it from

Susan's waist. She bent her head and bit him. He hit her in the face and she fell back on to the ground as Sue and Lesley, hand in hand, fled away and round the corner into Brindley Square. Mrs Trevelyan, who had watched the scene, astonished, from her dining room window, ran to open the door to them. She helped the nearly fainting Susan into the house.

In the car Sister Brook said, "No, Reg! Leave it! We done wot we was booked for. My God, Ben's downed old bossy-bones! Scram, love. Scram, you silly bugger!"

In a jerky start and a screeching acceleration Reg Bridge flung the Ruler's car into action and it had disappeared before Constable Torch arrived breathless, but quite ready for immediate action in this quick-flaring street incident.

A small crowd had begun to collect about the spot on the pavement where Ben stood, gazing down at Sister Manley, who was lying on her back, holding her blood-stained handkerchief to her nose, her grey uniform dress pulled down from her throat, the gold chain she always wore, its gold cross fallen behind her neck, also bloodstained, the narrow skirt, pulled up in falling, still in disarray above her knees.

Gripping Ben by the wrist Constable Torch asked sternly, "Did you strike this lady?"

Ben said, "Obvious, isn't it?"

The crowd growled a little. It had not understood the subtleties of the situation. Sister Manley sat up, causing a further flow of blood from her swollen nose. Dark shadows were appearing under both eyes.

Constable Torch, unwilling to free his prisoner, unwilling to secure him with handcuffs, for what might prove to be an accident, yet wanting also to help the injured lady, was relieved when Sister Gordon appeared beside her fallen colleague, saying, "Let me help you up, Sister Helen."

"Let *me* help, too," Ben said, shaking off the constable's hand from his arm.

Sister Manley shrank away with a little cry, but scrambled up and leaning on Cissie, head drooping, dropping more blood on the path and on her dress, reached the door and disappeared inside it.

"Now, young man," Torch said, recovering control of his suspect, "what was all that about?"

Ben told him, as briefly as he could, but it took long enough for Torch to get in touch with a patrol car while Ben was stammering out his account of the abduction attempt and his own unavoidable action.

"You wouldn't call it an unprovoked assault on your part, then?" Constable Torch asked.

"I would bloody well not. Rotten, bleeding — "

"That will do." Torch opened the door of the patrol car that had just drawn up beside them. He pushed Ben into the back seat through the door just flung open. "You tell it all at the station, mate, and see if they agree."

18

Mrs Trevelyan had watched the strange scene outside Holy Group House from her wide dining room window on the ground floor of her house. It was a restricted view across the right-angled corner of the end of Upper Polson Street. In fact she had begun to watch, with interest, when the small procession left the House, marched in single order down the path from the front door steps; but it faded out of sight, obscured by the arriving car and then by its stationary bonnet.

But the following confusion, the shouting, the blurred figures, above all, Cissie's high and piercing whistle, were alarming. When the two girls, hand in hand, easily recognisable, Lesley clearly leading, separated themselves from the tossing group and ran towards her she lost her stunned immobility and herself ran to her front door to fling it open and wave them in.

She could do no more than gesture to the girls to shut it again, which Lesley did and bolted it too, while Sue and the old lady sank upon chairs in the hall, overcome by their explosion of energy.

"Are you all right?" Lesley asked, bending over her elderly friend. She had no fears for Sue: she knew *her* limit, soon reached for sudden sprints, so seldom tested in the religious life at the Group, but often encouraged by herself in recent outings to Battersea Park. Sue's limit had not been reached, hardly tested, in their short run from Group House.

But they had run fast, even that short way. She herself had been hampered, too, by her right arm being fixed in a sling.

Mustn't pull those stitches, that clever wiping out of a shaming label.

"Well now," said Mrs Trevelyan. "Susan, what was all that about?"

Susan broke down and sobbed.

"They were trying to kidnap her," Lesley explained. "Under orders from that devil they call Ruler. I know the two in the front of the car. Sister Brook, the one who sent me to the Group in the first place last year and Reg Bridge, driving, the one she asked at Victoria to show me the way. They weren't in the schemozzle on the pavement. Not them. Drove away like a flea in the arse — "

"Lesley! Please!"

"Sorry, Mrs Trevelyan."

"If it hadn't been for Ben Shaw we shouldn't have got away," Sue explained, in an awed voice.

"That's right." Lesley's voice grew soft. "Poor old Ben, bless his heart, poor love. Must have been sent to get Sue into the car. Sister Manley was behind her, telling her to get into the car, saying she was with friends, she knew Ben and I don't know what-all. And he just jumped out and yelled to me to get Sue away to you and he went for Manley. I don't know what after that, couldn't look round. You were pretty smart on the door, Mrs T., we do thank you, don't we, Sue?"

"Oh yes, yes," Sue agreed fervently. "I think — I think, if I may use the phone, please, Mrs Trevelyan."

"Of course." The old lady got to her feet with an effort. "Your parents, dear. They must take you home at once. No possible reason for any more delay. Mr Grant seems to have taken leave of his senses! He must have decided to move you to another branch of the sect. I believe there are several. Delay and perhaps persuade you to change your mind. Ridiculous. Sad, of course, in a way. But dangerous. Terribly dangerous."

Still murmuring her disapproval of the Group and its methods Mrs Trevelyan took Susan away, leaving Lesley alone in the hall of the big house, wondering, not for the first time, if there was really no one else there and how the old dear managed on her own.

She understood in part when a figure in an overall appeared from a door at the back of the hall and said, "Oh! You come with the other young lady?"

"That's right. In trouble. But Mrs T's working on it."

"She would be. Doesn't like no interference. But we 'as to keep an eye, see she don't overdo it."

"Yes."

The woman turned to go away through the door, but paused and stepped back.

"I see Torch, that's Constable Torch, running up when you two girls left. Young feller socked that Miss Manley one — right between the eyes. Got hisself nicked for that. Quite right. What the kids gets up to these days . . . "

This time the self-styled guardian disappeared, closing the door behind her.

Lesley waited. She was there to help Sue, though with the news of Ben's arrest her heart was directing her to go at once to rescue *him*. All resentment of his treatment for her, all suspicion of his attachment to the Ruler had vanished. At the same time she could not suppress a wicked glee at the thought of Sister Manley overthrown. She walked with confidence to Group House and went in.

Sister Gordon was in the hall. Lesley said at once, "I've come for Sue's things," and waited.

"Have you indeed?" said Sister Gordon. "Why's that?"

"You know why."

"Wait here."

Lesley waited. Sister Gordon went into Sister Manley's office. She repeated Lesley's request, which sounded more like an order.

"Why is that?"

"You know well enough. Sue's father and mother are coming to take her home."

"When?"

"She didn't say."

Actually Lesley had answered when Sister Gordon had asked the same question, "Wouldn't you like to know, Cissie? Mrs Trevelyan said not to let it out here on any account." But

Cissie did not repeat this piece of impertinence to Sister Manley.

When she went back into the hall she saw Lesley beginning to creep up the stairs, but she ran to stop her.

"Not so fast, Miss Knowall. We're waiting for the doctor, to see Helen Manley. That young thug may have broken her nose. He's given her a pair of black eyes at any rate. Such a sight!"

Lesley could not suppress a giggle. Sister Gordon's face grew red with suppressed mirth, but she managed to say, "Get along then, you heartless bitch! I'm not sure it wasn't you did the kidnapping. That's what Manley says. She says that car was sent by the Ruler to move Susan Ford out of your influence because you are ruining her vocation."

"Good grief!" Lesley was astonished. "What'll he think up next? Has he been to see her here?"

"No," Sister Gordon said. "He's out of London today. Seeing some of the older brothers, Elder Brethren, he calls them, off abroad. From Dover, Helen thinks, but she isn't sure."

Lesley shrugged and went on upstairs. She found the Indian girl Nana, in Sue's room, taking her clothes out of the two suitcases with which she had entered the Holy Group and had been preparing to leave it, when the false call came that sent her down to the hall.

"Hullo!" Lesley said and stood puzzled. "What d'you think you're doing, Nana?"

"Putting Sister Susan's clothes back in the drawers."

"Why? Don't you know she's left here? For good?"

"Yes, I know. But she has not gone. Sister Manley says to put it all as it was before."

"Well I say leave it in the cases and we'll finish the job, Nana. Because Sue *has* gone and she'll never, repeat *never*, be coming back."

The Indian girl stared. She showed no surprise, no anger, no feeling of any kind, but she brushed her hands together as if wiping off any responsibility, any part in, this change of plan and then, with a little nod, went very quietly out of the room.

198

"Don't bother Sister Manley," Lesley called after her, "If you want to explain this, go to Sister Gordon."

But Nana did neither. She went to her own room, collected her own belongings and walked away from Group House. She knew where she would find her own people. The Holy Group had served their purpose, hers too, in food and lodging, for long enough. They would welcome her return. They would find her a new, a different, a young husband.

Lesley finished packing up Sue's belongings and carried the suitcases down into the hall. There was no one there, so she let herself out and completed her mission at Mrs Trevelyan's house.

After a good meal and a rest the party there decided that it was not necessary, or even desirable, for Lesley to be present when Sue's father came for her. As Mrs Trevelyan said, in private, to a very tired, but still willing Lesley. "We must let them be quite alone when they meet and I hope I can then urge them to get away in his car as quickly as possible, after as short an interval as possible. Don't you agree?"

Lesley did not know whether she agreed or not; such subtleties of behaviour had never come her way. But she did agree, rather thankfully, kissed her friend, hoped to see her sometime, received an unexpected hug and kiss from Mrs Trevelyan and was shown out by the guardian and her husband from the basement, who were, it seemed, on duty for the evening, with the coming drama of reconciliation and escape.

Lesley walked away feeling more respect and affection for Mrs Trevelyan than ever before. The old lady might be classed as a geriatric, but she had more wits about her than most people of her age. She knew how to meet 'situations' and how to take sensible precautions.

At Group House Lesley went straight to bed and to sleep. If she thought of Ben it was chiefly to decide he was at least safer in the nick than in the charge of the Ruler and that she would go to the police station in the morning and try to see him. She thought she loved him, but he was much too free with his fists, silly twit.

While Lesley slept matters had not rested in the Incident Room at the police station.

Ben Shaw was again afflicted by guilt, though this was modified by triumph in the success of Sue's deliverance, coupled with the overthrow of Sister Manley. He described these linked events with a barely concealed satisfaction to Detective Superintendent Walsh himself, with Detective Inspector Frost also listening.

"Mr Grant sent you in that car to bring Miss Ford away?" the Superintendent asked.

"That was the idea. Sue knows me on account of Les being my girl-friend. Or was — I told you before — "

"Never mind all that. We want to know your part in this attempted abduction. Miss Ford was to be moved away from Upper Polson Street. Where to?"

"They didn't tell me that. Just to make sure she got into the back of that car with me."

"Go on."

"I knew it wasn't on the level. When I saw them come out of the house, that Miss Manley edging off Les, I was sure it was a kidnap, as I'd suspected. So I yelled to Les to run to the old lady with Sue, which she did. Fast."

"And Miss Manley tried to stop you?"

"She — well, she got in the way, sort of, sir."

"You hit her?"

"I pushed her. She fell over backwards. She was very excited and angry. She — sort of tripped herself up."

"You socked her; straight in the face."

Looking very sulky and opening and shutting his big, heavy hands, Ben said he supposed it looked like that.

"You were arrested, very rightly, by Constable Torch, on the grounds that you had assaulted Miss Manley, done her genuine bodily harm and caused a public affray."

"I done what I said," Ben was roused to defend himself. "I don't see the public came into it."

Walsh changed the subject.

"Why was Mr Grant not in charge of this very improper operation?"

"He's been away, day before yesterday."

"Has he, indeed? Do you know where he's gone?"

"Not exactly, but I did hear he'd gone to a religious conference in the south somewhere, to meet some foreign members, branch Group or something, to see them off back abroad."

"*Abroad*! Where from?"

"How do I know? He did mention Dover."

"Who did?"

"Young chap driving that car. She — Sister Brook, in front with him, was talking about the Ruler on our way to Group House to get Sue. Sister Brook asked him where they were taking her and he told her to shut up and then said he had to fetch the Ruler back from Dover that night."

The two detectives exchanged quick looks and both jumped to their feet.

"Stay here!" Walsh ordered Ben and both disappeared. A third officer, beside the door, shut it after them and turned to Ben.

"Tea or coffee, mate?" he asked, stonily.

Ben's muddled, half-resistant, half-boastful revelations of the Ruler's probable movements were the first real meat in the very meagre dish the two detectives had cooked between them after the discovery of Perkins's laboratory in the cellar at Mangoes. They fell upon it with speed and hope.

Harbour authorities in several south coast ports were warned to look out for and hold at least three passengers, possibly foreign in some sort of religious garb, one of whom might be British and using the name Mervyn Grant. Probable destination France.

The Scotland Yard drug traffic and control department, who knew all about the Perkins story from its beginnings and had been engaged upon the little villain's latest exploit in running the underground lab at his shop, had been keen to learn how he disposed of his new product for street sale, made from those new ingredients that came from the Middle East with other less valuable so-called 'health' products.

This element at the yard had been active at the ports in

many ways for a long time. After discussion Detective Superintendent Walsh and Detective Inspector Frost decided that the latter had better go down to Dover at once, with all the latest detail of Perkins's death and of those in any way connected with the criminal chemist. Also with the sect calling itself Holy Group and the two youngsters, connected, however vaguely, but perhaps significantly, with other strange aspects of the case.

After Frost had gone off in a staff car, with a driver, Walsh went back to Ben.

"I'm not going to ask you any more questions now," he said. "I don't think you've any more useful things to tell me. I'm not going to charge you now, because I have not talked to Miss Manley, who is in no state to answer questions, being in a state of shock, I gather. Constable Torch saw what he believes to be the result of a direct blow from you, but he did not see you deliver it. So you can leave here now and go home, which is the Group place in Playhouse Road, I believe."

"That's right," Ben said, his spirits rising, telling himself not to bloody well lose his cool now, for chrissake. He even tried to smile.

"Get along, then," Walsh told him. "You may yet be called to account for that so-called 'push over', so don't run away. Get yourself a lawyer, more like."

Ben ran all the way back to Playhouse Road, where he arrived about ten o'clock and, like Lesley, went straight to bed.

Detective Superintendent Walsh waited for news from Dover. When it came it was much as he expected. Mr Mervyn Grant, with three companions, all wearing semi-religious gowns of grey cloth, with gold crosses on chains hanging round their necks, had gone on board a ferry for Calais at seven o'clock. But Grant came off it again almost at once and went to a nearby hotel, where he had a substantial meal before being picked up by a private car about half-past ten and driven away. Frost was now on his way back, following this car at a discreet distance.

Walsh got in touch with Interpol in France, whom he had alerted earlier.

On the following morning work went forward briskly in the Murder Incident Room at the station. While Detective Inspector Frost organised a round-up check on the known junkies in his manor and another of those useful grasses who had helped in the past over the source of supplies of the kind it now seemed certain that Perkins had set up from St Andrew's Place, Detective Superintendent Walsh went to the Group House in Playhouse Road and demanded to speak to Mr Grant.

The Ruler received him at once. It was half-past eleven in the morning.

"Coffee time," the Ruler said, smiling. And though Walsh refused the offer, coffee in two cups arrived. The Ruler sipped his slowly, waiting for the detective to begin the conversation.

"I have two important matters I am enquiring into," Walsh began. "It has come to my notice in connection with the late Edwin Perkins that he was pursuing an illegal trade in certain drugs. He had done this several times in the past and served prison sentences for it, too. But he went back to it each time when freed, the same trade run in much the same way. With associates, of course."

"Dear, dear," said the Ruler and waited to hear more, sipping his coffee and looking blandly at Walsh.

"Perkins's part in the trade was to act as a go-between, we think. I approached you before, as you will remember?"

"I do," said the Ruler, "and I gave you a full and I think a sufficient explanation of the parcels he made up for me and which young Brother Shaw fetched from the shop."

"Yes. It now appears that you spent most of yesterday in Dover with friends of your persuasion, that you saw them go aboard a ferry for Calais and that you were then picked up by a car, clearly ordered in advance and returned home, here."

"All that is true," said the Ruler calmly, with a serene smile. "There are brothers of our faith in France and Italy."

"On the other hand," Walsh went on. "Three men in your religious uniform did not leave the ferry at Calais."

He paused. The Ruler, still smiling said, "No?"

203

"No, Mr Grant. But three men in various clothes, not moving together, but separately, from different gangways, but with the passports they had carried on board at Dover, did leave the ship. One was an Englishman, the other two were Middle Eastern. You may be asked to identify them, Mr Grant."

Mr Grant said, from white lips, "I don't understand you."

"I think you do, but I will leave you to consider your own position. Perhaps you have been deceived by those so-called brethren. It is very possible. You will prove that, no doubt."

He got up to go.

"I am now going to see Miss Manley, to discover what lay behind the attack on her in a very curious argument on the pavement involving a car sent from here to fetch away a young girl who was not intending to leave by it."

The Ruler, who had appeared stunned a moment before, went very red in the face and spoke most forcibly.

"But who, we knew well, must be saved from wicked contamination by that evil creature, Lesley Rivers!"

"I will discuss all that with Miss Manley," Walsh insisted.

And he did. He found Sister Manley up and dressed, but far from well. However, she was in her office and was quite ready, in fact eager, to see him, Sister Gordon said, to explain the unfortunate misunderstanding of the day before and the accident to herself that followed.

"She does look a sight today," Cissie told him. "Two of the loveliest . . . " But they had reached the office and the detective, who had kept a very straight face up to this point, dared not risk it then, though a moment later he thought the younger woman's remark was fully justified.

Sister Manley's appearance was indeed alarming, wholly traditional, ludicrous, in one of her age and position, alarming. The detective expressed shock and sympathy, and went on:

"I won't tire you, Miss Manley but I'm afraid we must have your account of what actually happened before we can bring a correct charge against this young man. What he did is most reprehensible, but he is emotional, he is convinced he was preventing some sort of kidnap attempt on Miss Susan Ford."

"Poor boy!" said Sister Manley, though her swollen, discoloured face expressed the opposite of sympathetic understanding. "It shows the length to which that evil girl will go to get her own way!"

"To whom are you referring, Miss Manley?"

"To Marion Colbert, who insists upon keeping her false name, Lesley Rivers."

"And were you trying to move Miss Ford from here to another of your houses?"

"Temporarily, yes. For her own good. For her soul's salvation."

"In spite of the fact, the established fact, Miss Manley, that Miss Ford is of adult age by any count and has now rejoined her parents at her own request."

"Alas, I have been so informed. A good friend and supporter of our order rang me up, or rather rang Sister Gordon to say Sister Ford was with her, waiting for her father to come for her."

The old betrayer, Sister Manley moaned inwardly, the wicked, old sentimentalist . . .

"Misunderstanding on both sides," said Walsh cheerfully, "which does not excuse young Shaw from attacking you, or us from failing to bring him to court."

"Not that, not that!" cried Sister Manley. "I refuse utterly to have — to see our order — to explain — He was under an evil influence, officer; Lesley is the real culprit. It is she who ought to be in prison for her crimes — "

"*Crimes*, Miss Manley?"

"Theft, deceit, lies, perhaps — Poor Mr Perkins, how envious she always was of him, she showed it most plainly always, how wicked in her selfish, self-seeking ways — " Miss Manley panted to a stop, looking now as if she felt she might have gone too far, but did not know how to retract.

A star-class performance, Detective Superintendent Walsh considered it and very much the sort of thing he had hoped for. He thought it time to finish this interview. So he got up, thanked Miss Manley for her assistance, wished her a rapid recovery and, forbidding her to tire herself by getting up, let himself out into the hall.

Cissie Gordon, as he knew her best, was no longer there, but a short, stout figure got up from a chair and took a step forward, then stopped abruptly.

Walsh, astonished, amused, held out a hand to her.

"Polly!" he exclaimed. "Why, if it isn't Polly Smith! We haven't seen anything of you for *years*!"

Sister Brook, drawing herself up, in spite of her suddenly racing heart, said, "I don't know you, sir!"

"Oh yes, you do, Polly. You can't have forgotten young Constable Walsh taking back from you the wallet you'd just taken off him and keeping a hold on you, too."

Sister Brook stared at him. Then she said, very slowly, very precisely. "I think you must be off your rocker. I am here to see Miss Manley. Let me pass, please."

Back in the Incident Room Walsh found Detective Inspector Frost still writing up his report on the Ruler's movements and companions in Dover. Seeing the look of pleased satisfaction on his superior's face he asked what it meant.

"Meeting up with a very old friend," Walsh told him. "Twenty-five years ago she was young and slim and pretty and the cleverest dip in our divison. She made one big mistake when she nicked my wallet, for which I got her on the spot. Seems she was in the kidnap car to help take Sue Ford. Calls herself Sister Brook."

"I see," Frost was not amused, but he supposed very little helped.

Late that night Sister Brook, (Polly Smith) and her son, Reg Bridge (or Smith) drove north in Reg's motor cycle and side-car. No good pushing your luck too far, they were agreed.

19

With Sue's rescue achieved and her shameful scar most skilfully removed, Lesley, though still wearing a sling, went back to Group House to explain her plans for the future to Sister Manley and settle her account with the sect.

She had engaged the help of the young solicitor recommended by Mrs Trevelyan; he had gone into the legal side of a possible transfer to Lesley of the Mangoes shop and its contents, taking over the mortgage on the property held by the bank, provided no heirs were discovered to whom Perkins's good and chattels were due to be given. In the meantime the young man suggested that he would like to see the shop, which he suggested was still being held incommunicado by the police.

"They have the keys," Lesley told him. "We'd want to get those off them. Mr Walsh, that's the top one in charge, said he'd like to go with me if I wanted to see over again or show it to anyone."

"Very right and proper," the solicitor agreed.

Sister Manley refused to see Lesley, though it was now three days since the mishap over Susan Ford. Though Miss Manley's black eyes had now begun to fade into a sickly shade of green and her nose, fortunately not broken, had lost its bloated contour and shrunk back towards its own sharp, prominent outline, the blow to her morale, her belief in her method of governing her set of converts and disciples, had been very severely shaken. All due to Lesley's dreadful powers of disruption, that gift of hers for concentrating all her energy

207

upon a single purpose and following that aim with a terrifying force. No wonder the police were anxious to keep her under their close observation.

"She begins to frighten me, Sister Gordon," Miss Manley told her second in command. "I *dare* not see her."

"Rubbish, Helen," Sister Gordon said. "But just as you like. The cops haven't done with that shop, not by a long chalk. Looks like there was some very dicey work going on there and Perkins got across some of his old pals who rubbed him out. Even old Ma doesn't like to speak about it."

"We can hardly go by what a person of Mrs Dillon's character thinks and says. Or won't tell us."

"Pity then you used her shop for posting your private correspondence." Sister Gordon's voice was scornful.

Sister Manley felt she had lost influence with her assistant, as well as losing face generally.

"What'll I tell Les, then?" Cissie pressed again. "Now she looks like getting Mangoes. And if the cops aren't just playing her along, her and that Ben Shaw."

Sister Manley started, flushed, paled and said in a very different voice, "I'm not bringing any charge against that boy. It was an accident! I shall stick to that! We *won't* have the Group in the papers again, maligned, misinterpreted — "

"You may not be asked," Sister Gordon interrupted her. "So don't lay down the law where you don't have the power."

Sister Manley gave up. She felt weak: her face ached if she talked for long. No more argument! Let the awful Lesley stay at Group House until she found somewhere else to upset everyone else in, or until the police took the right action with regard to her.

Lesley accepted Cissie's word for her to keep her room a little longer at Group House and even paid for the current week out of her small savings. She arranged with the solicitor and approached Detective Superintendent Walsh again for an appointment to view Mangoes the next morning. They were to meet at the back door at nine o'clock.

During that night, almost for the first time since snatching

Sue to safety, Lesley found herself thinking about Ben. She had not seen him arrested because she was just reaching Mrs Trevelyan's house with Sue when Constable Torch arrived at the scene on the pavement in Upper Polson Street. But several people had told her that Ben had been handcuffed and pushed into a police patrol car with Torch. Nobody who spoke to her had seen or heard anything of Ben since; this was the third clear day since the kidnap attempt. Was he still in custody, poor love, waiting to go before the court, she was not sure which? Waiting to go to prison, perhaps?

She no longer held any anger, any longing for revenge. Why should she? The doctors had been marvellous; — particularly the surgeon. There was a new, quite light plastic cover for her forearm in place of the former plaster. She had seen the result, still pinkish, but smooth, no longer rough and puckered, certainly no longer of any significant shape, no T for Thief ever again. Fantastic. Super. She had to hand it to the surgeon and to that top copper, Walsh. Ready to change her mind about the Law. Not *all* were a menace. She'd get the low down about Ben when she saw Walsh at Mangoes and after she'd said how grateful she was for everything.

Lesley and the solicitor found Detective Sergeant Cole waiting for them at the back entrance of the shop. In her softened mood Lesley was prepared to forgive George, too, for all his deceptions. She introduced her solicitor to him and found, without much surprise, that they knew one another slightly already.

"We've met over mutual clients," her lawyer told her. As Lesley did not fully understand that phrase she simply nodded.

"I have our keys," George said, producing them and turning to Lesley went on, "The super sends his regrets but he can't get away this morning so he's sent me instead, because I know, well — the facts of the case from the start."

"And how!" Lesley replied, but without rancour.

They inspected the flat first, though Lesley refused to go into Mr Perkins's bedroom. Then they walked round the shop and she explained the former layout of the goods they sold there, the pay desk and wrapping counter, the little office at the back with Mr Perkins's larger knee-hole desk with drawers at either side.

The whole shop was quite bare, but the empty shelves and the sloping boards in the window space remained, also the empty furniture.

"It was some sort of shop before Perkins took it," George explained. "I wasn't in this division then, so I never saw it."

"Two years," said the solicitor. "I remember him fixing all the legal part with a friend of mine."

"Of course you would know," George said, quoting names and conditions. "That will make it easier for Les here to take over with your help, won't it?"

The solicitor smiled but said nothing. Lesley, again not understanding their conversation said, "Well, let's get on, shall we?"

"Of course." George moved away, saying as he went, "The cellar. Where they stored their bulk deliveries. This way."

The two men went ahead, Lesley following, propping open the cellar door from the little hall by means of a hook on a loop of rope to a ring on the wall.

"There's no light unless you put a bulb in," Lesley told them. "Old stingy Perks put one in for me when the carrier came with the sacks of new stuff."

They stood in the middle of the floor, their voices echoing. There was one ground-level small window, heavily barred and wire masked as well, in the wall facing the road outside. In the dim light Lesley and the solicitors could see that the cellar, too, was quite empty of goods for sale or any other use.

George Cole moved across to the far wall where the door, formerly hidden, was now in full view. He found the key on its separate ring, put it in the lock, turned and pushed.

Lesley moved forward quickly, grasped George's arm and said in a tense, low voice, "Stop!"

"Let go!" the detective said, annoyed by this recurrence of hysteria. "I only want to find the light switch!"

"I heard something!" Lesley shouted. "I heard . . ."

They all heard it. A weak, imploring, hoarse voice, saying,

"Don't put it on! Don't put — for God's sake, don't — "

But George had found the switch and pushed it down. Instead of light, hanging in a bulb above the central table, where George had seen it before, there was a plop, a brisk ignition, and a burst of flame running up and down a wooden chair that stood beside the table in a cleared space; that grew as it reached a plentiful dose of paraffin, that spurted and flamed, sending out choking fumes.

And behind the table a dark figure reared up, coughing, shaking too, falling, struggling, to get round the obstacle before it, too, took fire in one enclosed furnace.

"It's Ben!" shrieked Lesley, trying to push her way past George.

"Hold her!" he called back to the solicitor, as he leaped across the table to drag the caged man out.

Lesley, far too sensible and quick-witted to hamper a rescue when she understood its purpose, had given no trouble. When George came through the secret laboratory door, dragging the fainting Ben Shaw with him, she jumped forward to shut the door on the blazing room, before following the two men who were carrying Ben between them up the cellar steps out of the smoke and fumes.

They took him outside the back door and laid him on the pavement. He was filthy, smelly, with a three days' beard. He had lost his jacket, his t-shirt was torn, there were deep weals on both wrists and ankles, his jeans were split at the seams. But there were no major injuries.

In the open air Ben came round to find Lesley, sitting on the ground beside him. She took his head on to her lap; there were tears on her cheeks and her voice was as hoarse as his had been in his recent prison.

"Water?" George asked, when he saw Ben's eyes open.

Ben shook his head.

"Sink," he said. "Drip. Turned the water off, the devils, but didn't drain the cistern." He gasped and stopped speaking. In a few seconds he spoke again. "Didn't understand it at first. Wasted a lot. Nearly out when you came. Thought it was them. Thought — " He shut his eyes.

211

The ambulance arrived, picked up Ben and carried him away to hospital, with Lesley holding his hand and refusing to let go of it.

The fire brigade came, put out the fire in the cellar laboratory, left the scene cold but unsearched, as the police demanded. The firemen praised the action in shutting the door from the lab into the cellar, which minimised the amount of damage and prevented a spread that might have involved the whole house and even the whole of St Andrew's Place.

The Fire Brigade did not hear the whole truth of this fire until some months later, though they worked it out at a high administrative level after several appearances in the courts to testify to their part in the whole complicated story. The chair, wired to catch fire on the turning of the light switch, had been completely burned to ash, together with the lengths of flex, the fuse and so on. Perkins had taken out no insurance of any kind on the building or its contents. When he set up his mortgage to buy the shop he had taken on the current insurance, which had nearly a year to run. There was no evidence that he had paid any renewal demand and it had lapsed. No assessors claimed to examine the scene, so the cause of the blaze remained a matter solely for the police.

It was clear enough to them. A diabolic method of destroying Ben Shaw: either while he was still alive, bound to the chair and gagged, burned fatally by the turning of the room light switch, or in the disposal of his body after he had died of thirst, hunger, exposure, unrescued, undiscovered.

"There were three thugs set on me," Ben explained to Detective Superintendent Walsh. "Black clothes, hoods. Small car. Jumped me at the corner of Playhouse Road. I been waiting near Group House to see Les and make it up with her and ask after Sue, but she never came."

"Les Rivers never came?"

"No. I mean, yes. She didn't come out."

"Did you go in to ask?"

Ben reddened.

"Well, yes, I did. I was told she'd left Group House for good and they had no address for her." He paused and added, in a very reproachful voice, "I was fed up. I never thought she'd let me down as bad as that."

"Nor did she. But you know that now, don't you? There's been plenty of lies all round in this business, haven't there?" The superintendent's words were harsh, but his smile was friendly as he went on. "Never mind about your feelings. Go on about your kidnap. You were taken in Playhouse Road in the evening of the day after your assault on Sister Manley. Where did they take you?"

"To Mangoes. Back entrance. Straight down to the room in the cellar. They fixed me in that chair, but they weren't expert, I could see that."

"See? Was the light still on? Were you not blindfolded?"

"No, I wasn't. And yes, it was. At that stage. First bad mistake. They made a lot more in the end. I could mark everything in that room, the sink, the slabs, the table, no window but a ventilator and it was working, you could feel it."

"Go on."

"We'd played kidnap games at school. I knew how to swell my wrists when I was tied up and relax later to get free. They weren't experts, not professional at all. I thought I'd be able to get loose and I did. But I saw them wiring the chair to burn and that scared me proper."

"I bet it did. But you got loose from the chair, of course. Did that take much doing?"

"More than I expected. Even so, I expected them back, turning the switch to see me burn. I didn't think your lot would be looking for me yet. Just think I'd scarpered. Les, too."

"I'm wondering," Walsh said carefully, "how you found water in that tap at the sink. Our people emptied the cistern for the flat, after turning off the main."

"Must come off the main, independent," Ben said promptly. "I found it worked, soon as I got free of that bloody chair. Saved my life, that tap."

"Another bit of inefficiency. They can't have tried it."

"They didn't. Saved my life."

"I think it probably did. You were down there all of thirty-four hours before we found you."

213

"Only that!" Ben was astonished. "I thought it was getting on for a week!"

Walsh laughed.

"You'd be a damned sight weaker now if it had been a week. You look no different from the first time we had you at the station."

This was true. On arrival at the hospital Ben had refused to be put to bed. He had insisted upon having something to eat first and after a bowl of soup, all too small, he complied with having a bath and a shave and putting on clean pyjamas, followed by a real meal, taken sitting up in a dressing gown.

The doctor called to advise on these proceedings agreed to every one of them. It was after the second meal of scrambled eggs and ice cream, that his conversation with the detective took place.

"So now," Walsh said, "What are we going to do with you?"

Ben grinned.

"I'm on bail," he said, "for socking Sister Manley."

"So you are. But I can't let you go back to Playhouse Road. Mr Grant thinks you've scarpered, — right out of London. I want you where I can keep an eye on you until your date with the magistrates. You can't stay in hospital. There's nothing wrong with you."

"No more can Les stop at Group House," Ben began, but Walsh put up a hand.

"You don't know, do you, that Lesley was thinking of taking on the shop at Mangoes and running it chiefly for the West Indians and vegetarian students around here. Mr Grant will go right round the bend when he hears that, I think. Miss Manley too. She was going to move into the Perkins flat, Lesley I mean, if the sale to her went through."

Ben was silent, overawed by the news.

"So *I* don't want *her* back at Group House, either," Walsh concluded.

"Where's she got to?" Ben asked, vaguely looking round about him. "She was down in that cellar. She was in the ambulance. Where's she got now?"

214

Walsh turned to the officer who was guarding the door against the Press and gave a brief order.

A few minutes later Lesley was in the room. She gave a little cry and ran forward. Ben scrambled up with open arms to clasp her closely. But he tottered at the impact and they fell into the chair behind him, laughing and crying and kissing wildly.

Detective Superintendent Walsh said in a formal voice, "I'll arrange to have your belongings brought here in a couple of hours, Mr Shaw. After that, if you and Miss Rivers are agreeable, the officer who brings them will drive you both to suitable lodgings in a house we control, which is safe, but not secure, if you understand me."

He did not wait for an answer, but paused at the door to say "May I ask you both, direct you, I should say, not to speak a word of these arrangements to any member of the hospital staff or any member of the media who tries to accost you before you leave, or as you are leaving?"

Then he was gone.

It was Detective Sergeant George Cole who drove the pair to the authorised haven where they spent the next four days in total seclusion, reasonable creature comfort and a lasting peace neither of them had ever known before. They decided they must each find a new job of some kind, well away from any connection with the crazy sect, the altogether 'unholy' Group. It was obvious that the police interest in Mangoes, in its connection with the Ruler and his buddies outside the Group, of whom Mr Perkins had been one, went far beyond any kind of religious purpose and into the wide field of vice, collectively called 'drugs'.

"As long as they don't try to pin anything on me I couldn't care less," Ben declared at intervals in their speculation over their happy, but prolonged seclusion.

"Anyhow Mangoes is out," Lesley insisted. "I couldn't have anything to do with that rotten place now. Gives me the heeby-jeebys even to look down those cellar steps."

"Me, too. First thing, love, we better get married."

"As if we weren't already."

"You know what I mean."

"Yes, my darling. I know what you mean."

In the Incident Room dealing with the Perkins murder, matters were progressing well. Interpol had interesting news. When the cross channel ferry from Dover docked in Calais the French police picked up three travellers in religious dress who left the ship's gangway together, took their luggage towards the customs shed and disappeared. Later three individuals in civilian dress, one clearly European, two Middle Eastern, one in Arab dress, one in a western suit with a fez, each with authentic passports and other papers went through customs, but were picked up as they separately tried to leave the port.

Information extracted by the French from these people established a widening circle of drug smuggling operations, in which it seemed certain that both Perkins and Mervyn Grant were involved. Perhaps the little ex-chemist, ex-old lag, had been warned of danger and tried to get out of the circle. So which of these three would-be escapers had throttled him before going?

The newspapers, reporting the inquest on Perkins, had brushed up his history. They had made a good deal of it, since they were prevented from enlarging on Lesley's part by her total disappearance, chiefly in hospital, it was believed. All they could do was quote Detective Inspector Frost's obstinately held opinion that it was a case of gang warfare of a well-known type.

But after four days news came from Group House, conveyed by Sister Gordon, who saw the end of her post there and had already fixed most of her possessions in a room at the 'dollies' house in Brindley Square, though she had not yet given her notice to Sister Manley.

There was to be a big occasion in the Great Hall, a kind of farewell party, quite openly advertised, for the Ruler, who was going to open a new branch of the Sect in Belgium and was going to take his leave of them with a blessing and regret, but he was bidden to spread the word.

"It's *incredible!*" Walsh exclaimed, when this news was

brought to him. "Grant must be right round the bend by now. He'll have learned what went wrong in Calais. They'll drop him or go for him more likely. Up to us to get in first."

"What about those two young 'uns, Ben and Les?" Cole asked, when he was briefed on the coming meeting at Group House.

"Leave 'em be," said Walsh. He had more important matters to think about.

But Lesley and Ben had already thought otherwise. To them their own future was all important; it needed immediate attention. So they simply walked out quietly from the safe house, which was not secure, as they had rightly been told, and made their way back to London.

The Great Hall filled rapidly when the senior Sisters and Brothers threw open the double doors. Most of the inmates of the two halls of residence both knew and feared the Ruler. A few of the older ones, and the several chronically ill or deformed, who had found safety and a certain degree of care, at any rate no responsibility, no worry over shelter or food, these poor souls respected, if they did not like, him. Now he was going, taking his strange ways with him, going elsewhere to run a like establishment, it seemed. But who would take his place? There was a certain tension in the Great Hall as they waited for the farewell ceremony to begin.

When the lights were partially dimmed and a solemn procession came in from the far end of the hall, moving up to the central dais, excited rumours ran about the waiting mass: they grew into a low, continuing moan as more lights dimmed and the Ruler, in his black and gold robe of office, took his place before the great chair on the dais. He raised his hand for silence, but the moaning went on. He opened his mouth to speak. Another voice, one he knew and feared, and hated, rose shrilly above the moan.

"Murderer! Would-be bloody murderer!"

The Ruler screamed, leaping forward from the dais, pulling from under his hampering robe a long, thin, pointed knife. He knew the voice: His enemy, his battered, but unbeaten enemy!

217

At last she must be destroyed! Utterly destroyed! Must, must MUST! Now!

Sister Gordon, near the door and the light switches, plunged the Hall into darkness and slipped away to avoid the mass panic that would follow at once. In the outer hall Constable Torch signalled to the police outside, who left their cars and piled into the building.

The Ruler found his knife arm caught by Ben, twisted to drop the knife and broken above the wrist.

Lesley caught the other arm by the hand and threw the still screaming Ruler to the ground. She grabbed the knife from the floor but as she did so the panic rush began, brothers and sisters pushing and pulling one another in a mad rush for the only light glowing in the open doorway.

Lesley, still holding the knife, point downwards, fell to her knees. She thrust the knife, still point downwards away from her own body as she fell.

A wilder cry from Grant told her she had struck some part of him. She was elated, wickedly rejoicing, no concern for a true enemy defeated but a woman of the tribe defending her man.

The lights went up suddenly. The Hall seemed to be full of uniformed police, shepherding away the last of the Group.

George was beside her, moving her back gently. Ben was beyond George, another plain clothes man beside him, all staring down at the Ruler, who lay still now, his eyes closed, a crumpled right arm flung out on that side and on the other, the hand spread open, palm upward, pinned to the floor boards by the knife. It was fixed through the loose skin between the base of the thumb and the edge of the palm. There was no blood to speak of.

Quite suddenly Lesley felt sickened. She stooped towards the knife. George held her back. Detective Superintendent Walsh appeared behind George, who moved out of his way, still holding Lesley.

"The hand, sir!" he said. "The *small* hand!"

"Yes, sarge. That gives us the main answer, doesn't it?"

Lesley murmured to Ben, "What's he on about? I always knew the Ruler had small hands."

"Means he's the one croaked old Perks."

"Oh!"

Outside the Holy Group the cars began to move away. The Ruler's get-away van had been boxed in carefully and its driver held quite early in the exercise. The journalists and photographers were assured they would get full statements without much delay.

A message, by hand, came to Ben and Lesley from Mrs Trevelyan.

"Please come in as soon as you can. The Ford family are all here and anxious to meet you both."

20

Six months later the Holy Group affair, with its sinister history of oppression, torture, associated murder attempt and actual murder, though providing the media with first class entertainment in the shape of news, had faded in a few weeks from their pages and their screens and therefore from the minds of the general public, not all of whom took a really serious interest in the first place.

The main excitement had lain in the revelations regarding the sect. A controversy grew between those who approved of the undoubtedly useful harbour it provided for many who were incapable of managing their own lives and at the same time introduced them to a religious base for the first time, and those who considered the religious base, as shown to them, a travesty of the Christian faith, in fact a definite blasphemy. They demanded its abolition.

In fact, with Mervyn Grant serving a life sentence for murder attempted, following murder achieved, and a concurrent sentence for drug-smuggling; and with Helen Manley, acquitted of any direct part in the major crime, but guilty of conspiring to torture, physical in the case of Lesley Rivers and mental in the case of Susan Ford, the community in Upper Polson Street was broken up and the house lay empty for a year. Then it was re-opened with a new staff, organised with the help of Mrs Trevelyan, by the main original sect of the Holy Group, situated in the north of England. The old lady had been very much distressed by the fate of the Group, so near to her home and so near her late husband's heart and her own. She had used all her influence and some of her fortune to promote this development. The local council, horrified at having to take on a considerable number of dependent citizens in several undesirable categories, was overjoyed by the success of their retired colleague.

Miss Manley, after serving a short sentence, followed by a period of probation, left the area. She never forgot the appalling scene in the Great Hall and the exposure of the Ruler. She comforted herself with a belief that his behaviour was due to mental illness, not crime. She was told that crime was breaking the law, and major crime was all set down in the ten commandments and held as good now as in the time of Moses. Also that no place could be found for Grant in a mental hospital, that was also secure. The prisons were full, but people sent there had to be admitted. And nothing would be allowed to stop Grant from being shut up, hopefully for at least twenty years, if he lived so long. Miss Manley wept frequently, but in due course she went north, where she was not recognised, and where her experience and her organising and directing powers were badly needed in big industrial organisations. Later she found and held a job in a remote Social Service unit.

The death of little Eddie Perkins made no lasting impression of any kind. Murder in crime circles was an old, sordid tale. His atrocious killing was as unremarkable as his hard-working, perverted career had been. Detective Inspector Frost's original conclusion was borne out by all the evidence. Gang warfare. Mervyn Grant would not have survived much longer, after his buddies, guaranteed by him their getaway from Dover, had been rumbled at Calais, by his fault in setting up a super-grass in his complicated cover.

But George Cole and Amanda Drew, having proved their genuine friendship with Lesley and Ben, were invited to their wedding in the local Register Office, a fortnight after the final collapse of Group House and the arrest of the Ruler and Sister Manley.

Mrs Trevelyan was also present and a wedding luncheon was set up at the Swan by Mr Ford, who had already made it his business to advise Ben upon his future and to offer help in finding him a job where the lad's straightforward nature, great physical stamina and muscular strength could be used. With his known courage and persistence, if no great intellectual powers, he ought to succeed, if he could show more self-confidence.

The outcome of this was that the couple, after a blissful honeymoon in Devon, had decided to emigrate to Australia, where, with Mr Ford's help once again, an engineering job would be possible for Ben. It was left to Lesley, now Mrs Shaw, to find something for herself.

"She'll do that for certain," Mandy said, before she and George separated, when the taxi, smothered in confetti, drove away to Waterloo Station.

He nodded. They walked silently towards George's parked car. Before they reached it he felt for her hand and held it until he had to get out his car keys.

Then he said, "Bit of a let-down after all that's happened. What about another look at the country tomorrow. I'm off this weekend. What about you?"

"Have you forgotten? We both have extra leave as a sort of present for our part in the Mervyn Grant case success? Actually it was Les and Ben pulled it off."

"And nothing for your Cousin Madge and her friends, who helped a lot in finding and showing up the Colberts. I ought to tell them exactly what happened."

"Don't you dare! Horror stories would not go down well with any of them. But we might drive over and tell them how it all turned out for Les."

They had settled themselves in George's car by now. He took her hand again, to pull her closer.

"I'd like to meet her; again. I did meet her the time I really fixed the Colberts at Brockton. I went to Rugby to apologise for not stopping to see her when I dropped you off? D'you know what she said to me?"

"How could I?"

"She laughed and then she said how lucky I was to have you with me, helping, because that was how you always were and

222

never got in anyone's hair, either."

"To which you answered how wrong you can be, Miss Small."

George grunted a denial and moved his arm to her shoulder.

"We'll go to Rugby and take Cousin Madge and her buddies out to dinner. Then the next day we'll go west to the hotel I got pulled back from in a hurry. We'll spend the rest of our leave there. That suit you?"

"If you say so, Detective *Inspector* Cole," she answered, irritated by his crisp tone and calm assumption. But breaking down, as she turned her face to his, she said, with a break in her voice, "Oh George, if you really mean it!"

Cissie Gordon settled very comfortably in her new job, housekeeping and cooking for the girls in the flats in Brindley Square. She had followed the break-up of Group House: she had deplored its resurrection; but since she was in no way involved in this, she began to follow its altered fortunes and saw a good deal of improvement.

Ma Dill praised the new management, for the rules of the sect under a milder regime offered her considerably more custom of various kinds. Or so she told Cissie, when the latter came to pay her weekly bill for newspapers and magazines, cigarettes and sweets.

They too had waited outside the Registry Office with the usual crowd of photographers and journalists. They had both been touched and most grateful when Lesley had broken away from Ben to dash up to them and kiss each in turn, a gesture applauded by the crowd and shown on front pages and television, where a few papers only produced a group with Mrs Trevelyan in attendance on the bridal pair.

"Off to Australia," said Cissie. "Hope they'll make it, out there. Ben'll be all right, if he doesn't lose his temper too often."

"Les'll see to that," Ma Dill said.

"So long as *she* doesn't get over-excited," Cissie warned.

"How so?"

"Those attacks she had. They've put it in her passport and her diary. Anyway, her handbag, that she'll always have with her."

"Wot d'you mean?"

"After her name, address, age, blood group. The words about those attacks."

"Wot words?" Ma Dill plunged a moistened finger into the jar of sweets at her elbow.

"In capital letters. SUBJECT TO CARDIAC ARREST."

"Blimey!" said Ma Dill, dribbling a little.